WHERE

Fate

WHISPERS

WHERE

Fate

WHISPERS

E.G. TUDOR

★ ★ ★ ★ ★ ★
Inlustris

First published in the UK in 2022 by Inlustris Publishing, Wales
Text © E. G. Tudor 2022

Edited by Emma O'Connell ©
Cover designed by Inlustris Publishing © Map ©
Interior formatting and design by Inlustris Publishing ©

A CIP catalogue record for this book is available from the British Library.

Paperback ISBN 978 1 7395865 0 8

E-book ISBN 978 1 7395865 1 5

Hardback ISBN 978 1 7395865 2 2

For all those who dance their way through life…
and to those who catch them when they fall.

This is for you.

I was supposed to be a part of a Fated Pair – I was supposed to stave back the shadows with my union to my Fated Partner. But instead, our Choosing went wrong, and now I was destined to kill him... if he didn't kill me first.

Prologue

Three Years Ago

"Stop gripping my hand so tightly, Wen," Eva complained, pulling her hand away and rubbing at the reddened skin.

"I'm sorry. I'm just so nervous," I confessed, scanning across the Celestial Bridge and over to the group of assembled candidates from the realm of Sol. *There.* My eyes rested on Kai's grinning face. Even the Shadowmist swirling around him could do nothing to dim his light – well, any of the Solian candidates, really. Coming from the realm of the sun, they all appeared to glow from the top of their blonde- and white-haired heads, their blue eyes, ranging the spectrum of summer-sky blue to seashore cerulean, and their warm golden skin.

"Really, Wen, it's not as if you didn't see him only yesterday." Eva pouted as I glanced back at her. She tossed her long black braid over her shoulder and rolled her stormy grey eyes.

I flushed and dropped my eyes to my star-studded velvet slippers. Not especially practical in the mist, but the Council expected a certain ceremonial standard for their rituals.

Meuric – the Council head of Nos, our realm of night – walked over the bridge towards Sabra, Sol's Council representative. They bowed at each other, before placing their hands on the crystal podium set deep into the wide, circular centre of the bridge.

I pushed up on my tiptoes, craning my neck to see what was happening, and accidentally stepped on Eva's toe.

She hissed in pain. "You are so clumsy!"

"Sorry," I muttered.

Maxen, on the other side of Eva, looked at me with a grin. "Want me to lift you up?"

It was a slight sore point with me that I was shorter than all the other candidates. At fifteen, I was still the same height as I had been two years ago. My adoptive mother, Alys, kept telling me I would catch up, but I couldn't help but wonder when that would be – when another two Fate's Days had passed? Or more?

"No, thank you," I said to Maxen with as much dignity as I could muster, and turned back to hear what Meuric was saying.

"Nosian Candidates." He turned to gesture to our group of twelve girls and boys. We were all dressed in varying shades of black, purple, and silver, complementing our pale skin, dark hair and grey eyes. "You have been selected from your class for showing the skill, resilience, and intelligence needed to become part of the next Fated Pair. Fated to stand side by side and become the next rulers of our Twin Realms."

"Everyone except Ceridwen," I heard someone at the back mutter. I bit my tongue so I wouldn't retaliate. If Meuric thought I showed promise, then I deserved to be here as much as anyone else.

Fated Pair. A shiver ran through me, and I exchanged a look with Eva. As the daughter of the current Fated Pair, I knew she expected to be picked. Her parents had already ruled for seventeen years out of the traditional twenty-year reign. The last three years would be dedicated to helping train and mentor the next pair, and I was sure Eva's mother had her heart set on it being Eva – but it was up to the Fates to decide.

I turned back to listen to Meuric, but he had conceded to Sabra. The tall, slim lady with hair so blonde it appeared white cast a glance over the Nos candidates before turning to her own. "And candidates from Sol, I have personally selected those whom I have seen show great spirit, strength of character, and charm. The two names – one from each realm – will now be chosen. Whoever they are, know this. Your future union will strengthen the bond between the Twin Realms, staving off the shadows of the realm of Fog, the evil which seeks to devour our realms of sun and night. For if the Fated Pair are not bonded in union by the third Fate's Day from now, the Celestial Bridge will fall, opening the doorway to the realm of Fog… and what dwells within it will be unleashed."

"Way to sound dramatic," Maxen whispered loudly, causing the other Nos candidates to snigger, but my skin iced all over. I stared down into the swirling mists below, the mists that concealed the lower mysterious realm of Fog where the Shadowwraiths dwelt, then looked up and met Kai's eyes across the bridge. His usual cheeky grin slid from his face as his eyes pierced mine, and dizziness washed over me.

A sharp nudge to the ribs had me turning to Eva. Her grey eyes were intense on mine, but her face had paled. I looked beyond her to the other candidates; they were staring at me too, all traces of humour vanished.

"What is it?" I asked in confusion.

"Ceridwen Moonshade."

My blood ran cold. From Meuric's impatient tone, I assumed it was not the first time I had been called, and that was why everyone was staring at me.

I jolted, but I couldn't force my feet to move forward. It was if the bridge beneath me had turned into a river of honey, gluing my slippers to its surface.

"Go *on*, Wen." Eva pushed me none-too-gently forwards, and the momentum propelled me on.

I swallowed past the lump in my throat and, wiping my clammy hands on my black silk robe, began to walk across the Celestial Bridge towards Meuric and Sabra. I kept my eyes focused forward; I didn't dare look at Kai. I didn't want to appear too keen and have him thinking I was *wishing* he would be chosen. Still, a thrill of hope started burning within my chest. What if he *was*? He was my best friend, after all. I could imagine no one better to rule the realms with.

I could sense everybody's eyes on me, as though my thoughts were on show for all to see. My cheeks began to burn, and I wished the bridge would open up and swallow me now.

The walk towards the centre of the Celestial Bridge was agonisingly slow, but finally I reached Meuric's side. His pewter eyes rested on mine, and I squirmed uncomfortably before remembering myself and giving him a bow.

"Meuric—" I started, then broke off, horrified at my faux pas. "Master Meuric," I corrected myself, focusing on his long, grey braid instead of holding his gaze. My thoughts clouded with memories of long days of training and Meuric's exasperation at my clumsiness. I wondered if he was regretting putting me forward as a candidate now.

He clapped a reassuring hand to my shoulder, and I looked up at him in surprise. With a nod, he turned to Sabra and gestured for her to continue.

She stared at me, her turquoise eyes unreadable. I couldn't tell how she felt about my being Chosen. From the handful of times I had met her, it seemed that she usually kept her emotions hidden. Kai said she was a tough mentor and trained the Sol students hard.

Abruptly, she broke eye contact and looked down into the shimmering bowl on the podium before her. The Celestial Bridge mists gradually collected inside the bowl, and I could see churning, shifting flashes of light and broken images. Finally, they coalesced into two words which emerged from the mist and hovered in front of Sabra. I squinted, but I wasn't close enough to make them out.

At last I saw a spark of emotion in her eyes, blue flames flickering like a sunburst, and I wondered who had been chosen to evoke such a reaction in the serious Council leader. Her thin lips moved soundlessly, and a rushing in my ears blocked out her voice. I shook my head to try and clear them and my long black and silver curls fell over my eyes, obscuring my vision.

I pushed the hair out of my eyes and gasped as I saw who was walking towards me.

"Hi, Wen," Kai said as he joined us. His voice held the merest of tremors, and his usually sun-warmed face was pale as moonlight. If I put my hand to his cheek now, it would blend in.

My voice was husky. "Hi."

At almost sixteen, he was older and already a head-and-a-half taller than me. I hoped I would catch up to him soon. My head swam: I'd have a *lifetime* with him now to catch up.

"Lady Ceridwen, Lord Malakai, join hands over the bowl, please," Meuric instructed.

I gaped at the new title, but of course they came with our new positions as future Fated Pair.

Kai took a position opposite me and held his hands out over the shimmering bowl. Taking a deep breath, I moved to clasp hands with him, but paused when the contents of the bowl flickered with pulsing black sparks. Rumbles echoed around the cliffside, and the Celestial Bridge shifted beneath my feet. Disconcerted, I looked at Kai, but despite troubled shouts from the other candidates and Council members, he nodded encouragingly.

My heart pounding in my chest, I linked our hands. His were warmer than mine, and I sent him a tentative squeeze. He squeezed back, and immediately I relaxed. Nothing bad would happen with Kai by my side.

I was an orphan. Found as a newborn baby on the Celestial Bridge, I had been settled in Nos with Alys, healer to the current Fated Pair – Eva's parents – and raised by her. Still, I had sometimes felt like an outsider in my own realm, so often sneaked away into the Twin Realms' shared caves to visit the Fates' shrine. Last year I had met Kai there, and we had been firm friends ever since.

Sabra and Meuric moved around us, preparing the purple and orange twisted cord that would be wrapped around my and Kai's clasped hands, joining us – and the Twin Realms – together for all to witness. I swallowed nervously, remembering the day before, when Kai and I had met at the caves. We hadn't talked about today, or what our futures might hold. We had simply swum in the pool and visited the shrine and then shared overripe pears, getting slightly giddy from the heady taste.

Kai gave me a wink. My heart fluttered, and the last of my apprehension drifted away. I wouldn't want to be Paired with anyone else. This was something to be *celebrated,* not feared. I was excited to spend the next three years under the guidance of Eva's parents, learning how to rule the Twin Realms… with Kai.

A stronger rumble rang out around the cliffside, and I stumbled as the Celestial Bridge bucked beneath us. The Shadowmist thickened, and I hoped a Shadowwraith attack wouldn't happen – not today, of all days. I didn't want anything to spoil this moment.

"Do not let go," Meuric shouted as I fought to hold on to Kai. Was this normal? I hadn't been to a Choosing before; none of us candidates had. My hands slicked with a sudden sweat, but I clung on as tightly as I could.

"Let those here present bear witness to the candidates Chosen. Lady Ceridwen Moonshade and Lord Malakai Ostara are to be our next Fated Pair.

When they are of age, which will be the third Fate's Day from now, they will be joined in union to strengthen the bond of our two realms."

As Sabra spoke the words, the sun crested behind the horizon and the full moon shone down onto the bowl, illuminating the mist inside. She stared down into it, her eyes wide.

"No," she murmured, moistening her lips. "This is not right…"

"What is it?" Meuric asked as the Celestial Bridge moved again. Shadows shifted closer, and I shuddered. *Would* the Shadowwraiths attack today? There hadn't been an attack from the lower realm of Fog for some time.

Not much was known about the mysterious realm – not that was imparted to us candidates, anyway – but that would all change when Kai and I came to rule. The Council would share with us the knowledge of what lay below. Eva had overheard her parents talking about it once, and she had told me that there were actually people who lived there, though how they could exist in that murky world I didn't know – especially when it was home to Shadowwraiths too.

I pushed back my apprehension and looked over at Kai. What if the bridge fell? No, that wasn't possible. The Fated Pair's union strengthened it and kept the shadows at bay. Eva's parents were strong and ruled the Twin Realms well. The Celestial Bridge was stronger than ever… surely?

Misty images erupted from the bowl: two figures locked in fierce battle while the Celestial Bridge bucked and twisted beneath them, ominous mist creeping ever closer. As one figure plunged a dagger into the other, the bridge stilled, and all was calm once more. What was I seeing?

The vision dissolved, and as it did so a vicious crack split the bowl, racing down the crystal podium and across the surface of the Celestial Bridge, the force throwing me and Meuric back towards Nos, and Kai and Sabra onto Sol's side of the bridge.

Pushing up onto my hands and knees, I looked aghast at the scene before me. A jagged crack forked across the surface of the bridge where the crystal podium had once stood, now in pieces. *What just happened?*

"The Fates have spoken!" Sabra called out, her voice full of more emotion than I had ever heard from her. Immediately, silence reigned from both sides of the bridge. "Before the bowl broke, I saw... I saw what must happen. There will be no union this time."

Gasps and shouts echoed around the mountainside, and I stood on legs made of jelly. *No! Was what I saw in the bowl true?* I couldn't believe it. I wouldn't believe it!

Kai looked as devastated as I did. I tried to run to his side, but Meuric held me back.

"What do you mean, no union?" he asked Sabra, his voice surprisingly strong for someone facing something unprecedented. "There *must* be a union. How else will the bridge stand strong? How will we keep Fog at bay?"

I looked at the Celestial Bridge, at the crack in its surface. Had me and Kai being Chosen caused this?

Sabra gripped Kai's shoulder as she spoke once more. "I have seen it." She paused to take a shuddering breath. "The only way to repair the Celestial Bridge and to prevent the Shadowmist from overcoming both our realms is this: on the third Fate's Day from now…" She broke off to look directly into my eyes, her gaze piercing me like icy daggers even from the distance across the crack. "One of you must kill the other."

Someone screamed. As my legs gave out from under me, I realised it was me. Only someone who'd had their heart rent into a thousand icy shards could feel as much pain as I did in that frozen, horrible moment. I landed on my back, the bridge hard and unyielding beneath me. My vision greyed out; the full, glowing moon was the last thing I saw.

I came to as I was picked up in a pair of strong, gentle arms.

"They must be separated. Take her away." Sabra's insistent voice cut through the smoke in my head, and I struggled feebly.

"Kai," I tried to call, but my voice was merely a whisper, as insubstantial as the mist now swirling around me, trying to claim me as its own.

"Please, let me go to her… let me check she's all right!" Kai's voice reached my ears and I tried to hold out a hand to him, but it was in vain. Meuric carried me away, and Sabra urged Kai back to Sol. His candidate friends pulled him with them. My vision greyed again as my best friend, my soulmate, was removed once and for all from my life.

The terrified voices of the other candidates surrounded us as Meuric started the long climb up the five hundred steps up the mountainside to Nos. Situated at the pinnacle of the mountain, it nestled amongst the stars, whereas Sol spread out in the lowlands, the golden sands and the seas at its front and leafy forests behind.

"Let me tend to her, Ric," I heard Alys' soft voice say.

Gentle hands smoothed my brow, and I willingly gave in to the darkness.

One

Present day

"Come *on*, Ceridwen – how will you ever beat Malakai if you give up because, and I quote, 'I'm tired'?" Maxen scowled at me from across the training yard in exasperation. "Do you think *he's* having an early night?"

I stopped myself from retorting that yes, actually, he probably was. Kai liked to train with the sunrise.

I couldn't keep going on at this pace. I was so very, very weary. For almost three years, I had been relentlessly training both body and mind. Although my muscles were honed and ready, my mental state was not. Time was running out, and I still couldn't accept the fact I would have to fight Kai – and I had yet to master the art of fighting to *win*.

A metallic taste in my mouth, I threw down the two swords. They clattered onto the stone floor of the training yard

"I'm done," I said, holding a hand to my brow.

Maxen opened his mouth to protest but I walked away from him, calling softly for my mothling. "Lunara."

The palm-sized mothling fluttered over to me, her purple feathered moth-like wings whispering gently. She settled on my shoulder with her four clawed feet, and I took comfort in her furry body pressing close to my cheek. Her antennae twitched in concern.

"It's all right," I told her. Her body rumbled, and I chuckled. I could never fool my pet. Usually she waited for me at home, but she must have sensed my swirling emotions today; she had firmly attached herself to me as I left the cottage earlier.

Lunara on my shoulder, I headed away from the training yard, passing through the stone archway and along the cobbled path. Set high above the main city, the realm's training yard had been a second home to me these past three years, but at times I felt suffocated there. Feeling the need for some quiet, I didn't stop walking until I reached the winding trail leading to the temple ruins. Hundreds of years before it had been the main place for Nosians to worship Arianrhod, the Moon Fate, but a newer temple had been built closer to the city and this one had fallen into disrepair. It was the place where I was most at peace in Nos. Here, I could be alone with the star-strewn sky and my thoughts with no interruptions.

Or so I had thought.

"You never came," a silky voice accused from the darkness. Lunara rumbled in happiness on my shoulder.

I turned swiftly around, searching the hidden alcoves for the source of the voice. A tap on my shoulder made me whirl back.

"Too slow," Kai said, his full lips widening in a smirk.

My heart pumped in my chest, but I slid a grin of my own onto my face. "Thought I'd let you win this one."

The smirk vanished. "Where were you? I waited for you."

"So, you thought because I didn't turn up, it was safe to sneak into Nos? If anyone found you here…" I trailed off as Kai let out his full, rich laugh – the one that made me tingle all over. I gave myself a mental shake. *Focus, Wen!*

For the first six months after the Choosing had gone wrong, I had been inconsolable. It had taken many talks with Meuric, potions from Alys and visits from Eva and Maxen before I could even leave my room. They were the darkest memories of my life. But I couldn't fool myself that the dark days were over. Darker ones crept ever closer.

The first time I had felt strong enough – thanks to one of Alys's tonics – to leave my room, I had sneaked away across the Twin Realms' shared farmland into the orchard, and Kai had been there. I let the memory wash over me…

My breath laboured in my chest; I sprinted as if I could out-run fate itself. But who was I fooling? Fate – my fate – had already been set in stone. There was only one other person in the whole of the Twin Realms who could understand what I was feeling right at that moment – and he was the only person I *couldn't* see.

Without thought or direction, my feet pounded over the grass, and before I knew it I was clambering

22

over the stile and into the quiet orchard. The branches hung bare. As I stood, panting, I stared at them at shock, before remembering it had been six months since I had left the comfort of the cottage. The picking season was long over.

The back of my neck began to tingle, and my breathing slowed as an immediate, calm awareness came over me.

"Wen…"

I froze, the blood in my veins turning to ice despite the warmth of the tone.

"Turn around, Wen."

I continued to stand, rooted to the spot, while the trees danced in front of me, black spots pinpricking my vision.

"*Please.*"

My body relented. I turned slowly, my gaze working its way up from brown boots to the tightly-fitting leather trousers and caramel-coloured tunic. My heart began to thud sluggishly as I continued my trailing gaze. Where my eyes usually would have stopped, I needed to continue. Kai had grown since I'd seen him last.

I finally landed on his tanned face; his blonde hair waved around his cheeks to settle on his shoulders. I met his eyes. I could have crumbled right there and then at the pain I saw there. A reflection of my own?

Dizzily, I turned away from him to collapse on a straw bale, my head in my hands.

A warmth pressed next to me. Suddenly, Kai was pulling me into his arms, rocking me as I wept.

I ranted incoherently, and he let me. Everything I'd kept bottled up inside me these last horrid months was released in a torrent of grief. We sat together for what felt like hours, but finally I straightened, and a charged silence fell between us.

I sniffed and focused on a point over his shoulder. "I'm sorry."

Kai gently tilted my chin up so my eyes were on his. "Don't you *ever* be sorry for your feelings, Wen. Fate knows how many times I've given in to mine lately." He held up a hand, the knuckles covered in bruises.

Immediately, I took it into my own hands and rubbed my thumb softly over them.

"I waited for you," he told me. "Every day, I came – either here or the caves... hoping you'd show up. But you never did. I even debated storming up to the Celestris' manor and demanding they arrange an audience with you." He gave a crooked grin, and my heart melted, imagining him confronting Eva's parents.

"Kai, I—" What could I say? That I had been too caught up in my own grief and fear to consider that he had been going through the same?

"It's all right. You're here now." He smiled, his eyes lighting up, but my heart sank. Didn't he realise it could never go back to the way it was before? Things were different... we were different.

I gently let go of his hand and stood, needing to create some distance between us. Both physically *and* emotionally.

I sensed the moment he realised something was amiss.

"Wen, no," he breathed out slowly. "It's still me – Kai, your best friend, the one who makes you snort-laugh at silly jokes... who can juggle four pears. And you – you…" He trailed off as my eyes locked onto his. "You're my Wen, *my* best friend, the one who I lose track of time around, the one person in the whole realms that I can be myself with!"

He stopped abruptly as I shook my head, my curls billowing around my head like a desolate cloud. Two and a half years seemed so far away, but still not long enough. It would never be long enough. How could I ever prepare myself to lose him?

He stepped up close and gripped my hands, and I realised again how much he had grown. His muscles had filled out too – and I was still, scrawny, small Wen, a shadow in his sunlight.

"We don't have to think about it. We can just meet up, like old times." I wavered. "Just once a month. I can't lose your friendship." His voice cracked.

My mouth opened, and I said, "All right," and pushed back the inner voice demanding whether I had lost my mind. I would rather lose my mind than lose him right now. He was the only one who understood, and I needed to cling to that. There was still time…

"Twin Realms to Wen." Kai waved his hand in front of my face, and I blinked away the memory.

I released a puff of breath. Since that moment we had met in secret every month – avoiding the caves in case we angered the Fates further – but lately it had got so much harder to push myself to go. Leaving him every time was breaking my heart, piece by tiny piece. Now it was time for me to be the strong one.

"I think it's best if we stop meeting up."

There: I had said it. I should have been proud of myself, but the desolate look on Kai's face had me questioning my decision.

"Whose idea was that? Maxen's?" he ground out, then shook his head, an unreadable look crossing his face.

Maxen? "Of course not. No one knows I still meet with you!" Was Kai *jealous*? A warm sensation grew in my chest, but was doused by ice-cold realisation. What good would it do if the friendship he felt for me had grown into something more? It was not fated to be.

Kai stepped closer, his face back to his usual sunny expression. "I'll make a deal with you. You continue to meet up with me, and I'll train with you. Perhaps you'll learn my weak spots," he teased.

We had never talked about training; the conversation had always steered clear of what our future held. We had simply been two friends sharing pears and jokes over the years.

Hope flared. Perhaps this way we could both come to terms with what we had to do, and by training with him, I could learn to distance myself and see him as what everyone else told me he was: my enemy.

But no. I knew that no matter how many times he knocked my feet out from under me or held a sword to my throat, I could never see him as that. To me, he was my Kai, and always would be... whatever happened.

But... I owed him this. He had held me while I sobbed in his arms that first time we had seen each other after the Choosing. He'd hidden his own grief at our forced separation and foggy future, while allowing me to give voice to my own. If he wanted to still meet so badly, then it was the least I could do. Perhaps we could, just for a few more hours, forget what our future held.

I nodded, and his eyes lit up with warmth. My cheeks burning, I was grateful when Lunara fluttered off my shoulder and landed on Kai's to croon and grumble at him. She never wanted to be left out.

"Ceridwen, are you up there?" Alys' soft voice floated up towards us.

I looked at Kai in horror. "Go! You can't be found here."

"I'll go, but promise to meet me tomorrow?" Kai handed Lunara back to me.

"Yes, yes, I'll be there," I promised. "Now go."

He reached out and tucked a stray curl behind my ear, and my skin ignited where his fingers lingered. I fought hard not to lean into his touch. "I'll see you tomorrow at noon," he said, and rounded a pillar, disappearing as if he'd never been there.

"There you are," Alys puffed out from behind me. "Maxen told me you headed off in this direction."

Pasting an innocent smile on my face, I turned around. "I needed a break," I told her, and she nodded sadly.

"I forget the burden you are carrying sometimes," she admitted. "I think we all do. The Council keep impressing on you how the fate of both realms lies in your – and Malakai's – hands. But it isn't fair. I don't know why the Fates did not favour your union. You should have been able to choose your own destiny." Her lips pursed angrily, and she came over to pull me into her arms. Lunara fluttered away to the top of the broken temple roof as I returned Alys' hug.

Cool tears pricked the back of my eyelids, but I could not let them fall. I had vowed never to cry again, not after that time when I had almost broken in Kai's arms. If I started crying I might never stop, dissolving the armour I had placed around myself.

Taller than Alys now, I pulled back and looked down at her. Much to everyone's surprise, I had caught up with, and then passed, my peers. Only the men were taller than me now.

"I'm tired," I told her, not acknowledging what she'd said. There was nothing more to be said about it. We both knew what must happen.

Even those amongst the Council who had questioned the prophecy had eventually had to come to terms with it all. Sabra had been questioned over and over, but she had been adamant about what she had seen. A powerful Seer and noble of Sol, no one had any reason to doubt her – especially as the survival of the realms was at stake. It was now accepted that, for the first time in the Twin Realms' history, a Fated Pairing had – for reasons unknown – been frowned upon by the Fates. Fated blood *must* be spilled to seal the rift in the Celestial Bridge, instead of being joined together. If it wasn't the bridge would fall, and Fog would no longer be held back.

"Come on. I've put some chocolate on the stove – I added your favourite ingredient," she wheedled, accepting my silent plea to change the subject.

My smile was genuine. Moonpepper did add a bit of a bite to Alys' famed hot chocolate – exactly how I liked it. With Lunara flying after us, we walked the trail back down to the city and to our small cottage, on the edge of the current Fated Pair's estate. They would now continue to rule until the next Fated Pair's union.

A pair usually ruled for twenty Fate's Days after their union. Chosen at fifteen, they had three years until they came of age to prepare to rule, learning etiquette and leadership skills from the current Fated Pair and the Council. I had none of that, merely continuing with my training with Meuric.

Knowing Eva's mother, she would relish in ruling until the Celestial Bridge had been repaired and a new Fated Pair chosen, trained and joined in union. She especially seemed to enjoy the pomp and glamour that came with overseeing the Council and ensuring the Twin Realms remained harmonious by setting out laws, handling disputes, and creating opportunities for prosperous trade. With a shudder, a small part of me gave thanks that I hadn't had to be mentored by her. I was sure we would have had vastly different ideas on what made a good ruler.

Would I get to see the balance restored after this next Fate's Day? Or was I to be a victim of fate? Either way, my future would not be a happy one – whether short-lived, or long and desperately lonely… and filled with guilt.

With a sigh, I followed Alys into the cottage and breathed in the spicy aroma of bitter hot chocolate. With the kitchen and living area one big space, the scent filled the whole lower floor and comforted me. Hopefully it would permeate my small bedroom in the attic too and stave off the nightmares, at least for one night.

Lunara gave a little rumble and fluttered over to her perch near the small kitchen window. She looked at me expectantly.

Chuckling, I dipped a thimble-sized cup into the chocolate and blew on it, before offering it to my mothling to drink.

"You spoil her," Alys said, but her eyes twinkled. I refrained from telling her that I had seen her dip frostberries in sugar and leave them out for Lunara only the day before.

"Al," I began. "When – if – I don't ma…"

I trailed off in surprise when Alys' eyes unexpectedly filled with tears. She had been stoic over the last few years, except for that one time she had demanded an audience with the Council. At first she simply couldn't accept that there wasn't a way around the prophecy. Eventually, she had been convinced by others that the Fates were not to be trifled with and this was their will. She never broke down in front of me, but the walls were thin; sometimes on nights I couldn't sleep and headed down to the kitchen, I heard her sobs and knew she had never really come to terms with it.

I turned away, guilt churning in my stomach, and filled up two more cups of chocolate. As Alys ran a hand through her closely cropped black hair, I held one out to her.

She took the cup with a trembling hand. "Don't be up too late. You have training with Meuric in the morning," she said softly, and I nodded in resignation.

I always had training.

Two

The moon dipped low in the sky, and I decided I would get up. Despite the soothing hot chocolate, sleep had eluded me. I had traced the moon's journey with my finger and watched not one, but two shooting stars arc across the sky. I hadn't bothered with wishes. Wishes were for the hopeful.

After doing my daily stretches, I pulled on my leather training trousers and tunic before stuffing my cold feet into thick socks and steel-toe-capped boots. If I was training with Meuric himself today, I had to be prepared. He wouldn't go easy on me.

Lunara, from her leafy nest on my bedside table, opened one tiny black eye, grumbled at me and fell back asleep. I watched her affectionately for a moment, wishing I could sleep as easily. But since I was up, I might as well start the day off right.

I crept down the steep ladder and into the kitchen area, not wanting to awaken Alys. Moving quietly, I made myself some porridge and left a few frostberries out for Lunara in case she woke before Alys. That wasn't likely – Lunara did like her sleep. Mothlings were nocturnal; Lunara had slowly adjusted to my sleeping patterns, but she usually liked to sleep in while I did my daily training.

I was rinsing out my dishes when a soft tap on the cottage door made me sigh. Wiping my hands, I walked over to answer it. Maxen leaned against the doorframe; his long blue-black hair was tightly braided in rows along his crown, leaving the rest to fall down his back in a silky waterfall. His steel-grey eyes regarded me warily.

"Morning," he said. "Ready for training?"

I grimaced. "Always."

I grabbed my leather jacket and joined him outside. Frost sparkled over the grass, and the air had a nip to it. It was always chilly in Nos in the morning, even during mid-spring as it was now. I was actually looking forward to working up a sweat and warming up a bit.

"Sorry I pushed you so hard yesterday," Maxen said as we walked along the path towards the training yard. "I'm worried about you."

Guilt prickled along my neck as I thought about seeing Kai last night. If Maxen knew I was still meeting him, I didn't think he would be so eager to keep helping me train.

"It's fine," I said, more gruffly than I intended. "You won't be working me as hard as I'm sure Meuric will today," I continued in a lighter tone.

"True. I don't envy you. Meuric was in a foul mood yesterday after the Council meeting. I think he and Sabra clashed again." Maxen raised one eyebrow at me and shook his head, then lowered his voice to a whisper. "She's demanding updates on you."

I stopped in the arched entryway to the yard. "How did you find that out?"

Maxen's gaze slid away from mine. "Eva – she overheard her parents talking about it."

"Why didn't she tell me herself?" I asked in confusion.

"She thought it would be better coming from me... she said you've been avoiding her."

The guilt was back, this time covering me like a shroud. I *had* been avoiding Eva since she'd come of age and stopped training with us, but not because of that. To be honest with myself, I was avoiding everyone. I only bothered with Maxen because he was like my shadow lately.

"I'll talk to her later," I promised, "but tell me what Sabra said." Why was the head of the Sol Council keeping tabs on me? Surely she wanted her own candidate to win. Malakai was the literal golden child, and everyone believed he would win. Even my own classmates.

"If you two are quite finished gossiping?" a voice remarked, and a shadow fell over us as Meuric stepped in front of us.

"Later," Maxen assured me, and moved into the yard with a bow for our mentor.

Frustrated, I watched him join the other young men and women in our class. Most of them would be coming of age soon and would begin looking for a trade or a union with another. That was not in my future. I turned eighteen in three weeks, and six days after that would be Fate's Day, when my destiny would be sealed.

"Lady Ceridwen?"

Meuric jolted me out of my thoughts, and I followed him into the yard. I *really* wished he would stop calling me that, but he always spoke formally to me when the others were around. I ignored the scornful looks from some of them. Their opinion of me hadn't changed much in the last three years, and I hadn't done a lot to try and improve it. I had bigger things to worry about.

"I'll be training Lady Ceridwen one-on-one today; Maxen, you can pair up the others to work on their drills," Meuric announced.

A harsh laugh came from the back of the group, followed by "Good luck with her," and Meuric's eyes flashed. "Gus, you can start with ten laps up and down the steps."

Now it was my turn to hide a laugh, as Gus scowled darkly. He pushed his way through the group. His jet-black hair had been cropped close to his head; that was new since yesterday – perhaps he thought it made him look tougher. His watery grey eyes flicked over at me as he sullenly made his way out of the yard.

I'd probably pay for that next time I was paired with him, but for now it gave me satisfaction to know that however hard Meuric trained me, he still had my back. I turned to give him a grateful smile, but the sword pointed at my throat made me falter.

"*Always* be on your guard," Meuric told me tightly, and tossed another sword towards me. With a clash of metal, we began.

I tried my best to ignore the others training behind me, but as Meuric and I continued our slightly clumsy dance – the clumsy part being mine – I became aware of the silence starting to surround us as they stopped to watch.

Sweat dripped into my brow, and I wished I'd had the foresight to braid my unruly curls instead of tying them back loosely. I sidestepped a particularly deadly thrust and felt a thrill run through me. Despite having trained hard since almost three years ago, I hadn't made a lot of progress. Secretly, I hadn't wanted to. Excelling in swordfighting would have been like accepting the fact that I intended to fight Kai. I would never be a match for him, even if I *wanted* to be.

But maybe, despite it all, I was inadvertently getting the hang of it. As I twirled away and leapt up onto a stone bench, my chest heaving, I parried and caught the edge of Meuric's blade. He lost his grip, and the sword clattered to the floor.

I crowed with delight as adrenaline surged through me. Pausing, I held out my hand to shake Meuric's at a good fight, but tripped off the bench and landed flat on my back. Meuric's upside-down face peered at me as he held his sword to my chest. I could see the exasperation in his eyes, but he didn't voice it.

Someone else did, however. "Fates above, she's getting worse not better."

"Ten more laps, Gus," Meuric said without breaking eye contact with me.

I heard a huff and boots stomping away.

"Take a break," Meuric told me, helping me up.

I grabbed my sword and strode from the training yard without a backwards glance. Gus was right, I *was* getting worse; I wasn't fooling anyone, especially myself. I walked away from the yard and over the grassy cliff top, swishing my blade through the tops of the grass.

I looked up at the sky, where the sun was climbing higher. I thought of my planned meeting with Kai and hesitated. I shouldn't go. I should go back to the training yard and work with Meuric. Time was running out. Meeting Kai would only distract me.

But as I stood looking below me to Sol and its blinding beaches, my hesitation disappeared. I missed him. I missed my best friend, and the fact that I could be my true self around him.

Determined, I turned around and headed to the realms' shared fields. I'd tell Meuric I had felt unwell and gone home.

I kept to the hedges – I didn't want any of the workers tending to the crops spotting me. Who knew who reported back to Meuric... or Sabra, for that matter? She already had eyes on me. I climbed over the stile, my sword in its scabbard banging against my leg.

Jumping down, I landed hard, and mud splattered up my trousers. Great. Grabbing a large leaf and wiping the worst of it off, at first I didn't notice the two figures a little distance away in deep discussion next to a large pear tree. Dropping the leaf, I realised it was Kai and a girl.

The girl was facing away from me; her long, straight, sunny blonde hair hung down her back. She was obviously from Sol. Nosians and Solians took on the appearance of the place where they were born, the Fates blessing them with the traits and appearance of that realm. Solians practically glowed with their various shades of white, blonde or golden hair, blue eyes, and tanned skin. Right now, I felt woefully inadequate with my Nosian black hair, silver-grey eyes, and pale skin. The girl gestured wildly, her hands moving rapidly, then jabbed a finger at Kai's chest. He backed up with a laugh, rubbing at the sore spot. With a gesture of exasperation, the girl threw up her hands, before pulling Kai close in a hug.

My stomach somersaulted as I watched Kai return the embrace, rubbing the girl's back in a placatory gesture. Unsettled, I remembered him doing the same with me.

I ducked behind a tree as the girl headed my way. She passed close by, her long hair shielding her face from me. A warm, floral scent met my nostrils as she passed by. *Not only does she have amazing hair, but she smells great too*, I thought in dismay. Looking down at my mud-splattered trousers, scuffed boots and chipped nails, I sighed, then peered around the tree. Kai sat on a stack of hay bales, his legs swinging, a pile of pears next to him.

My heart skipped a beat, and before I knew it my traitorous legs were walking towards him. Perhaps I imagined it, but I was sure his bright blue eyes lit up as I approached. He threw a pear at me, and for once I didn't fumble it, but actually caught it one-handed.

"Nice," Kai said.

My tongue tingled with the urge to ask who the girl had been, but I didn't want him to think I'd been spying on him... and I certainly didn't want him to think it actually bothered me. But it did. Blindsided, I realised it bothered me to the point of pain.

"How's training going?" I blurted out, then fought an eye roll. Of course training would be going well for him.

Kai grinned and hopped down from the hay. "Why don't I show you?"

His tone was teasing, but his eyes had turned serious. His sword whispered as he withdrew it from its sheath and took a stance in front of me.

Slowly, I dropped the pear and withdrew my own sword. The effect was somewhat marred when it got caught on the edge of the leather scabbard. I laughed nervously as I planted my feet evenly.

His eyes boring deep into mine, Kai sidestepped before thrusting forward. My nervousness must have a lit a fire within me, as I met it with a clang and pushed back, moving his sword out of range.

"I always enjoyed watching you fight at the joint candidate training sessions. Your moves almost have a dance-like quality," Kai mused as he parried, then ducked.

I gaped at him, almost losing my footing as I thought back to the days before our fateful Choosing, and how the candidates from both Nos and Sol had trained together once a fortnight. All Twin Realm teenagers were trained in combat in case of a Shadowwraith attack – until they came of age at eighteen and either joined the Guard or started another trade. They could also join in union with another from within their realm. As tradition dictated, only the Chosen Fated Pair couples were one from each realm, their rule a symbol of the Twin Realms joining together.

"I know what you're trying to do, but distraction won't work," I told Kai.

"It's true. You've always been graceful to me," he countered, his voice growing husky. Without warning, his sword was against mine; with a flick he had my blade flying through the air, landing with a swish in the hay bales. He stepped up close to me, his breath blowing the curls from my cheek, his sword hanging loosely by his side. "And are you sure distraction won't work?"

His eyes locked on mine; my breath hitched. I moistened my lips, and his gaze dropped to follow my tongue's progress. Heat curled low in my belly and I closed my eyes. Immediately, my mind was filled with the memory of the girl who had just left the orchard.

I stepped back and scowled. "Nice trick," I said, and stomped over to get my sword.

"It wasn't a tr—" Kai started, before another voice filled the air.

"What do you two think you're *doing?*"

Three

Sabra, in robes of sea-blue, strode across the orchard towards us, her eyes fierce and her face livid.

I pulled my sword from the hay and tried to hide it behind my back, then swallowed hard and moved away from Kai. He raised one perfect blonde eyebrow at me, but he didn't look the slightest bit flustered at being caught by his mentor.

"I will ask you again, what do you think you are doing?" Not giving either of us a chance to answer, Sabra continued, "How long has this been going on?"

"Long enough," Kai said with a shrug.

My head whipped around to stare at him questioningly. What did he mean by that?

"Lady Ceridwen, return to Nos at once. I will be speaking to Meuric about this. I cannot believe the *stupidity*, the risks! Do you want our realms to suffer? There is a way this must be done, and you two making light of it in this way is just deplorable!" Sabra marched up and down in front of us, her eyes sparking blue fire. "You cannot chance spilling each other's blood now."

A flush of shame worked its way up my cheeks. Of course I didn't want to risk the realms.

"I'm sorry, Mistress Sabra," I said, hanging my head. I didn't want to see the accusation on the older lady's face, and I couldn't bear to meet Kai's eyes – not when the next time I would be looking at them might be when we came face to face to fight for real in a few weeks' time.

I moved away from them both, only pausing when Kai said, "Wen..." His voice was full of anguish.

Without looking back at him, I shook my head and moved on, sheathing my sword with an angry thrust – one that would have made Meuric proud and Gus' eyes widen in shock.

As I was climbing over the stile, I saw the blonde girl hovering nearby. One look at her face, and her guilt was plain for all to see. I didn't recognise her; she'd never attended training with the other Sol candidates.

"I'm sor—" she started, but I didn't give her chance to explain.

"Save it." I hated the way my voice cracked. They were welcome to each other. I was fed up with Kai's tricks and Sol's perfect citizens. I longed for my cool realm and the midnight sky.

My legs ate up the ground, fuelled by my anger; before I realised it, I was back at the now-empty training yard. Everyone else must have broken for lunch.

I placed my sword into a rack on the wall and sat with a huff on the bench to wait for Meuric. It would probably be better coming from me. I hoped Sabra hadn't had the chance to send a message yet.

I guess that would be a yes, I thought as Meuric strode towards me, his long grey braid flapping behind him, his pewter eyes like storm clouds.

He tossed a creamy scroll of parchment at my feet. "What is the meaning of that?" He gestured as if it were one of Sol's poisonous sandsnakes.

Stupidly hoping it was an invitation to a party at the upcoming Fate's Day Festivale, I hunkered down, picked up the scroll and read Sabra's scathing summary of what she had witnessed in the orchard.

"Ah," I murmured.

"Ah, indeed. Come on, Ceridwen. I thought you were cleverer than this. Don't you see how he – and perhaps others – could be manipulating this situation… your feelings for him?"

I looked up sharply. How did he know? Was it that obvious? Did everyone know? Questions and embarrassment battled in my mind, but anger made a swift appearance and won out.

"Perhaps *I* was using the situation!" I seethed, but even to my own ears it sounded false.

Meuric's mouth clamped shut as he looked at me, various emotions rippling across his face. After a moment, he sighed. "Whatever it is, you are both called before the Council tomorrow. You can explain it to them."

"The Council?" I sat back down and stared into space. How could I possibly explain what was going on when I didn't understand it myself? Recently Kai's behaviour had changed – instead of the teasing, joking boy I knew, he had been more intense and tactile. I had half-hoped it was because he was beginning to feel what I had always felt, but now I was wondering if Meuric

42

was right and it was all a ruse, a tactic to throw me off guard. Well, if that was the game he was playing, then he'd already won. I was too weak to resist him; I always had been. One look at that bright wide smile and I was lost. Perhaps it was fate.

Meuric took a seat beside me and patted my leg awkwardly. "Try not to worry about it now. Go for a run, spend time with your pet or with Alys." He looked uncomfortable, and despite the situation I had to hold back a grin. Meuric was your go-to man when you had a weapon question or needed advice about which stone would build a better barricade... but anything to do with emotions and he was all at sea.

"Knock, knock," a bubbly voice said. I looked up to see Eva tapping against the stone archway.

"Ah, Miss Eva. Perhaps you could cheer up Lady Ceridwen," Meuric said in a relieved voice, standing up. "I'll – ah – go and clean the swords."

Eva sauntered over to me, all voluptuous curves and shimmering hair in a waterfall of midnight black. Her grey eyes were worried. "What's up, Wen?"

I played with the frayed cuff on my tunic, before answering her. "Oh, you know, the fact that I either have to die or become a murderess."

I wasn't sure why I didn't tell her the truth. Perhaps it was because ever since she had turned eighteen and gained more freedom, I sensed a chasm growing between us. She went out with the other girls, shopping for dresses, going out on dates... planning for her future. A future I couldn't even dream of having. My dreams had died three years ago.

"Right, that's it – no more wallowing. You are sleeping at mine tonight." She held up a perfectly manicured hand as I opened my mouth to protest. "You can bring Lunara, she can keep Aruna company."

Lunara had been a gift from Eva's parents the Fate's Day after I had been Chosen. They had hatched a pair from their own mothlings; the purple one had been given to me, and the navy blue one to Eva. Only the most elite of Nos owned such rare pets.

Knowing Eva would only continue to nag, I gave in. "All right. I'll be up later on."

"There's a good girl." Eva nodded in approval, and I fought not to roll my eyes. "Oh, come for dinner. It will give me some company – Mummy and Daddy have business guests over."

Despite being the realm's current Fated Pair, Eva's parents didn't rest on their laurels; their vineyard made a special blend of mead made from night-blooming grapes and the honey from nocturnal bees only found in Nos. The honey had a smokier taste to it, thanks to the flowers they favoured. The nectar from the Lady's Starlight flower was perfect for creating a uniquely flavoured honey.

"Sure," I agreed. "Anything to keep Eva happy."

"No need to be snarky," Eva admonished, so I leaned over to give her a quick hug. "Watch the hair," she said, pulling back. "I just had it done at the salon."

"It looks nice," I said in an attempt to be more friendly. And it did. I wished my hair could look so sleek and stylish, but my mass of curls could never be tamed like that.

"Oh, the salon gave me some serum – we can use it on your hair later and try out some styles to wear at the Festivale." Eva had the uncanny gift of always knowing what I was thinking.

I smiled weakly. The last thing I wanted was to think about the Festivale – the weeklong festival that ran up to Fate's Day, filled with rides and stalls and events; it was the perfect chance for both Nos and Sol citizens to get together and enjoy each other's company. The Shadowmists beneath the Celestial Bridge mysteriously disappeared for that one week. The Festivale had been created to celebrate the fact the citizens could enjoy the shared lands without fear of the Shadowmists swirling in and making them lose their way.

"Sure," I repeated.

"Perfect!" Eva exclaimed. "I'll see you at six."

I waved at her; she sauntered out of the training yard, giving her cat-that-got-the-cream smile as a few young men walked in and gave her their usual open-mouthed stares. This time I did roll my eyes.

"You two made up then?" Maxen asked as he joined me. He never looked at Eva the way the other men did – at the moment his eyes were all for me. It made me uncomfortable. I could never feel about him the way I suspected he did about me.

"We're fine. I'm staying over at hers tonight," I told him, and he smiled in relief. He always hated to be stuck in the middle. Restless, I suggested, "How about a race up the climbing wall?"

"You're on." He followed me over to the stone wall at the side of the yard. Pegs stuck out at intervals for hand and footholds, but for the most part you had to use skill and strength to make it safely up the wall.

"I can't watch," Gus told the others melodramatically, but a few of the girls shouted up encouragement.

Throwing a grin over my shoulder, I started climbing. I might be clumsy on the ground, but climbing was my strength. Maxen knew this, so I knew he was only humouring me, but it still felt good when I reached the top first. To the sounds of whoops and "Go, Wen!" from below, Maxen pulled himself up behind me and sat with his legs dangling over the edge.

"I think you've got even faster," he said good-naturedly.

"I think so too," I agreed, and for a few minutes we sat in companionable silence.

It was broken by Meuric shouting up, "Are you two going to come down at any point? These swords won't clean themselves."

"Last one down is on cleaning duty!" I sing-songed, before putting my foot on the rope and sliding down.

"Hey, not fair!" Maxen shouted, but I was already at the bottom.

"See you tomorrow," I called, and tried to do a fair impression of Eva by sauntering out of the yard.

The smile slid from my face as a boot appeared out of nowhere and tripped me up. "You are so clumsy," Gus said, with a smirk hovering around his thin lips. His small eyes peered down at me in mock sympathy.

"Yeah, well, apparently people fall over if you trip them up," I shot back, clambering to my feet.

Immediately, his expression changed. "Just let Malakai kill you and do everyone a favour. Nos doesn't need you."

I watched him go with my stomach churning. The worst part was, he was right. What could *I* offer Nos?

All I would do, come Fate's Day, was embarrass the realm when everyone saw how easily Kai defeated me. All this training was useless. In the end, everyone knew Kai was a far superior fighter... and the far superior person to survive. He would bring honour to his realm, and he was so beloved by all that no one would be angry at his victory. No one, save a few, would mourn my loss.

Even I knew he was the better option.

Four

"Best behaviour, Lunara," I murmured to my mothling as I pressed the large gold bell on Eva's parents' manor front door.

I had enjoyed the long walk up the path from the cottage. The stars were coming out, and peacefulness flowed over me beneath the moonlight. The flowerbeds full of Lady's Starlight soothed my senses with their smoky aroma, so I was almost content by the time I stood at the large black-and-silver double door.

Crane, Eva's family's butler, opened the door and peered down solemnly at me. "Good evening, Lady Ceridwen."

"Good evening, Crane," I replied, and entered the foyer. I took a moment to look up at the domed ceiling, where a mosaic of the constellations was featured. The focal point was the constellation Celestri, for which Eva's family were named. A prominent noble family, a large proportion of the realms' Fated Pairs had come from this line. The same went for Malakai's family—it appeared the Fates favoured those two lines… but not *my* Pairing with Malakai.

Heels click-clacking down the wide central staircase caught my attention.

"Oh, I thought it was our guests." Salomé Celestri, Eva's mother, didn't bother to hide her disappointment upon seeing me standing in the entrance hall. Her turquoise eyes glared down at me from her heart-shaped face, surrounded by bright blonde hair, while her full red lips pursed into a pout.

For some unknown reason, she didn't like me. She barely tolerated my presence, in fact, and frowned upon Eva's friendship with me. Eva's father was the complete opposite. It would have been easy to assume that *he* was from the realm of Sol, and not his wife, with his sunny disposition and good nature.

"Eva is in the drawing room," Salomé carried on.

"Thank you, Lady Celestri." I nodded politely. As the older lady's eyes narrowed on Lunara, I made a quick getaway, heading down the long, marbled hallway towards the drawing room and leaving Salomé to berate Crane for not announcing me. "I know, I know," I told my mothling as she grumbled in my ear. "She doesn't like us – that's why we need to be on our best behaviour, all right?"

I entered the drawing room and saw Eva standing by the open stained-glass doors, nursing a wine glass full of purple liquid – no doubt a superior year from the Celestri Vineyard.

"Oh, good, you came. I was beginning to think I would have to endure this tedious dinner alone. Hi, Lunara," Eva purred at my mothling, tickling her furry purple belly. Lunara preened happily as Eva placed her on a perch next to her own navy-blue mothling, Aruna. The pair chirped happily to one another.

Apparently, I was distinctly underdressed. Eva wore a long, blue-black sheath dress of silk, with sky-high glittery silver heels. I stared down at my black trousers and blouse. At least my boots were clean, I conceded with a grimace.

"Drink?" Eva didn't even wait for my answer before pressing a glass into my hand. "You're going to need it," she muttered, and I wondered how many she'd had already.

"Eva, darling, please wait for dinner." Salomé appeared and took the glass from her daughter's hand, setting it down with a clink on a nearby side table. She threw a tight smile in my direction, as if it was my fault Eva was drinking already.

"Oh yes, the business dinner – or should I say barter dinner?"

Tension filled the air as Salomé shot daggers at her daughter before giving me a pointed look.

I put my untouched drink down and hefted my overnight bag. "Perhaps I should go…" I trailed off as Eva pulled me to her side, took my bag and set it down again.

"Absolutely not. I need some moral support tonight. My parents are trying to pair me off with the son of their business partner."

"Yes, well, a young lady should make a satisfactory union," Salomé said. Though her words were innocent enough, I knew they were directed at me. My and Kai's Pairing had been far from 'satisfactory'.

"Ugh, Mother," Eva said, and rolled her eyes. She picked up her glass and drank deeply. "Can't I at least be trusted to make my own Pairing? It's not as though it will go as horribly wrong as—" She stopped abruptly as she realised what she had said.

This time *I* downed my drink, and said, "I need to use the bathroom."

"Wen, I'm sorry," Eva said, her face stricken. She looked down at her wineglass as if it had left a sour taste in her mouth.

But it wasn't the wine; it was her words that had been sour. "It's fine," I murmured and left the room, avoiding looking at Lady Celestri. I could sense her avid scrutiny of me. Her amusement at my discomfort had claws – ones that reached out to cut me.

I walked as fast as I could without breaking into a run, heading down the hallway and into the downstairs powder room, locking the door behind me. I gripped the scalloped basin until my knuckles turned white and stared at my reflection in the gilded mirror. My silver eyes looked enormous in my pale face. What had I been thinking, imagining I could get away from my problems for a few hours? They followed me wherever I went. I should have stayed in my room and read a good book instead.

A soft knock sounded on the door. "Wen, are you all right?"

I took a deep breath and forced a smile onto my face before unlocking the door. Eva leaned against the door frame, her eyes wary.

"I'm fine. The mead just went to my head," I said, not meeting her eyes.

"You always were a terrible liar," she said, linking her arm through mine and walking us back to the drawing room. "I've told Mother to behave, and I won't have any more wine. It tends to get me into trouble."

I gave her a sideways look – that was an understatement. At her Coming-of-Age party she had almost broken her neck by taking a dare to climb down the mountain into the Shadowmist-strewn valley. The drop alone was deadly, never mind the risk of a Shadowwraith attack. Luckily Maxen and I had talked her out of it.

As we entered the drawing room, Crane came up behind us and announced the Celestri's guests. "Master and Mistress Ostara, and Lord Malakai Ostara."

I stopped cold at the announcement and looked accusingly at Eva, who paled. "I didn't know who was coming, I *swear*. Mother told me they were new business partners and their son!"

Bile rose in my throat, and I hurried forward to grab my bag, then looked at the perch. Aruna sat alone on the perch, and the previously opened double doors were now tightly shut.

"Where's Lunara?" I demanded, my voice unnaturally high-pitched.

Salomé raised an airy hand. "Oh, I think she flew out, but I was cold, so I closed the doors."

"What?" I seethed, all pretence at good manners out the window. "I have to find her!"

Eva gave me a jerky nod. Over her shoulder, I watched a gorgeous pair of sunny Sols enter the room, their inner glow lighting up the space, followed by Eva's father, Cosimo, and… *Kai.*

The honeyed wine threatened to escape up my throat. I backed away, but not before Kai's laser-like blue gaze landed on me, almost pinning me in place like a moth on a specimen board.

Eva's father opened his mouth to speak to me, but I turned away, opening the drawing room doors and escaping out into the garden. Lady Celestri's scathing words followed me. "Really, for a Lady of the realm, that girl has no manners…"

My bag bumping along my back, I hurried down the glowing gravelled moonstone path, calling for Lunara. I raged inside. I knew Eva's mother didn't like me, but to lock my pet outside was beyond even what I had thought she was capable of. I didn't believe Lunara would go fluttering off, either – not when she had been cosied up to Aruna. Perhaps she'd thought I had gone home and had gone looking for me. Whatever had happened, I needed to find her before a night predator got to her.

I didn't want to think about Kai and Eva, and their parents plotting and planning amongst themselves, but it was hard not to fixate on it. Everyone knew Kai had a future before him, and they were already preparing for it. But what about me? How could Eva go along with her mother's schemes? Was I so easily forgotten about – discarded? *I* was the other half of Kai's Fated Pair. It should be me he was preparing for.

No doubt Lady Celestri had no intention of allowing me to stay for dinner; she had just wanted to humiliate me first. I shook my head, my curls bouncing around my head like an angry cloud, as I moved through the neatly trimmed gardens. "Lunara!" I called, my voice taking on a desperate edge.

A voice like warm butter made me turn. "Lost something?"

I pursed my lips as I looked at Kai, Lunara nestled up against his neck, standing against a stone arch.

Sneaky little mothling, I thought. But I wasn't really angry; I was just relieved to see Lunara safe. Although the way Kai was looking at me, I didn't know if *I* was. There were more than Nos predators in the garden tonight.

"Lunara, come," I said softly, and after a final nuzzle of Kai's neck, she swooped over to me and grumbled on my shoulder. "We will have words later," I whispered to her.

More settled, I looked back at Kai. "Shouldn't you be getting back to your dinner party?" I didn't add *with your intended future in-laws*, but the words hung in the air, hovering between us, sharper than any swords we could wield. Kai's eyes flashed.

"I would rather be out here," he said pointedly. *With you*, my treacherous heart added, and a blush burned my cheeks.

"It is a lovely night," I said innocently, gazing up at the full, lavender-hued moon.

His breath warmed my cheek as he stepped nearer. "It is indeed." But his eyes were on me, and his face was close, too close, when I turned his way.

"Malakai, darling. Do come in," a warm, rich voice called from the patio.

Kai sighed. "Duty calls," he said to me, before answering louder, "Coming, Mother."

I edged away. "Don't let me keep you," I bit at him, my voice filled with a revealing hurt.

"Aren't you—?" Kai gestured to the house.

"No." I shook my head. *Absolutely not.* There was no way I was going back in there to spend a torturous evening watching Eva flirt with Kai; she couldn't help herself when a handsome young man was nearby, even if he might be the cause of her best friend's death. Would she stoop that low? I just didn't know who to trust any more.

"Well, goodnight then," Kai said. "I'll see you tomorrow." He smiled at me and turned away.

What? Did he actually think I would meet him after what had happened today? "Tomorrow?" I demanded, jerking my shoulder up in confusion. Lunara groused at me as she clung on with her tiny claws.

"Yes, tomorrow. The Council meeting, remember? Both of us have to be there." He stared at me in concern as if I had gone crazy.

Perhaps I *had* gone crazy, because I had completely forgotten about it, but it all came rushing back. Sabra's disapproval and Meuric's disappointment. How could I have forgotten? Maybe my brain had tried to block it out. Our mentors knew us well, but the other Council members not so much; what would their reaction be at us meeting up in secret – potentially jeopardising the Fates' prophecy, and the future of the realms? My stomach churned at the possible ways we could be punished. But what could they do that was worse than our fate?

I swallowed hard. "I'll be there," I told him. What choice did I have? "Go on. They're waiting for you."

Kai hesitated as if he wanted to stay, but what was the use in drawing out this moment? One of our futures was soon to be cut short. What was the point in any of it? As tinkling laughter filtered out from the drawing room doors, my heart clenched. I didn't belong here.

I walked away without a backward glance, but from the absence of crunching gravel, I guessed that Kai watched me go.

Five

I paused outside the cottage door. What could I tell Alys? She thought I was spending the night at Eva's.

I was about to push open the door and face the music when voices on the other side made me drop my hand. I could make out Alys's gentle tones, but the deeper timbre had me racking my brain for who might visit her at this hour. I didn't intend to eavesdrop, but my name being spoken piqued my interest and before I knew it, I had cracked the door open to peep inside.

Meuric sat with his back to me at the small wooden kitchen table. Alys was out of sight behind one of the old beams that held up my attic room.

"It's not fair, Ric," Alys said. "She's been training so hard, but I fear it's all for naught. She doesn't stand a chance."

Even you, Alys? I thought sadly.

"Don't give up hope. She might surprise us all," Meuric said, and took a sip of his drink.

"This is all my fault." Alys moved into view, wringing a cloth in her hands. "I should never have allowed her benefactor to pay for her to join your class. I should have kept her here, safe, and trained her myself in the ways of Healing. Then she never would have been picked as a candidate."

"Then the fault lies with me. I thought she would make a good ruler for the realms; that's why I put her up as a candidate. You mustn't blame yourself, Alys. You thought you were doing the best for her – we both did. Placing her alongside the children of the other noble families in the hope of being Chosen – it was a great honour. Well, it should have been… I still don't know what went wrong."

My head reeled. I had a secret benefactor? I listened closer. Lunara adjusted herself on my shoulder and nestled into my neck. Apparently, she didn't find this as fascinating as I did.

"You haven't found out anything more?" Alys took a seat opposite Meuric, and I drew back a little. I didn't want to be caught now, not when I was hearing so many revelations about my own past – and future.

"No. I've been trying to work closely with Sabra, but she prefers to work alone, so it's a battle to get her to share information sometimes. She has always had what seems to me like a direct path to the Fates. They favour her with their visions, and although hard to decipher at times, they usually come true." Meuric set down his cup and pushed back his chair.

"So Ceridwen *will* have to fight to the death, then?"

Meuric stood, and a long, telling pause filled the small area. "It certainly appears that way."

I scuttled backwards into the shadows as the door opened wider and Meuric stepped out, Alys following.

Hidden from view, I heard Alys say, "I can't lose her." Her voice cracked with emotion, and my heart broke a tiny bit more.

"I will do everything I can to stop that from happening," Meuric promised, laying a hand on Alys' shoulder and giving it a gentle squeeze. His voice rang with a steely certainty that had me questioning what I'd always thought about Meuric's belief in me. Perhaps he knew of a way I could actually win.

But did I *want* to win? Of course I didn't want to die, but did I want to live, knowing what it would cost? Not only would I lose my Fated Partner, but I would lose a piece of myself – a piece that, once something so hideous had been enacted, would cease to be. I would die myself, inside.

Lost in my thoughts, I hadn't noticed Meuric leave or the door to the cottage close. I sat in the shadows long enough for my feet to go numb from my cramped position. Lunara grumbled at me, and I realised she was probably getting cold, or more than likely hungry. The downstairs light clicked off; Alys must have gone to her room. That made it easier – I wouldn't have to come up with an excuse for why I was home early.

I rifled in my pocket for my key, knowing that Alys would have locked the door if she had settled down for the night. Letting myself in, I locked the door behind me, moved quietly through into the kitchen, and put together a dish of frostberries and nuts for Lunara. I grabbed some bread and cheese for myself and took it all up to my room.

Exhaustion hit me, so I transferred Lunara to her nest, kicked off my boots and lay on my bed, food forgotten. I needed to close my eyes for a moment.

Swirling mists cloaked me, cutting off my vision. I searched about with my hands, but couldn't grab on to anything. I knew I had to keep going, so I shuffled cautiously along, my feet sliding on the slick surface beneath me. *I'm on the Celestial Bridge,* I realised as the mists parted briefly and I made out the long stretch of it before me. Shapes moved in the distance, and I wondered who it could be.

"Go back, Wen!" a voice shouted.

Another added, in jeering tones, "You don't belong here."

A hand roughly gripped my wrist, nails – painted a dark, fiery red – digging in deep. "You should have perished on this bridge when you were a baby – but no matter. You will perish on here soon enough."

I gasped, the words cutting deeper than the nails did. "You're wrong! I deserve to live!" I cried, trying to make out the face in the mist.

Long, white – no, was it blonde hair? – whipped in front of me, but the face remained obscured. Whoever it was, they were trying to stay hidden, but the voice felt eerily familiar.

Lunara swooped in, diving for the mysterious figure's face. With a screech, they let go and I was free, but to my horror Lunara was batted violently away and plummeted over the bridge, her wings unmoving.

"*No!*" I woke up screaming and sat bolt upright in bed, desperately searching for Lunara in the dim light. I saw her tiny, furry body curled up safely in her nest and breathed a sigh of relief. "Just a dream," I comforted myself.

Lunara opened one eye, grumbled, and then went back to sleep. I ran a gentle hand over her to confirm she truly was safe and whole before I lay back down. With a curse, I realised I had probably awakened Alys, but no gentle face peeped above the ladder. Curious; she usually came when I had a nightmare. Sitting back up, movement outside my window caught my attention. Alys, in a hooded cloak, walked down the path leading from the manor. Her face was mostly hidden, but I couldn't mistake the two silver tracks of tears working their way down her pale face.

Where had she been? And why was she crying? This felt different to the eavesdropping last night. This felt like it shouldn't be witnessed by anyone – it was personal, it was powerful, it was grief.

I withdrew from the window and sat back on my bed, listening as the door opened and closed softly. A light flickered on, and the sound of water running filtered up to me. As the aroma of chamomile and heartsbane wafted up the ladder, I knew that whatever ailed Alys was troubling. That remedy was the cure for heartbreak.

Nibbling on my lip, I debated whether to go down, but Alys decided for me. "You can come down, Wen. I can sense your indecision from here."

She always did have an uncanny knack where I was concerned. I scooted off my bed and padded over to the ladder. Lunara didn't stir.

Down in the kitchen, I looked sheepishly at Alys. "I didn't stay at Eva's," I said.

"I can see that," Alys said, and took a fortifying sip of her drink.

"Everything all—" we said at the same time and broke off, laughing. I gestured to Alys to carry on.

She set her cup down and came over to draw me into a hug. "Anything you want to talk about?" she asked.

It was on the tip of my tongue to mention what I had overheard yesterday – my curiosity at who my secret benefactor was and why they were helping me. But after a moment, I shook my head. "No, just the usual worries," I told her, stepping out of the hug.

Sadness swirled in her eyes for a moment before she smiled. "Well, seeing as we're both up, how about some breakfast?"

I gave her a grateful smile back. I didn't like having secrets between us, but I was actually scared to find out the truth. Would it even change anything? My future was set in stone, unless a miracle happened; knowing that a secret someone had been looking out for me wouldn't change the outcome of my and Kai's destiny.

Soon the small area was filled with the scents of honeyed batter and chocolate. "There you are." Alys plated up the pancakes and set them in front of me with a bowl of frostberries.

My stomach grumbled appreciatively, and I picked up a juicy, plump berry. Before I could take a bite, a whirring of wings warned me of an impending ambush. Lunara whipped the berry from my fingers with one of her four taloned feet and swooped away to her perch.

"Cheeky mothling!" I admonished, while Alys burst out laughing.

Lunara grumbled back at me from around a mouthful of frostberry and I shook my head. Feeling lighter, I finished my breakfast and looked at the clock.

Alys followed my gaze, and her face fell. "Do you want me to come to the Council chambers with you?" I didn't ask how she knew about the meeting. Meuric had always been good at keeping Alys updated of my progress, where I tended to skip over it.

I shook my head and took my dishes to the sink, dumping them in the soapy water. "No, it's fine. I think I'll take a walk first – clear my head a bit." I forced a bit of inflection into my tone, not wanting it to come out hollow, the way I was feeling inside.

"All right," Alys agreed. "But come and find me afterwards. I'll be in the forest today, collecting herbs and flowers; my stores are running a bit low."

"Will do," I replied, ignoring the knots forming in my stomach. Perhaps the third pancake had been a bad idea. I ducked into the small washroom and splashed cold water on my face. The pallor of my skin made me grimace; I wasn't going to make a good impression with the Council members looking like this. I rifled through the cabinet and found the makeup set Eva had gifted me last Yule.

I tried to tame my curls, but it was like fighting a losing battle, even with the hair cream Alys made for me. In the end, I left them loose – I was more comfortable that way, anyway. I added a touch of blusher and a little mascara. I still wanted to look like me, but less like a sleepy ghost. *Ugh, that will have to do*, I thought, replacing the tiny brush back in its pot and tossing it back into the case. I was putting off the inevitable. It was time to go.

Lunara fluttered onto my shoulder as I left the washroom. "Look after Alys, all right? I'll be back soon," I told her. Lunara knew I usually went to training, but she must have sensed something different about today.

With a grumble and a nuzzle she flew off and settled against Alys's neck. I looked into Alys's eyes for a moment, fortifying myself with the strength I saw in hers.

"You are a Lady of Nos. Hold your head high," she said.

With a determined nod, I squared my shoulders, tossed back my curls and left the cottage.

Six

I walked slowly down the winding path towards the city of Nos. I loved that our cottage was set on the outskirts, nestled against the forest. The Fated Pair always had a large estate away from the hustle and bustle of the city, and as the Pair's healer, Alys – and I – enjoyed a level of privacy most Nos citizens didn't have the luxury of. Except from a few noble families who had larger residences, most lived in humble dwellings, though still beautiful. All Nos architecture was.

I looked out over the city, seeing the ornate, black-stoned buildings with intricate carved roofs and cornices. I found the largest building, set in the centre of the city square. As tradition dictated, the Fated Pair's home would alternate. Currently it was the turn of Nos, so the Council's main base was settled here, using rooms in the old library. If my and Kai's Pairing had gone well, after we were joined it would have been Sol's turn to host the Fated Pair and Council, and I would have had to move to Sol.

I had never had to think about how I would feel, moving from my beloved Nos with its cool moonlight and star-strewn skies. Fate had intervened.

I weaved through the quiet streets; it was still early yet. A few traders moved about, setting up their fruit and vegetable carts and flower stalls. The blacksmith's forge was going, and I could smell fresh bread coming from the bakery.

I kept my eyes averted – I didn't want to converse with anyone right now – but everyone was too busy to notice me. Arriving at the square, I looked up at the building dominating the area. Twisted spires stretched towards the sky, and stained-glass windows depicting the various stars and planets above threw muted light onto the wide steps leading up to the double doors. They were a mahogany so dark they looked black, with silver fretwork over the glass.

At the rumble of carriage wheels, I turned to see a silver carriage, pulled by four sleek ebony stallions, coming into the square. I recognised that carriage: Eva's parents. Of course; as the current Fated Pair, they would be attending the Council meeting too. Eva's mother certainly wouldn't favour anything *I* had to say.

I tried to duck out of sight, but it was too late. Cosimo Celestri, not waiting for the footman, jumped out of the carriage before helping his wife out. Salomé was dressed in a glittery black trouser suit, her blonde hair pulled back into a glossy chignon, while Cosimo favoured the full military dress of Nos, black jacket with silver epaulettes. A thin rapier hung at his hip. His thick black hair was smoothed back from his handsome face.

"Ceridwen!" Cosimo exclaimed. "We could have given you a lift." They walked over to join me at the foot of the wide steps to the building.

Salomé pouted. "I don't think that is seemly, darling," she said, linking her arm through her husband's. "We do not want to be seen favouring her, now, do we?" She gave him a pointed look. Something unreadable flashed momentarily through his silver eyes, but after a moment he nodded.

"Quite right, my dear," he said tightly.

I couldn't resist – I gave Lady Celestri a bright smile. "That's all right. I actually enjoyed the walk."

She stared down at my mud-splattered boots, disdain shining in her turquoise eyes. "Oh, Eva enjoys walking too. In fact, she and dear Lord Malakai had a *lovely* walk around the gardens last night." Her smile was quick as a viper's bite.

My heart tilted in my chest. So much for not favouring one of us over the other. It was clear who Lady Celestri's champion was.

"Sal!" Lord Celestri hissed, but the damage was done. I knew exactly my place now. Alys was wrong; I could never be a true Lady of Nos. Eva's mother knew precisely how to quash any ideas of grandeur I might get.

Lady Celestri raised one eyebrow innocently at her husband, before stalking up the steps.

"Sorry. She is severely lacking in tact sometimes," Lord Celestri said, staring down at me in concern.

This time it was my turn to raise an eyebrow, but I bit my tongue. I couldn't exactly insult the Lady of the realm, especially to the *Lord* of the realm.

"Cos, darling, they are waiting for us," she called down, and Lord Celestri gave a grimace.

"Shall we?" He offered me his arm, and with wobbly legs, I took it gratefully. A glimmer of satisfaction filled me when I saw the look on Lady Celestri's face. It lit a fire in me – one that got me up the steps, through the doors, and into the large, domed Council chamber without collapsing to the ground.

Lord Celestri patted my hand as he withdrew it, gave me a small, respectful bow, and took his seat beside Lady Celestri in the centre of the other Council members. Almost giddy, I took in the sunny Sol members on the left and the moody Nos on the right. It was like a visual representation of day and night in one place. A few members I recognised from Nos – parents of some people I trained with – gave me nods, but the Solians, despite their usual warm disposition, regarded me seriously. But what else could I expect? They didn't know me well.

Meuric approached me and guided me to a crescent-shaped table, with four chairs around it, in the centre of the mosaic star-burst floor. We took our seats, and I wondered where Kai was. I didn't have long to wait. He and Sabra entered through a side door.

I dropped my eyes as he took a seat next to me, and Sabra beside him. His heat warmed my arm, and for a second the full force of his searing gaze branded the side of my flushing cheek. I lifted my chin, hearing Alys's voice in my head. *Hold your head up high.*

Lord Celestri stood and spoke to the room. "As this relates to both Chosen, we will be chairing to show impartiality."

My stomach dropped to my boots as I looked at the smirk on Lady Celestri's face. *Impartiality – ha!* My fingers clenched on the edge of the table, and Meuric patted my arm. Immediately, I released my grip and stuffed my hands under the table. Kai's eyes were on me again, but I refused to look his way.

"Lord Malakai, could you please tell the Council why you and Lady Ceridwen were meeting in the orchard?" Lord Celestri inquired, taking his seat.

"Stop worrying," Kai whispered to me as he made a show of pushing back his chair to stand.

Right, I thought. It was all right for him to say; he was the golden boy.

"We – I – thought we needed to take the prophecy seriously. I invited Lady Ceridwen to meet, as a parley of sorts. This is not about us; this is about the realms." Kai walked up and down in front of the Council, throwing a dazzling smile out here and there like Festivale candy. "I must admit, I did have ulterior motives. I'd heard Lady Ceridwen's prowess in the training ring had improved drastically. I wanted to see what I was up against." As he turned away from the Council, he tossed me a wink.

I stifled a groan. *Really, Kai?* I thought he was overdoing it a bit.

"Preposterous! I have heard the exact opposite!" one stocky Nos Council member called out.

I pursed my lips. Gus' father – *Of course,* I thought sourly. He *would* tell his father how lacking I was. I couldn't deny the accusation, but with the scrape of a chair, Meuric stood and gestured for Kai to sit.

"If I may?" he directed at Lord Celestri.

"That went well, I thought," Kai said in an undertone to me as he sat, his fingers brushing my bare arm.

Really? I actually looked at him, my eyes wide in shock.

"Got you to look at me, didn't it?" He grinned his sunburst smile, and a smile of my own twitched at the corners of my lips.

Sabra tapped the table next to Kai and he sat up straight, huffing a sigh. The humour had gone from his eyes, and his body tensed as his mentor leaned in close to speak to him.

I turned my attention back to Meuric, who had been granted permission to speak.

"Lady Ceridwen *has* improved. She has been working exceptionally hard to better her skills. She knows that the fate of all within both realms lies in her and Lord Malakai's hands." Meuric looked over at me, and I was shocked at the pride shining on his face. "She knows that should the bridge fall, horrors from Fog will overrun us. She knows what needs to be done."

"Yes, but does she realise how utterly foolish it was for her to meet Lord Malakai? What if one or the other had got carried away and seriously hurt the other? The prophecy *must* be fulfilled on the Celestial Bridge. If Chosen blood must be spilled, it must be spilled to heal the bridge." Sabra was on her feet, and hadn't even waited for Lord Celestri to acknowledge her.

Lord Celestri held up both hands as Meuric turned angrily on her. "Mentors, please. I am certain Lady Ceridwen knew the risks, however questionable her reasons for going..." He broke off to look at me closely, his silver eyes intense. Was he disappointed in me? "Perhaps she was scoping out her opposition too," he concluded, as all eyes turned speculatively on me.

Uncomfortable, I wriggled in my seat, feeling the question in Kai's look. That wasn't why I had gone, but I could hardly announce that to the Council. I didn't want Kai to think that *had* been the reason, though, so I looked him in the eye and hoped he could see the truth.

"Well, whatever their motives… perhaps it is time we showed them." Sabra looked past me and Kai to spear Meuric with her blue stare.

There were mutters and rumbles amongst the Council members. "I think that would be an excellent idea," Lady Celestri said with a wave of her dark-tipped nails.

"Show us what?" I asked Meuric.

Meuric frowned, but Sabra cut in. "You will see presently."

Everyone rose, leaving me and Kai sitting at the table in confusion. Lord Celestri dismissed the Council members. I was grateful no punishment had been set, but what could they possibly have to show us that would be worse?

"Shall we?" Sabra invited us, and Kai stood, following his mentor. I joined Meuric, and together we were all led from the chamber by Lord and Lady Celestri.

"We shall take our carriage," Lord Celestri told us.

Inside the sumptuous carriage, I took a seat on the padded black velvet seat next to the window, Meuric at my side, Lord Celestri next to him. Sabra, Kai and Lady Celestri sat opposite.

"So, Kai, did you enjoy your evening at Celestri Manor last night?" Lady Celestri purred. "We are so

71

excited to have your family's cider under our prestigious name."

Pears — of course, I thought. No wonder Kai had a fixation with pears, if his family produced cider. A reluctant smile hovered about my lips as I thought about long, sunny days in the orchard, nibbling on pears together. A few years back the reality of our situation had seemed so far away, and I had actually kidded myself that this Fate's Day would never come.

My eyes flicked over to Kai; his eyes were eerie in the dim light of the carriage. I wondered if he too was thinking of those days, but my hopes were trampled on as he turned to Lady Celestri. "I enjoyed myself very much. Please give my regards to Miss Eva."

Lord Celestri frowned, but his wife tinkled a laugh. "I most certainly will." Her gaze was triumphant as she looked my way.

A hand patted mine, and I realised Meuric was trying to offer some moral support. At least I had someone on my side. But still, I couldn't wait to be freed from the carriage. I tried to focus on taking deep breaths, but a tight band seemed to encircle my ribcage.

The road beneath the carriage wheels became bumpy, and my mouth dried up like the sand on Sol's beaches. I knew this route. *No*, I thought in horror, as we stopped with a sudden bump.

Seven

With trembling legs, I dismounted from the carriage. I clutched the side of the door and waited for the dizzy sensation to pass.

"Meuric," I tried to say, but no sound came out.

"What is the matter with her?" I heard Lady Celestri ask, although her voice sounded as if it came from the end of a long tunnel.

Gentle hands moved me away from the carriage to sit on a rock. "Breathe slowly... in and out," I was told. The voice was soothing and calming, and immediately my heart-rate began to settle.

"Really, Cos, let her mentor see to her."

I realised it was Lord Celestri tending to me. My eyes refocused, and I looked up to see expressions of concern from the men. Sabra and Lady Celestri, however, wore twin looks of disdain.

"If this is how she reacts to being back at the Celestial Bridge, then it will be an easy victory for you, Lord Malakai," Lady Celestri said.

"Nothing about this is easy," Kai muttered, so low Lady Celestri probably didn't hear him. I did, though. Perhaps it *was* hard for him too – or was I being manipulated again?

"How are you feeling now?" Lord Celestri asked, helping me to stand.

I didn't feel good. I could never feel good here. This was the place where all my hopes and dreams had been shattered – but I wouldn't give Lady Celestri or Sabra the satisfaction of seeing me crumble again, so I said, "Much better, thank you. I didn't eat a lot this morning."

The lie didn't sit right, especially to kind Lord Celestri, but I needed to come up with something to explain my dizzy spell. I didn't want them to know that every time I even thought about stepping foot on the Celestial Bridge, panic overwhelmed me, and I believed I would die.

"Shall we do this? I have an appointment at the salon in an hour," Lady Celestri said, tapping the toe of one silver stiletto heel impatiently. Was she actually going to walk down the five hundred steps in those?

Seeing my look, she smiled knowingly. "My dear, I could out-run the Shadowmists themselves in these."

That I didn't doubt. She was all about self-preservation. I was surprised the Fates had chosen her as one half of the union that would oversee and help protect the realms. But then, who was I to question the Fates? They didn't favour me.

Lady Celestri took Lord Celestri's arm, and with an encouraging smile, he led her over to the steps. Sabra and Kai followed, leaving me and Meuric to bring up the rear. I took a deep breath as I peered over the edge.

The last time I had seen this place, I was being carried away by Meuric, my heart bearing a crack as lethal as the one in the Celestial Bridge.

My breath lodged in my chest at the devastation below me. The crack had deepened – that much I could see even from this distance. The Shadowmists boiled beneath the bridge in angry shades of gunmetal, obsidian and puce.

"We will stop here!" Lord Celestri called up.

We all congregated together on the resting platform halfway down the steps and looked out over the black metal railing. Silently, we observed the bridge. Kai slanted a look my way. Things had got serious; we both knew it.

Sabra broke the silence. "So, you see, your little war-games must stop."

The bridge was almost rent in two. Only the part holding the circular platform was intact. The part where Kai and I would have to fight – the part that would run with blood from one of us. Only that, Sabra had told us, could fuse the cracks and restore the bridge.

Nausea rose up inside me, and the bridge whirled in my vision as if it had become part of the Shadowmists themselves.

"If the prophecy is not fulfilled on Fate's Day, then the bridge will fall, and what lurks within the mists will overrun both Nos and Sol. There will be no stopping it." Sabra's chest heaved. "The Celestial Bridge has linked our Twin Realms for millennia. Hundreds of Fated Pairs have staved back the horror of Fog; its very foundations block the entrance to that monstrous realm, and if you think for one tiny second that I will allow it to fall, you are sadly mistaken." She

75

turned first to Kai and then to me. "Do. You. Both. Understand?" she said slowly, enunciating every syllable as if we were children.

But we were no longer children, and my childhood hopes and dreams were nothing but a fantasy. It was time I faced up to the reality of the situation. If I didn't do this, everyone I cared about would die. *No!* They would live if I died – but if I lived then Kai would die. What could I do?

"Of course they understand, Sabra. Stop being so hard on them," Lord Celestri burst out. "Where is your compassion, your empathy? That's right – you have none."

Everyone stared at Lord Celestri. Lady Celestri appeared stunned into silence. Sabra narrowed her eyes and spoke. "You forget yourself, Cosimo."

"Perhaps it is time I remembered who I am, then." Lord Celestri gave a jerky bow to me, Kai and Meuric and broke into a run up the steps like a sure-footed mountain goat. He reached the top in minutes, leaving the rest of us in an uncomfortable silence.

Lady Celestri pulled Sabra to one side and talked to her in hissing undertones. I watched the two Sol women for a moment, for the first time noticing how alike they were.

I didn't have to time to dwell on it; Meuric took my arm. "Perhaps we should leave too. You've seen enough."

I trembled; the adrenaline from my earlier panic attack had dissipated, leaving my body shaky. He was right, I needed to get away. The gloom hung heavy in the air, permeating my very soul.

"Master Meuric, may I speak with Lady Ceridwen for a moment, please?" Kai asked formally.

Sabra and Lady Celestri still argued off to the side, so perhaps Meuric saw no harm in allowing us to talk for a few minutes. Perhaps he knew this would be the last time; perhaps he could sense the gap widening between us, a mirror to what was happening below.

We moved towards the steps, and Meuric leaned over the railing, giving us some semblance of privacy.

"Wen" – Kai reached out towards me, but appeared to think better of it – "I don't want this to be it. We should try and find another way…"

"Are you crazy?" I demanded, gesturing over to the bridge as Sabra had. "There *is* no other way!" But maybe I was the crazy one – the one barely holding on to the threads of her sanity. I'd had almost three years to prepare for what must happen, but I hadn't truly accepted it. Denial had been my cloak of protection. Seeing the dire situation of the Celestial Bridge had ripped that cloak to shreds. This *was* happening to us.

This time Kai did grip my arm, heat radiating off him to create a golden bubble around us. "I won't do it; I refuse to fight you. I will not be responsible for your death." He leaned in close, uttering the words fiercely.

"Kai," I murmured sadly, "you won't have a choice. We *must* fight."

"For once, I agree with the girl. The Fates will not accept a martyr. You must fight because you want to save your people, not each other or yourselves." Unseen, Sabra had moved up to join us. Lady Celestri was nowhere in sight. *Probably gone to join her husband*, I thought.

Meuric looked thoughtfully at Sabra. He seemed surprised by the Sol mentor's words.

"The Fates ask too much of us!" Kai snapped back.

A boom of thunder rocked the air, and Kai scowled up at the sky before he too turned to climb to the top, his white tunic rippling as he moved and his brown boots making short work of the steps.

Sabra shook her head, her blue eyes flashing, but she shot one apprehensive look up at the clouds above. "Leave him to me. Come Fate's Day, you *will* have your opponent," she announced, and glided after him, her long golden robe flowing. I didn't know whether she was speaking to me or the Fates.

"Come. Let us leave this Fate-cursed place," Meuric said, guiding me up the steps. I was eager to leave; the absence of Kai's Sol warmth left me covered in goosebumps. His smile flashed into my mind, the one he saved for after one of his corny jokes, and my heart fractured a little more. I was beginning to hate the Fates, but I wasn't brave enough to say it out loud. Kai certainly beat me on that score – it felt blasphemous merely thinking it. I glanced warily up at the sky, but no further thunder rumbled overhead to reveal the Fates' displeasure. I would need to visit the temple soon and leave an offering.

At the top of the steps, weak sunlight burst through the clouds. The carriage had gone, and Sabra and Kai had vanished too. It looked like everyone had deserted us, but I was glad. I couldn't bear to sit in a carriage with Sabra or Lady Celestri again, and I needed to start to distance myself from Kai. *Now is a good a time as any*, I thought as the last of my heart crumbled away into dust.

Meuric and I walked the long distance back towards the city. A few times he looked as though he wanted to say something, but stopped himself. As we neared the forest, I turned to him to say goodbye.

He looked sadly at me. "Ceridwen, know this: I will do all that is in my power to help you. I have a lot of respect for Lord Malakai, but you are my student, and my loyalty is to you and the realm of Nos. You must put your feelings aside; you *must* do this. It will help... afterwards. If your heart is not engaged, then the burden will be easier to bear."

I heard what he was saying, but my mind refused to acknowledge the words. I needed to detach myself from everything. It wasn't only my heart that must cease to feel, it was my whole being – my very soul. Because after this, if I survived, I wouldn't be the same person. I would be a mere shadow of myself. If Kai was my Fated Partner, then him dying would take half of me with him. The best half.

I hugged my arms around myself and nodded. "I need some time."

"Of course you do. Go and find Alys, I'm sure she'll have something soothing in that magic bag of hers." Meuric patted me on the arm, and I knew what it cost him to speak so openly with me. This was way out of his comfort zone. "I'll see you tomorrow for training."

He left me standing on the edge of the forest, standing half in the sunlight and half in the shade of the trees. A shiver of foreboding worked its way down my spine as I turned to find Alys.

Alone, I could give rise to my emotions. I wanted to *feel* one last time. I let the sensations come.

Wave after wave of grief washed over me, and before I knew it cool tears were pouring down my face. I stumbled as my vision was obscured, my chest heaving and my breath coming out in gasps. A tree root tripped me and I tumbled to the ground, not caring enough to save myself. I lay there sobbing until a pair of gentle hands pushed my curls from my face.

"Oh, my precious girl," Alys said, near to tears herself.

I threw myself into her arms, and she rocked me as I wept and raged, the grief giving way to anger. Anger at the futility of the situation. Anger at my chance of a long and happy life being cut short – whatever the outcome, I knew I would never experience true happiness again. I don't know how long she held me, but it was long enough for the anger to turn to numb acceptance.

I knew what must be done. *I* had to be the strong one and train harder than I ever had before, because if Kai refused to fight against me, he would anger the Fates and jeopardise everything – and everyone – in the Twin Realms. I could not let that happen. In that possible but extremely likely circumstance, I would have to do what must be done.

I would have to kill Kai.

Eight

"Wen, stop!"

Maxen pulled me off the makeshift training dummy. One of its arms dangled limply by its side, barely hanging on by a thread.

No, I wouldn't stop, not until it was nothing but dust. As if at that thought, the side seams split, and sawdust began to pour from the body. With a nod of satisfaction, I stepped back and inspected my knuckles. Blood seeped out, but I didn't even feel the pain. Numb – exactly how I wanted.

Maxen handed me a cup of water and stared at me through narrowed eyes.

I took a long gulp. "What?" Maxen had been hovering even more than usual; I was sure Meuric had asked him to keep a close eye on me.

"I think you're overdoing it a bit," Maxen said with a wince, taking the cup off me and setting it down before I could throw it at him.

Admittedly, I had been a bit spiky this past week, barking at anyone who came near me. Even Gus had kept his insults to himself, and no one wanted to fight with me anymore. Well, that was fine – I was better on my own anyway. I couldn't afford to waste time with inane chatter and jokey asides.

"Max, I could train night and day and still not be anywhere near as good as Kai. There's three weeks until the Festivale. I have to train harder and get fitter."

Maxen held up a placating hand. "Then let me and Eva help you!" he repeated for the hundredth time. I started to shake my head as always, but this time a thought popped in my head.

"Does Eva still go to dance lessons?" I asked, Kai's words coming back to me. *Your moves always reminded me of a dance…* Perhaps I needed to use what limited skills I did have.

Maxen frowned, puzzled. "I think so. My cousin, Larissa, still dances – I'll ask her if she sees Eva at the dance academy… didn't you use to go too?"

I nodded. "Yes, Eva and I went together on a Saturday morning." I had thought Eva's parents had paid for me to go, to keep Eva company, but now I was wondering if it was my secret benefactor all along. I'd stopped going to the lessons after the Choosing; my heart wasn't in it anymore. Eva tried to get me to come back, but eventually she gave up asking. Maybe it was time to return. I had three weeks. I might as well spend it doing something I used to enjoy, especially if it would improve my fighting prowess.

Maxen looked relieved at my enthusiasm. "Great, I'll go and speak to Rissa now." He waved over to his cousin, a willowy girl with her black hair caught neatly up in a bun on top of her head. She stood to one side with a group of others. They looked carefree and relaxed, despite the gruelling training session Meuric had put them through. *It must be nice to switch it off.*

Maxen talked to Larissa for a few moments, then returned with the slightly younger girl at his side. I hadn't spoken much with Maxen's cousin before, and seeing her wary expression made me realise that although I had been training with these people for years, I had always kept my distance.

"Hi," I said, making an effort to be friendly. "I was wondering if Eva still attends dance classes. Max said you might have seen her around?"

Larissa nodded. "Yes, actually, I told Max you might catch her now if you go to Madame Stella's academy."

I looked up at the clock on the side of the yard. "Perfect," I said. "Tell Meuric I'm calling it a day." With only an hour before Meuric dismissed the others, I didn't think he'd mind if I sneaked away early. He'd been nagging me to take it easy, anyway.

Maxen looked bemused but nodded. I gave them a wave and left the training yard, a spring in my step and intent in my mind. For the first time in a long while, I allowed optimism to fill me. This was a productive use of the moments I had left… *if* I could get Eva to agree to teach me.

We hadn't exactly spoken since the night of the fateful non-girls'-night. Not that Eva hadn't tried. She'd come knocking on the cottage door the night after the Council meeting, but I told Alys to tell her I was sleeping. I didn't want to listen to her apologies and explanations about the dinner with Kai, and I certainly hadn't wanted to hear about their moonlit walk in the gardens.

Stop thinking about him.

The city centre was bustling, and I had to sidestep a carriage full of giggling girls no doubt headed to the local dressmaker's to pick an outfit for the Festivale. *Ugh.* I grimaced, looking down at my black trousers and grey T-shirt. You wouldn't catch me dead in a dress.

Dead, dead, dead... The word rang hollowly around my mind, like a bell clanging the final hour, and my heart skipped a beat.

The girls' laughter became shrill as the carriage moved on and dark clouds rumbled overhead with ominous thunder. I clapped my hands over my ears and darted down an alley, where I sucked in deep breaths, fighting back the overwhelming panic of everything crashing down on me. I refused to let it take hold; I would never again break down the way I had last week.

With a growl, I pushed off the wall from where I had slumped and marched out of the alley, head held high. I was a Lady of the realm, and I would act as such.

People ducked out of my way as I walked with purpose towards the academy. Set back from the hustle and bustle of the street in a fragrant garden, the academy rose in an elegant, pillared building of traditional Nos stone. I let myself in through the front door and was immediately greeted by beautiful, lilting strains of piano music.

"Well, look what the cat dragged in."

I turned to see Eva leaning against the frame of an open studio door. Sweat beaded along her brow and down the deep vee of her black leotard; a wispy, silvery skirt floated around her shapely calves.

"Hi," I said.

The silence drew out between us while Eva dabbed herself with a towel. She was going to make me say it, I thought with resignation.

I blew a stray curl off my forehead and conceded. "I'm sorry, Eva."

"Good. Now that's out of the way... I've missed you." She skipped over to me on her pointe shoes and linked her arm with mine. "What brings you here?"

"I need you to teach me some dance steps. I want to be light on my feet and agile." Not clumsy and uncoordinated, as I felt I usually was when I fought.

Eva tinkled out a laugh. "But you gave up dancing years ago! There's no way I could teach you in... never mind," she caught herself hastily, before adding, "Why?"

Why? Because when I'd danced, I had felt light and free, like I could pirouette across the air and touch the stars themselves. Nothing had weighed me down: no prophecy, no not knowing who I really was or where I came from; none of that mattered because when I danced, I became my true self.

I huffed out a breath. "Because, my friend, I have a fight to win."

Eva stared at me with wide eyes. Her lips pinched into a grim line, and I wondered if she thought I was scuppering her future plans – her mother's future plans. I didn't want to know if she had come around to the idea of the Celestris joining the Ostaras through their children. Kai hadn't been an option for me for a long time, but I refused to feel guilty at robbing Eva of *her* chance. She had plenty of men to choose from.

A sly smile reminiscent of Lady Celestri's worked its way across Eva's face. "I'll agree" – she held up one dainty hand as I grinned in return – "*if* you go dress shopping with me."

The memory of the girls' giggling laughter was back in my head, mocking my earlier thoughts. "Eva!" I groaned. Yep, she was definitely punishing me in the best way she knew how. "You want clothes advice from *me?*" I asked, un-linking our arms and doing a poor version of a pirouette of my own.

She looked me up and down from the top of my wild curls to my mud-encrusted boots, lingering briefly on my cut knuckles, and said, "I certainly do. If I take my mother or any of my other friends, they'll just tell me I look good in everything. But you – you'll tell me straight. You're the closest thing to a sister I have, and siblings, I'm told, are brutally honest."

"Brutal." I nodded; I liked the sound of that.

"Then it's settled. I'll meet you in the old temple ruins for dance practice after your training finishes tomorrow, and then the next day, you and I are shopping." Eva smiled her cat-like smile. "Now, I have to finish my class." She waggled her fingers at me and danced into the room, doing a series of complicated little steps.

I rolled my eyes, but a surge of affection lanced through me in spite of myself. I could never be angry at her for long, and I knew the same went for her with me. I was lucky to have her... and Alys, Meuric and Maxen too. They never gave up on me, even when I gave up on myself.

The walk back to the cottage was uneventful, but I had a definite spring in my step. I don't know whether it was because I had made up with Eva or the fact that I had a plan in place, but I didn't dread going to sleep that night. Hopefully, my dreams would be easier, and no crushing nightmares would haunt me. It was funny – I shouldn't actually have any nightmares when I had essentially been living one for the past three years.

Shaking my head at my dark humour, I entered the cottage and was greeted by a fluffy projectile as Lunara launched herself at me.

"Hi, girl," I murmured, and my heart twisted at the thought of possibly leaving her behind. If I died, she would surely pine away for me. Stroking one of her velvety, feathered wings, I listened to her affectionate grumblings and determined not to think of it... for now.

Alys wasn't at home, so I decided to make dinner. A pile of root vegetables and mushrooms sat on the side and I found diced beef in the cold box, so I set about making a stew, adding some of Alys's myriad of herbs from pots on the windowsill. Soon the cottage was filled with a deliciously savoury aroma, and I sat at the table and poured myself a drink from the amber glass bottle on the table, thinking it was one of Alys's many cordials to have with dinner.

Immediately the tart flavour of honeyed pears burst on my tongue, and I almost gagged as I realised what it was and where it had come from. I wished I had spat it out. I took a closer look at the label: *Celestara... a merging of flavours.*

That's not all they want to merge, I thought darkly, imagining Lady Celestri toasting Mistress Ostara with their new Cider Mead.

Tempted to toss the rest of the bottle down the sink, I thought better of it. Alys might actually enjoy it. I, however, took great delight in pouring what was left in my glass away. I watched the liquid drain, disappearing down the plughole, leaving no trace behind. Would that be how it would be after Kai, or I, was gone? Or would our passing leave a residue, a blot on the realms – one that could never be washed away?

It was a question only one of us would ever find the answer to.

Nine

I tripped over my untied lace for the second time, and Eva sighed in exasperation.

"Really, Wen, I remember you being far more poised than this when you attended lessons with me."

"Well, I wasn't wearing steel-capped boots then," I replied snidely, kneeling down to re-tie my lace in a tight double knot. "Ballet slippers tend to add a certain poise by their appearance alone."

Eva tilted her head, pondering my words. "There is some truth in that," she mused. "Boots, however, lend themselves to toughness and brutality."

There was that word again: *brutal.* I gave my boot a tap and straightened up. *Let's see if I can become a mixture of brute force and grace.* Now that would be something Kai had never seen. Perhaps it would inspire him to fight back. He had to fight back; I couldn't kill in cold blood.

My own blood zinging, I looked at Eva. "Ready?"

She smiled a slow smile, tucked her braids over her shoulder and stretched. "Absolutely." She lunged at me with her long sword, and I twirled out of reach, just as we'd practiced. "Nice – now jump," she instructed as she swiped at my legs. I leapt cat-like up onto a rock and gathered my balance. "Kai won't give you time to do that," she sing-songed as she lunged again, almost catching my padded leather trousers.

"Jetée!" she called, and I leaped from the rock and rolled as I missed my landing. I flipped up and cartwheeled out of her way.

"That's new," she said, impressed.

Taking advantage of her pause, I skipped in close with my own sword and thrust forward, tapping the blade against her side. "Thanks – I came up with it myself." I grinned.

"Ouch." She pouted.

I rolled my eyes. "You're wearing the best protective gear your parents can buy. But, seriously, I've told you a million times – you would do well in the Nos Guard. You have more skills than most of them."

"Yes, well, as daughter of the Fated Pair, I'm not destined for the Guard. I am expected to make a noble match." She inspected her nails as she spoke, not meeting my eyes.

Her words lit a fire in me. "Let's go again," I said stiffly, placing my feet in second position. I bent at the knees and pirouetted out of her way as she made a sudden movement.

Despite my heavy boots, the movements Eva and I had been working on for hours slotted into place, and I could see how I could use them all to my advantage. I could almost predict where Eva would move, I knew her so well. Perhaps I could observe Kai in the same way. I might not be able to meet him, but that didn't mean I couldn't sneak into Sol.

"What are you smiling at?" Eva asked through heavy breaths. She managed to swipe at my legs; caught off-guard, I fell flat on my back, the mossy ground cushioning my fall. Winded, I lay there for a few moments until her face appeared above me. "Having a nap?"

"Haha, very droll," I said, "and I'm smiling because I think I'm getting better at this." I sat up and gestured at the swords.

Eva nibbled on her full bottom lip. "I hope so," she said quietly, and I met her eyes. We shared a long, unspoken moment, before I leaned over to clasp her hand.

"Promise me you'll look after Lunara for me… if the worst should happen." *The worst for who?* a voice whispered in my head.

Eva got up from her crouched position and turned away. "Let's not talk about that."

I stood. "Please, Eva, you have to promise," I insisted, taking her arm once again. "I can't do this if Lunara won't be safe. If I risk everything, I have to know going in that she, at least, will be looked after. I know Alys would care for her, but she doesn't understand mothlings the way you and I do."

Eva let out a long sigh. "Fine, I promise I will look after Lunara…"

"Say it, please," I said.

"…if you don't make it," she finished in a rush.

I pulled her in for a hug. After a moment she gripped me back tightly, her heart thundering through her toughened leather breastplate.

"I think we should leave it there. I need a bath," she said, pulling back. The Eva-twinkle was back in her eyes.

I took a big sniff and grimaced. "You can say that again."

"Watch it," she said through narrowed eyes, brandishing the sword at me, but a small smile hovered around her lips. "Are you coming?"

I shook my head. "I'm going to sit here for a bit and catch my breath."

"If you're sure?" At my nod, she collected both swords. "I'll get these back to Maxen to sneak back into the weapon store." She left with a wave, and I watched her sashay down the path, her two long braids swinging.

I couldn't help the sigh that broke free. Jittery from the adrenaline, I walked over to the edge of the broken temple wall and watched the sun descend over Sol in the distance. Dying rays shot out across the city and turned everything to molten gold. It was a beautiful sight.

"Fates, I thought she was never going to leave."

I closed my eyes at the voice, and this time the sigh that worked its way out was a long-suffering one. I should have known he couldn't stay away. I felt the pull too. My resolve, to do what was right for the Twin Realms, crumbled.

Annoyed at my own weakness, I slowly turned around, and even though the sun was behind me, I was blinded. Kai stood before me; his thick blonde hair tousled as if he had just run one of his sun-kissed hands through it. I stared – I couldn't help myself – and his smile grew wider.

To break the spell, I spoke harshly. "I thought you had a 'lovely time' with Eva the other night."

I thought that might turn his smile into a look of guilt, but I was mistaken. If anything, his smile turned predatory.

He stepped up close, and I was surrounded by his spicy yet fresh scent. Immediately I thought of the tart Celestara cider, but instead of enticing my tongue, it was my other senses that were assailed. Every nerve ending zinged as I breathed deeply, inhaling him.

"Wen, do you trust me?" Kai asked, reaching out and twining one of my loose curls around his finger.

Did I? Three years ago, I wouldn't even have questioned it – my answer would have been a resounding yes. I trusted Kai with every fibre of my existence. Now, I was so uncertain. But Kai would always be the chink in the armour I had woven around my heart... my one true weakness. My mind weaved back and forth, debating what to say. He knew the risk to the realms; he knew what was at stake, and I also knew Sabra would be using every trick in her mentor book to convince him to do the 'right' thing by the Twin Realms. So, *could* I truly trust him?

My head started nodding without my permission, as if some undeniable instinct had taken over.

"Then come with me." He linked his fingers through mine, and with a brief look back towards Nos, I allowed him to pull me away from the temple ruins.

We walked in silence as the first stars began to twinkle overhead. Uneasily I looked about. Shadowwraiths from Fog chose the in-between twilight minutes to materialise, though thankfully there hadn't been an attack in years.

"Star light... star bright..." Kai murmured, squeezing my fingers and looking up.

I wish I may, I wish I might, I added in my head – before I remembered wishes were for the hopeful.

We walked a familiar path along the glowing clifftop trail, down through the fields and orchards and... towards the caves. I stopped cold.

"I can't... Kai—" I pulled my hand away from his grip and stumbled back a few steps.

"Please, Wen. We need to speak to the Fates."

"No, Kai – we mustn't do anything to anger them further. What would Sabra say?" I stared at him, my heart thundering in my neck. "This is not the answer."

"It might be the *only* answer. You have to trust me on this." He put his hand in his pocket and withdrew a glowing Sunstone.

"Where did you get that?" I gasped, reaching out a tentative hand. Heat radiated from the stone, pulsing and glowing like a miniature sun. I knew the answer to the question already, though. There was only one stone like this particular one. He must have taken it from Sol's City Temple. Nos had its own version – an egg-sized Moonstone. Only high-up Council members and the current Fated Pair had access to the stones; only they could use them to speak to the Fates. Kai was going to get us in so much trouble.

"I did what I had to do. Come on," he coaxed.

Acutely aware the Fates themselves might be watching, I squared my shoulders and joined him. He had set us on a path there was no turning back from now. What was done was done; I might as well discover if the Fates *could* help us.

We reached the dark caves and Kai held up the stone in front of us, illuminating the path to the pool inside. I hesitated in the entrance, remembering all the times we had met there and when we had all been selected as candidates for the Choosing, and had made a pilgrimage to the Fated Shrines to pledge our acceptance. Those times the atmosphere had felt welcoming and right; this time the caves felt eerie and... wrong. Off, somehow. Kai and I had avoided the caves since our Choosing had gone amiss, meeting instead at the orchard.

Pushing down my trepidation, I joined him at the edge of the pool. His eyes on me, he pulled off his tunic and kicked off his boots. If he thought I was taking *my* tunic off, he was mistaken; my leather training jacket would suffice. He raised one golden eyebrow, and I turned away, a blush staining my cheeks.

Toeing off my boots, I slid my legs over the edge of the pool and looked down into the inky water. Kai joined me, and together we took a deep breath and slid beneath the surface. He moved ahead of me, and instead of the special jar-lanterns we usually would have used to guide us through, I followed the light from the Sunstone.

Diving deep, Kai guided us through the underwater tunnel, and we emerged into another cave. I pulled myself out of the water and stood trembling on the smooth stone pathway surrounding the pool. I hadn't thought this through.

Kai came up behind me and wrapped his arms around me, and immediately I jerked away. "What are you doing?" I said through numb lips.

He gave his husky laugh, before pulling me back to him and enfolding me in his powerful arms once again. "Warming you up," he said.

Immediately, liquid warmth pooled inside me – but it had nothing to do with Kai being a Solian; this was simply how he affected me. If I looked up, would I see steam rising from us? My cheeks heated at the thought.

"Better?" he asked as a sigh of contentment escaped me. I could sense the amused curve of his lips.

Fates above, I thought, pulling back as nonchalantly as possible. I pushed my damp curls off my face and nodded, not meeting his eyes. "Thanks."

"My pleasure," he said, so meaningfully I didn't doubt it. "Come on." He walked over to the altar beneath carvings engraved into the cave rock. Two stone deities stood tall and proud, both reaching up to the open roof of the cave, where the stars twinkled down on them; the sun Fate, Belenos, and the moon Fate, Arianrhod. Broken mosaic tiles still adorned the floor beneath the wide stone altar. The wax from thousands of long-burnt candles dripped down its sides like stalactites, and I wished I had thought to bring an offering. It felt wrong to come empty-handed.

Kai toyed with the Sunstone for a moment, rubbing its glowing surface. I bit my lip, knowing what would happen if he placed the stone into the sun-shaped indent. His hand hovered over the hollow, and I quickly darted forward to pull it back.

"Are you sure you want to do this?" We had, for reasons unknown, angered the Fates enough that they had not blessed our names being Chosen. What if this caused more anger, and they turned their wrath on the realms? It was such a great risk. Was it worth it?

Kai obviously thought so. His words were earnest, yet solemn. "We have to ask why – why they are not honouring our union. I need to know if there is a way around it."

The pain shining in his bright blue eyes was plain to see, but a sudden thought occurred to me. "But without the Moonstone, we can't call on Arianrhod."

Kai's eyes turned briefly speculative. "It's all right. We're just going to speak to Belenos… for now."

Before I could voice any further concerns, he placed the stone into the indent.

Ten

Immediately, the whispering started.

The first and only other time I had heard it, I had been curious, but this time it was disconcerting. It was like the whole cave had filled with hundreds of ghosts. Gentle breezes tugged at my hair, and indiscernible words floated past my ears.

I looked over at Kai, but he was unconcerned, or distracted by something else. I looked up to see what he was gazing at and saw that the statue of Belenos was lit from the glow of the Sunstone. The way the light undulated, it appeared the statue was standing on a platform of flickering flames, licking up the sun Fate's robes. Belenos's stone face rippled and morphed, and I took a step back as a fierce face regarded us.

"Who summons me?" it rasped.

My hands clenched on the altar, but I pulled them back and rubbed them on my trousers. I remembered Gus's snide voice telling me you shouldn't show weakness in front of a Fate, or they would smite you down. It was an absurd thought, but I wasn't going to take any chances, so I held my head up high.

"The Lord Malakai Ostara and Lady Ceridwen Moonshade," Kai announced.

The whispering grew louder, swirling around me and making my head spin. I thought I saw Belenos's eyes widen, but that could have been a trick of the light.

"And what do you demand of me, sun child?" Belenos asked, focusing on Kai and ignoring my presence.

"I – *we* – need to know if we have angered you in some way, and what we can do to put it right," Kai said clearly, throwing a glance my way to include me.

Belenos laughed, flames flickering from his wide mouth causing me to take a step back. "Put it right?" he mused, before falling silent. His eyes closed, and I wondered if he had gone.

But with a sudden grimace, Kai clutched the sides of his head, screwing up his eyes. "What is it?" I asked, looking from him to Belenos, but both of their eyes remained closed. Helpless and alone, I froze, not knowing what to do.

Kai fell to his knees. The whispering intensified, the myriad of voices rising to a crescendo as if they were now inside my head. Perhaps they were.

"*Do not listen… you cannot trust…*" The voices separated, and coherent words took form. *Trust who, or what?* I thought, trying to latch on to a voice, but they were like smoke, dissipating as my thoughts reached them. Who were the voices?

I shook my head to clear the cloud-like sensation and turned my attention back to Kai. He was now on his hands and knees, panting heavily as sweat dripped down his forehead and torso. I reached out to clutch at his shoulder, and my breath hissed out at the scorching pain in my fingertips.

"Kai!" I shouted, trying to rouse him, but he continued to pant. I looked up at the statue of Belenos. "Whatever you are doing to him, you must stop it... *please*!"

Looking around for a way to help, my eyes landed on the glowing Sunstone. I rushed forward and pulled the stone from the socket. I thought I heard a roar of rage as the light dimmed; the stone sat heavy and warm in my palm.

The statue of Belenos stood still and silent, no arrogant features glared down at me. With a sigh of relief, I joined Kai on the stone floor. He shivered uncontrollably, so I used my body to comfort him as he had me.

I stroked his face gently until he opened his eyes. "Are you all right?" I asked softly as his clouded eyes searched mine.

"Never invite a Fate into your mind," he joked feebly, running a trembling hand across his face. "Especially the sun Fate."

If Belenos could cause a reaction so severe in a citizen of Sol, I could only shudder at what would happen to one from Nos. We would be turned to moondust in an instant. "What did he tell you?"

Kai licked his cracked lips and struggled to a sitting position.

"You cannot trust him..." The wispy voice floated through my mind, but I pushed it away. I needed to hear what Belenos had told Kai. Both our futures could depend upon it.

"We were wrong… the Fates are not angry at *us*. There's something else at play, something far bigger than we could ever imagine. But the Fates talk in riddles and never give a straight answer."

"Well, you're not exactly giving me a straight answer," I pointed out, the first stirrings of unease rolling through me. How could I know what Belenos had actually said? He was not *my* Fate. If only Arianrhod had appeared too, then we could have got a balanced dialogue.

"I need to go," Kai said abruptly. "I must speak to Sabra." He stood and headed for the edge of the pool. Was he going to leave me here with no real answers? After *he* had proposed coming here in the first place?

"Kai… wait!" But he had already dived into the pool, the silky water closing over his golden form.

Shocked, I watched his rippling shadow disappear. Only after I had stood in disbelief for a few minutes did I realise I still held the Sunstone in my hand. My heart dropped to my feet. How was I going to get this back to Sol's temple now?

With nothing else to do, and apprehensive at being in the shrine alone, I followed him into the pool and lit my way with the stone. I hoped Kai had come to his senses and was waiting for me in the other cave, but when my head broke the water, I saw with dismay there was no sign of him. Watery footprints led from the pool over to where my jacket and boots remained.

With a huff of indignation, I pulled myself out, stuffed the stone into my trouser pocket, and pulled on my boots and jacket. Honestly, the man was sending my head into a meltdown. Not content with breaking my heart, he appeared to be set on breaking my mind too.

I sprinted out of the caves in the hopes of catching up with him, but the path was empty. He could certainly move, I thought with a frown. And I should too – it wasn't safe to be out wandering alone at night.

On the edge of the shared lands, I debated with myself. Did I risk sneaking into Sol, or should I go home and wait for Kai to come and find me? No doubt he would realise his mistake and come looking for the stone.

Yes, that was the best idea, I decided. When he came looking, I would be ready, and this time he wouldn't evade my questions. Patting my pocket to make sure the stone was still safe, I headed back to the cottage. My stomach growled; I hoped Alys had dinner cooking already. It had been a long day of training, sparring with Eva, and swimming through pools, not to mention navigating tricky Fates and contrary young men. I was ravenous.

A sudden clanging noise came from behind me in the direction of Sol. That was new. Curious, yet with a feeling of impending doom, I hurried home, keen to ask Alys what the noise meant.

I entered the cottage to find her staring down into a scrying bowl. I stopped short. Since when had Alys had scrying skills? I knew she was a gifted healer, but I had only heard of a few who could scry in our realm, and Alys hadn't been one of them.

She hastily placed a thin piece of cheesecloth over the bowl and gave me an overbright smile. "Hi, sweetheart!"

Lunara flitted over to me and nuzzled my neck in greeting. Reaching one hand up to caress her furry head, I wondered bemusedly what to ask first. "Hi…"

"Are you hungry?" Alys moved over to the stove and began dishing up the pie warming on the top.

"Well, I am, but..." I trailed off as the chicken pie aroma hit me in the face. I could talk and eat, couldn't I?

I sat down and placed Lunara on the back of the chair next to me before diving into the pie with gusto, scooping up peas and the meaty, gravy filling. Alys watched me with a wary smile on her face, her own food untouched.

I set down my cutlery after a few moments. "What's the matter?"

"Oh, nothing," she said, but it sounded forced.

My eyes wandered over to the cloth-covered bowl, wondering what she had seen, but I found I couldn't ask her. It felt like prying into business that didn't concern me, much like when I had seen her walking back to the cottage with tears streaming down her face. There was so much I didn't know about Alys, but it wasn't my place to intrude.

Instead, I asked about the clanging noise.

Alys' eyebrows rose and her lips pursed. "I have only ever heard that noise once before – around the time of the Choosing before yours." Her eyes grew thoughtful, and she appeared lost in recollections; when I touched her hand gently she looked at me, unseeing. Memories swirled in her light grey eyes for a moment before she refocused on me with a small sad smile. "Someone stole the Sunstone from the temple of Belenos. The Solians had lost their connection to their Fate; Sol was in uproar for weeks. Then, suddenly, it was back. If it had happened again, they will not look kindly on the perpetrator..."

My blood ran cold, and the pie congealed in my stomach. The stone in my pocket dug into my hip, its heat searing through my thigh. I stood, knocking my chair back. It clattered onto the flagstones, making Lunara flutter up to the roof beam in alarm.

Nausea roiled through my stomach. *Kai has been found out* was my first thought. How was I going to get the stone back to him now? Waiting for him wasn't an option any more.

"Ceridwen, are you all right?" Alys asked in concern.

What could I say? That the stone had been stolen *again*, this time by Kai, and I had it right now in my pocket? No. I couldn't drag her into this.

"I – um – I just remembered something. I was supposed to be meeting Eva," I lied, my eyes flicking away from hers.

"Well, she won't mind if you're a little late. Finish your food," she said, bending to right my chair.

The pie taunted me; the glistening chunks of meat and lurid green peas caused bile to burn up into my throat, closing it. I imagined Kai thrown into the Sol dungeons, closed off from his beloved sun. Surely they wouldn't keep him there for long – he had a prophecy to fulfil, after all. But I knew he had a family. What would happen to *them*? I needed air.

"I'm full," I told her, backing away, my hand clenching over the stone in my pocket.

"All right… I'll see you later." Alys tilted her head as if she could see through my lies, but I turned to hurry away, wrenching open the door. Lunara didn't follow me.

Moonlight washed over me, and immediately it soothed my senses. I took in three deep breaths... *in and out... in and out... in and out...* until my stomach stopped churning. I needed a clear head.

If Kai wasn't coming to me – or *couldn't* get to me – then I had to find a way to get into Sol, avoiding the Solian guards, get into the temple, and restore the stone back to its place. *Easy*, I thought wryly.

Kai had always snuck into Nos; I thought he liked the challenge. I had never had to go looking for him – he had always come to me. Perhaps he had left the stone with me on purpose. Perhaps he wanted to see if I would come to him... to see if I had the courage, or even if I cared for him enough.

Whatever the reason, I had to return the stone – but if I was caught with it, it wouldn't look good. I sent a silent plea up to the moon. I hoped Arianrhod was on my side.

Eleven

I crept stealthily through the fields and orchard, but I needn't have worried about being spotted. The workers had retired for the night, and the area was still. Moths and fireflies flitted above the crops and flowers, and I thought guiltily about Lunara. My outburst had startled my friend. I spotted some frostberries and picked up few; hopefully they would do as a peace offering for when I returned… if I wasn't caught red-handed.

On the outskirts of Sol, I hovered by a large carved archway. A full sun with long, spiky sunbursts was set into the orange-and-red-veined marble at the top, with runes and carvings adorning the side. I ran my hand over the stone. Despite the moonlight, it was warm to the touch.

Two Solian guards marched up and down the main street leading into the city centre. Ever since the bridge had cracked, the Council members feared a possible Shadowwraith attack and ordered that no civilians could cross between the Twin Realms at night. But the Celestial Bridge still held, and as there hadn't been an attack for years, I thought the Council were being overly cautious. Perhaps in reality they simply feared Kai and I would fail in our duty and allow the Shadowwraiths to be released, overrunning both realms. Some said they would become lands of never-ending twilight – neither day nor night. I never dwelled on that; I had to focus on what I needed to do. I couldn't afford to think of the alternative.

I pulled out the Sunstone and studied it. I couldn't believe this little thing had caused so much trouble.

Putting the stone back into my pocket, I waited until the guards were both turning before edging around the arch and blending into the shadows. When the one closest to me moved away, I sidled along the edge of a yellow-bricked building and into an alleyway. I didn't have a clue where I should go, but if Sol's layout was anything like Nos then its most important buildings would be in the centre.

A few citizens moved around the streets, heading home from workdays or off to one of the many taverns I passed. I wondered if they stocked the new *Celestara* cider. I didn't really care, I told myself, but a full-bodied aroma wafted out of a nearby tavern window, and my mouth watered. *Stop it*, I told my traitorous tastebuds.

I scooted back out of sight as the tavern door opened and a couple of guards emerged, holding a drooping young man between them.

"Mistress Sabra was right. She said he'd gone off to drown his sorrows," the taller guard said.

I did a double-take. The man they were holding was Kai! I knew he liked pears, but I couldn't believe he'd had the time to drink himself into a stupor since I had seen him last. *What sorrows?*

Shaking my head in exasperation, I followed the trio, keeping back, but close enough to see where they were going. After ten minutes or so, they arrived at a tall, thin building. It was made out of the same marble as Sol's entrance arch, but had gold pillars lining the wraparound terrace. The windows were covered with ornate gold half-grills, depicting the sun in its full, blazing glory.

One of the guards tapped on the door, which opened, letting the three in. I let out a frustrated breath. What was I going to do now? I glanced around. Maybe the temple was nearby.

I didn't have to look too hard. Opposite the door the guards had entered was a splendid gold building I had been too intent to notice. I kept to the railings running the length of the building, peered around the metal gates, and stopped short. A row of gold-jacketed guards stood in front of the temple, next to a large gong. That must have been the clanging I'd heard. Well, I wasn't getting in there.

I turned back to the building Kai was in. I needed his help. *He'd* stolen the stone and by the Fates, he could help me put it back again.

Letting determination overcome my fear of being caught, I sneaked up to one of the windows and peered in through the glass behind the grill. It appeared to be some kind of meeting room, with a round table and red velvet chairs. The next window showed an unoccupied office. I was about to move on when the door to the room opened and Sabra stalked in. *Aha*, I thought, and waited. Sure enough, Kai was escorted in by the guards and placed on a hardbacked chair, which he immediately slumped down into.

Really, Kai?

I watched covertly as Sabra tried to rouse him; she shook him and offered him water, but he continued to be unresponsive. Finally, with a gesture of annoyance, she had the guards lay him on his side on a sofa in the corner of the room, and they all left.

I tried to prise open the grill to see if I could open the window, then stared in shock as Kai rolled off the sofa and sprang nimbly to his feet. He walked over to the door and put his ear to it. After a moment, he headed over to Sabra's desk and rifled through the drawers.

What was he *doing?* I jolted myself into action and tapped on the window. Kai jumped and whirled to the interior door. I tapped again, and finally he turned to the window. His eyes widened as I held up the Sunstone. I couldn't be sure, but I thought he groaned.

"We have to put it back," I mouthed, but he pointed behind me with a look of terror on his face. I turned around – and came face to face with the two guards. I hadn't heard them opening the door to leave.

I whipped the stone down and shoved it behind my back. Now it was my turn to groan. *Caught!*

"What are you doing here? And what's behind your back?" the short guard said, eyeing me suspiciously.

"Hey, aren't you that Moonshade girl?" the taller one chimed in.

"Nope, not me – I, um, came into Sol for a dare." I knew a few of the younger Nosians sometimes sneaked into Sol after dark.

"Is that so. What's your name then?" Suspicious asked me.

"Oh… Eva," I replied, with the merest of winces. Lady Celestri would kill me if she knew I was besmirching her precious daughter's name. *Sorry, Eva.*

"Come on then, *Eva*. We'll escort you back to the border," the tall guard said with a smirk at his companion, and I breathed a sigh of relief. They were letting me go? At least Kai knew I had the stone. He could come and get it tomorrow and return it himself.

"Hang on a second, Aelius. No one is to leave Sol until the Sunstone is found," Suspicious said in a conversational tone, before turning his eyes my way at my small intake of breath.

"What shall we do with her then?" Aelius asked, leaning on his sword.

"I shall deal with her, thank you, guards," a cold female voice said. This time my wince was pronounced.

The guards backed off, their eyes wide, as I met Sabra's ice-blue gaze. I wished I could melt away as easily as they did. As surreptitiously as possible, I slid the Sunstone into the back pocket of my trousers and feigned surprise. "Good evening, Mistress Sabra."

"What are you doing here?" Sabra hissed, with not even a pretence at manners. She threw up her hands. "Did you not learn *anything* when we took you to the bridge? You cannot keep trying to meet with Lord Malakai. It is outrageous behaviour." She narrowed her eyes. "It looks like you're stuck here until the thief can be found."

I raised one eyebrow. "Thief?" I tried for an innocent tone, but it came out with a nervous laugh.

Sabra gave the window behind me a thoughtful look. A sly smile crept across her face. "Perhaps I *can* arrange a meeting with Lord Malakai, since you have come all this way to see him."

This about-turn threw me. "Ah, no, thank you. I'll find somewhere to settle for the night until I can contact Meuric in the morning."

"No, no, I absolutely insist. We cannot have a Lady of Nos wandering around unchaperoned and sleeping outside."

Actually, I wouldn't mind it. Many a night I had lain on the broken stone wall of the old temple with Lunara, watching the moon skip across the sky and the stars twinkle out a glittering staccato.

But with little choice in the matter, I allowed Sabra to lead me into the city hall building. She closed the door behind me and turned the lock. A ripple of unease worked its way down my back. I didn't like being trapped in Sol, especially with the Sunstone in my pocket.

"This way," she said tightly and glided past me, her muted gold robe whispering across the orange, red and yellow tiled floor.

She opened the door to her office. I expected to see Kai bolt past me, ready for escape, but he was once again reclining on the sofa. I blinked a few times to check I wasn't seeing things. Had I actually seen him get up and ransack Sabra's drawers? One surreptitious look at her desk showed that it was neat and orderly. *Kai's good,* I thought, once again questioning how well I really knew him.

"You will find him most scintillating company, I'm sure," Sabra said with a flick of her hand at him. "I am afraid he overindulged this evening."

As she turned away, I thought I saw Kai's lips twitch. No doubt he found this whole situation highly amusing.

"Please, have a seat, Lady Ceridwen," Sabra invited me, and I sat in the hardback chair Kai had been in earlier. I could understand why he'd slumped; drunk or not, it was most uncomfortable. I tried to wriggle into a more comfortable position, but the Sunstone dug into my behind. I couldn't very well remove it, so I tried to keep the pained expression off my face as Sabra leaned forward in her chair to rest her elbows on her desk. Steepling her fingers, she regarded me through narrowed eyes.

"Let us speak plainly," she said. "I, too, am a woman. I understand that you are letting your emotions override your common sense. We have all done it."

The back of my neck itched, and despite his closed eyes, I could sense Kai listening closely. My lips twisted; I didn't believe for one second that Sabra had let her heart rule over her head even once. She always came across so cool and composed.

I shook my head. I needed to stall for time so I could come up with a plan. "That is not why I came."

Kai tensed; I was surprised Sabra couldn't sense it too. Perhaps it was the connection Kai and I shared.

"Then why, Lady Ceridwen? What else could have possibly brought you into Sol on so beautiful a night?"

What could I say? Did I admit my guilt at having the Sunstone in my pocket? Or did I tell her what she wanted to hear – that yes, my heart pulled me towards Kai. *That yes, if there was a way I could be with him, then I would do it.*

112

My hand flew to my mouth at the sudden and revealing thoughts. Where had the numb feeling I had worked so hard to cultivate gone? I had to fight not to push back my chair and flee like I had done earlier at the cottage. I met Sabra's eyes, and she smiled. She was enjoying this.

"I don't feel well," I told her weakly, and a mask of concern slipped over her features.

"Let me show you to the guest quarters, where you can rest. I am sure this has been a most trying time."

"Guest quarters?" Uneasily, I wondered why Sabra was being nice to me.

"Yes. This is not only the city hall, it is also my place of residence," Sabra informed me.

I swallowed. I was trapped in Sabra's *house*?

Twelve

Sabra stared at me expectantly, so I managed a weak, "Thank you."

A groan from the sofa made Sabra turn. "It looks like our friend is returning to us," she said dispassionately.

Kai sat up and made a show of looking blearily about him. Was Sabra fooled? I stared at him, and he had the good grace to look sheepishly down. "That was some strong cider," he slurred. "Where am I?"

"Hmm," Sabra said, and walked over to a drinks cabinet to pour him a glass of water. "You are in my house. Drink this while I show our guest to her room."

"Hi, Wen," Kai said enthusiastically, toasting me with his glass and sloshing water on the carpet.

"Kai," I replied through gritted teeth. He was just overdoing it now.

Sabra looked from me to him and pursed her lips. "This way."

She led me from the room, and I shot an exasperated look over my shoulder, mouthing, "*The stone.*"

Kai gave me a thumbs-up, but Sabra turned to see what was keeping me, so I could only hope it meant he had a plan.

Sabra led me up the wide staircase dominating the foyer. I gripped the gold handrail tightly.

"Here we are," she said, pushing open the door to an opulently decorated room. A four-poster bed with gauzy cream drapes and brocade bedding sat against a painted feature wall of fiery sky and fluffy clouds. "Bathroom is through there; I recommend the juniper berry bath soak – does wonders for tired muscles... and minds." She opened a closet set into the wall next to the bathroom door. "Clothes, toiletries, towels."

I nodded wordlessly. Why was she being so kind?

"After you are rested, we will continue our little chat," she concluded from the doorway of the room.

Ah, that's why.

She left the room and pulled the door closed after her. I thought I heard a tiny click and waited a minute before checking. Yes; she had locked it. I moved over to the window and rattled the handle, but that too was locked. Funny way to treat a 'guest'.

My limbs weary, I sank onto the bed. Perhaps a bath *would* be a good idea. I headed into the bathroom and turned on the taps, letting the hot, steamy water fill up the copper clawfoot tub. Perusing the scents, I disregarded the juniper; I did not want to smell like Sabra. I found an unopened bottle of moonflower and happily added a liberal dose. *Much better.*

I left my clothes in a pile on the floor before sliding into the fragrant water. My muscles became fluid, and my breathing eased as the knot in my lungs untightened. I allowed myself to relax against the tub, lying still with my eyes closed, relishing in the fact that in this suspended moment I had nothing to fear. I could forget about my worries and just exist.

I don't know how long I lay there, but becoming aware of the water cooling around me, I roused myself to soap up my now chilled body.

I ducked beneath the water, slicking my curls back, then emerged and grabbed the bottle of shampoo I'd left on the small table next to the bath. I lathered up my hair, grimacing at the thought of not having my own special hair cream. This would have to do. I ducked my head back under to get rid of the soap.

Calmer, I got out of the bath and grabbed the thick towel to wrap around myself – and felt my heart give a double beat as I saw that my pile of clothes had gone, the stone with it!

Water dripped on the rug as I hurried into the bedroom and over to the door, but it was still locked. Someone must have entered the room when I had my eyes closed. What was I going to do now?

The door handle rattled, and I watched as the door opened and Kai slipped inside. I gripped the towel tighter around my body, and my mouth worked soundlessly for a few moments as he looked me up and down.

"Quick! Where's the stone?" he asked, giving his head a shake as if to clear unwanted thoughts.

I groaned. "It's missing! It was in my trouser pocket and now my clothes are gone." I shrugged helplessly.

"What a shame," Kai said with a crooked smile.

"Kai – focus!" I admonished, striding over to the closet to look for something else to put on so I could stop feeling exposed and vulnerable. I grabbed a silky top in dull gold and matching wide-legged trousers and headed back into the bathroom.

I pulled on the clothes, grateful they fitted, before scrunching most of the water out of my curls with a towel and finger-combing them. I quickly braided them into a loose fat braid and secured it with a piece of copper ribbon I found in a crystal dish on the vanity table. My hair would be a frizzy mess tomorrow, but Alys's wonder cream would help with that.

Back in the bedroom, I found Kai lounging on the bed. "Haven't you rested enough?" I asked snippily.

"Hey, I had to find a way to get into Sabra's office without her suspecting anything," he said, standing and coming up close. "Gold suits you."

"Stop distracting me," I said, stepping back, and he laughed, a twinkle in his eyes.

"Nice to know I still can."

I rolled my eyes. "Why did you need to get into Sabra's office? What were you looking for?"

His eyes turned serious. "Belenos let me see something – something I need to prove for myself. I had suspected for years something wasn't right about the Choosing, and Belenos confirmed it. Sabra—" He broke off as the door handle turned again. Without missing a beat, he dived under the bed and pulled the cover down to conceal himself.

I turned in time to see Sabra enter. "Feeling better, I see," she said, looking me over. "Come and join me for a drink on the terrace."

Fates above! Would I ever find out what Belenos had shown Kai? And what were we going to do about the stone? I slipped my feet into beaded slippers and followed Sabra out into the corridor, once again leaving Kai. I *really* hoped he had a plan.

On the terrace, Sabra poured me a drink of golden liquid. I fervently hoped it wasn't *Celestara* cider; thankfully, it was wine. I sipped it slowly, keen to keep my wits about me.

"You might be wondering where Lord Malakai is," Sabra said, and I shook my head innocently. "I had my healer make him a restorative tonic, and now he is doing a little errand for me. He will be along shortly."

Errand? What errand could she possibly have him doing? I took another small sip of wine, stalling the need to say anything.

"Ah, here he is now." Sabra set down her glass and walked over to Kai as he stepped through the double doors onto the terrace. "Is it done?" she asked in an undertone.

His eyes flicked to mine, and he gave a jerky nod. The pit of my stomach burned as I wondered what was going on.

"Excellent," Sabra said. "Right, well, I trust you two know not to kill each other... well, not yet anyway," she added with a little laugh.

I stared at her. That was low, even for her. Kai looked the way I felt.

"I have a little matter to attend to," she went on, "then we shall see about getting you back to Nos, Lady Ceridwen."

"But I thought I had to stay until…" I trailed off, not wanting to mention the Sunstone.

"Oh, that other little concern has been resolved," Sabra said airily, and went back into the house.

"How—?"

Kai cut me off. "Listen, Wen, don't believe her. She's out to drive a wedge between us. Don't let her do it," he said urgently, taking both my hands in his.

"What are you talking about? Kai, you have to stop talking in riddles. You need to let me in on what you know."

"I will, I promise. I need to make sure I'm right before I make any accusations. Come on – take a walk with me. We haven't got much time." He pulled my hand and led me down the terrace steps into the garden. The moon shone brightly on the path, and we followed its circular route.

My head whirled; there were so many questions I wanted to ask, but I also didn't want to spoil this moment. I could almost imagine that in another time, in another life, we were preparing for our union. That I hadn't had to learn how to fight to the death these past three years, instead learning etiquette and how to be a good ruler of the Twin Realms. I would have been planning to move into a mansion – much like this one – and learning to love the sun as much as I loved my Fated Partner. But that was something I didn't have to worry about… although I might have to say goodbye to Nos in a different way.

Perhaps Kai was thinking along the same lines. He abruptly stopped and turned to face me. "What if this is it, Wen? What if all we have is this moment, right here, right now?"

My heart pumped hard in my chest as he looked at me with the most intense expression I had ever seen. No crooked smile, no twinkling eyes – just pure blue intent, like a perfect summer sky. My lips parted and my breath hitched.

"What if it is?" I whispered.

"Then we should make it count."

And suddenly we were standing a shared breath apart. His hands on my hips were featherlight, but my skin burned through the fabric of my trousers. Time stopped. I could see my eyes reflected in his, like a galaxy swirling with a thousand shooting stars. Perhaps, after all, I could wish on these.

His mouth lowered to mine, and I leaned forward to welcome him home.

"No! What are you two doing?"

I was wrenched away from Kai before our lips could meet, but the promised heat still lingered on mine. I stumbled and landed in a flower bed.

I looked down at the streaks of mud on my trousers, and a flashback to the Nos training yard and my boots, splattered in mud, rose in my mind. What was I doing here? I didn't belong in these clothes, and I certainly didn't belong in a grand house like this one, dreaming of a future with Kai that could never be.

"Leave her!" Sabra hissed as I struggled to my feet, the cage closing around my heart once again.

Kai stood poised to help me up but backed away, his face unreadable, at Sabra's urging.

"I'd like to go home now," I said flatly.

Sabra gave a curt nod. "Your clothes are upstairs." I looked at her sharply, but she regarded me with an innocent expression, and suspicions slowly started falling into place. I had been found out.

I hurried from the garden as fast as the beaded slippers would allow. One slipped from my foot, and with an angry gesture I pulled off the other one, retrieved the lost one and carried on barefoot. The anger propelled me on, but I stopped short as I entered my room.

My clothes were folded neatly on the bed, freshly laundered, and my boots on the floor were polished to the extent that I could see my face in them when I picked them up. I expected Sabra had an army of servants to do her bidding. *Stealthy ones*, I thought, remembering how quickly my things had been removed.

I checked the pockets of my trousers, but the stone, as I had feared, was gone.

"Looking for something?" Sabra stood framed in the doorway, the Sunstone glowing in her outstretched hand. "I knew there was another reason you were in Sol. Silly me, thinking you were here to tempt Lord Malakai's heart. Although that little display in the garden had me fooled for a second."

I looked past Sabra to where Kai had come up behind her. Wasn't he going to say anything?

Sabra turned her head slightly. "But he was most helpful. He told me *exactly* who had stolen the stone."

What? No! Had he set me up?

"Kai," I breathed. But he wouldn't meet my eyes.

Thirteen

The warning from the whispering voices returned into my mind with a vengeance. *You can't trust him...* Had they actually meant Kai?

Finally, he met my eyes. "Wen, remember what I said in the garden."

Sabra narrowed her eyes as I racked my brains. Which part? The part about Sabra trying to drive a wedge between us... or the 'let's make it count' moment where I had nearly given myself over to him? I shook my head at my own naiveté. I got his message loud and clear: that moment in the garden *had* been all we'd ever have.

With a choked sob, I gathered up my clothes and stormed into the bathroom. I almost ripped the delicate gold fabric of the Sol clothes as I removed them, but I didn't care. I hastily dressed and pulled the copper ribbon from the end of my braid, letting my damp curls loose. I studied myself in the mirror; now I looked like me.

The bedroom was empty. *Coward!* my mind screamed. The door hung open, so I left the room without a backwards glance, clattered down the grand staircase, and wrenched open the now unlocked front door. No one tried to stop me.

I was jogging down the entrance steps when a prickling sensation made me glance up at one of the windows on the second floor. Kai stood there, staring down at me. I stared back. And I knew that this time, we were truly saying goodbye.

The first to break eye contact, I turned away and ran as if Shadowwraiths themselves were on my tail.

I didn't stop running until I got to the Solian archway; not even the guards could have caught me as I raced by them. One stood in front of the arch, so I launched myself up the carved posts, and with their shouts ringing in my ears, vaulted over the top. Climbing was my best skill, after all.

As soon as I reached the orchard, tears burned the back of my eyes, but I *refused* to give in to them. Instead I got angrier. A bushel of pears sat to one side, and I vented my anger by overturning them and launching them one after another at a tree. A scream of rage tore from my throat. Kai had *tricked* me. He had led me to believe he was working on a way to solve this whole mess, but no, all along he had been lulling me into a false sense of security and doing Sabra's bidding.

"Stupid, tempting cider-lips—" I muttered darkly.

"I mean, pears are not for everyone, but I didn't think anybody could hate them this much."

Startled, I dropped the pear I was holding. "Lord Celestri!" I exclaimed. "I was just, uh… practicing."

"Cosimo, please, and practicing for what?" he asked, picking up a pear himself and tossing it from one hand to another. He was dressed in casual attire – faded black trousers and a black, long-sleeved T-shirt. His short hair fell in ripples over his brow.

I slumped onto a barrel. "My aim," I said, and Lord Celestri laughed.

"Well, it's working. I wouldn't want to be on the receiving end of it." He took a seat next to me and bit into the pear.

I frowned, imagining Kai's head in the branches of the tree. It helped to picture it with pear splattered all over his pretty golden face.

Lord Celestri shifted to look at me. Concern shone in his silver eyes. "Ceridwen, is there anything I can do for you? You appear to be out of sorts."

The anger melted away, replaced by desolation. "Thank you, my lord, but no one can help me with this particular problem." *Kill or be killed.*

"It is so unfair, isn't it? Such a burden shouldn't fall on one so young. Especially you, my dear."

What did he mean? Did he think I wasn't up to the task?

"Oh, I didn't mean you can't handle it, but you deserve a better life than this. Everything is wrong." Lord Celestri frowned and rubbed a hand over his face.

I had never had such a deep conversation with Lord Celestri before. As Eva's father, I knew him, of course, but he had always been someone I looked up to... a hero of sorts. To see him so open was disconcerting.

"I've resigned myself to my fate," I told him, and he whipped around to look at me again, quicksilver eyes searching my face. *Curious*, I thought. Was that grief I detected in them?

I stood after an awkward pause. "I should get back to Alys. She'll be wondering where I am."

"Alys," Lord Celestri murmured. "Yes, of course. Give her my regards, won't you?"

"I will," I promised. "Goodnight."

"Goodnight, Wen," Lord Celestri said quietly.

I left him staring pensively at the trees. I wondered what had brought him so far away from his manor this night, but put that question aside to focus on my own problems. I should have trusted my earlier instincts and separated myself from Kai completely, but he had an uncanny knack of pulling me back to him. We were like magnets. Perhaps I needed to find a way of repelling him for good.

I shook my head. The damage had already been done. He had set me up, for some reason I couldn't fathom right now – but I actually didn't care what the reason was. That he had done it at all sealed the deal.

Relief filled me as I neared the cottage. I needed to see Lunara. *The frostberries!* I remembered. They had been in my trousers too. It felt like a lifetime ago when I had left in terror about what might be happening to Kai. Thinking he had been caught... but instead I had walked right into his – or Sabra's – trap.

I pursed my lips as I let myself into the cottage. At least *now* I could focus on the task at hand. I could concentrate on what needed to be done and not get distracted by hope of another way. If Kai wanted me off-kilter, well, he was mistaken. I would not be taken for a fool again.

A fluffy torpedo whirred into me, and I caught Lunara as she unleashed a barrage of grumbles.

"I know, I know, I'm sorry I scared you earlier." She grumbled harder. "And yes, left you for hours… where's Alys?" The cottage was quiet and empty.

I made myself a drink and looked for a note, but there wasn't one. Perhaps Alys had gone to see a friend, thinking I'd decided to spend the night at Eva's. The day had taken its toll on me. I needed to sleep.

Up in my room, I tugged off my boots, changing into soft sleep shorts and a T-shirt. Bit of a difference from the gold silk I had worn earlier, I thought sourly.

Placing Lunara into her nest, I burrowed down beneath my covers and was soon fast asleep.

Gentle singing woke me before morning, and for a moment I couldn't remember where I was. I sat up and looked over the wooden railing. Alys was down in the kitchen, singing softly to herself. I was glad she appeared happier than the last time she had gone on a midnight outing.

My mouth dropped open as she unpacked a basket full of… *pears.*

All right, Wen, don't jump to conclusions, I told myself sternly. There were plenty of places she could have picked the pears… No, there weren't – there was only the orchard. The orchard I had been in earlier, having a conversation with Lord Celestri. I sat back on my heels. My mind whirled with a million possibilities, none of which made any sense.

It's none of my business. I refused to acknowledge the suspicion I kept circling back to.

Stroking Lunara, I lay back down and drifted off into a sleep crowded with whispers that buzzed inside my mind like angry bees, as silky gold water closed over my head. Kai stood above me, doing nothing to help me as grasping, dark-nailed hands slowly pulled me down.

I awoke, my heart in my mouth, and watched the moon slowly dip out of sight. It looked like I would have to save myself.

There was no time like the present, I decided as I got up and stretched. I dressed in training gear and smoothed a slumbering Lunara on her head. Despite the events of yesterday, energy zinged through my veins, and I was eager to get to training.

The reason for my energy soon became apparent as I entered the kitchen to the scent of peppermint and rosemary washing over me. It was coming from a small dish hanging above a squat red candle.

"Morning, sweetheart. I thought you could do with a little pep up this morning." Alys came in from the small garden, holding a handful of rosemary and gestured over to the candle, before setting a pan on the stove to warm.

"Yes, um, sorry about running off yesterday. I didn't want to be late for Eva." I ducked my head and took a seat at the table.

"Funny thing about that is – Eva came looking for you. Told me to remind you about your shopping trip today." Alys took a seat opposite me.

"Ah," I said.

"Ah, indeed. Would you like to tell me where you really were? I know you're almost of age, and I don't like to pry, but I'm worried about you. We all are."

"We?" I returned, and Alys flushed.

"Yes, you know, Eva, Meuric, Maxen… all your friends."

I nibbled my lip, and before I could stop it another lie emerged. "I was with Maxen."

"Maxen?" Alys repeated, disbelief evident in her tone. She stood and cracked a few eggs into the pan. "Why did you tell me you were going to see Eva?"

"I'm… not sure. I didn't want you to worry if you thought I was meeting up with him." I cringed at the unintended meaning behind my words. I didn't want her to think there was more to my friendship with Maxen, but if it got me out of admitting where I really had been…

"Oh, but I thought…" She trailed off. "Never mind. Well, that's lovely, but no more secrets, ok?"

She placed the basket of fruit on the table, and the fresh, glossy pears caught my eye. I looked up at her.

"Sure, no more secrets." *For both of us*, I was tempted to add, but something stopped me. *None of my business*, I repeated in my head, before digging into the scrambled eggs Alys placed before me.

We ate in silence until there was a knock at the door. Alys answered it, and I heard hushed voices. She opened the door wider and let Meuric in. I pushed my plate away at the serious expression on his face.

"I thought I'd walk you to training this morning. We can have a talk."

"All right." I glanced at Alys and got up. "I'll see you later – I might be a bit late. Shopping with Eva always takes longer than it should."

Alys grinned. "Don't rush. You should enjoy yourselves."

Hmm, enjoyment or torture? Shopping with Eva could be a painful combination of both. "Right," I said with a grimace.

Alys laughed as I left with a sombre Meuric. He didn't say anything until we were a good distance away from the cottage, but when he did, his words were the last ones I expected him to utter.

"Would you mind telling me what you were doing in Sol last night?"

Fourteen

I stopped dead. "Good news travel fast," I stalled, attempting a joke, but Meuric's expression didn't even flicker.

"I had an interesting message from a friend of mine. Told me they saw you running from the city hall. Do you know anything about the Sunstone being stolen?"

I couldn't stomach telling any more lies, and Meuric's expression was fierce. I didn't want to disappoint him again. I nodded.

He raised one grey eyebrow and waited.

"Kai thought he could speak to Belenos and see if there was a way around the prophecy. But… he tricked me and blamed me for stealing the stone." As I spoke, Meuric's eyebrow rose even higher.

"The young man surprises me. It wasn't a bad idea," he mused, staring off into space.

I gaped at my mentor. "Didn't you hear what I said about him blaming *me*?"

Meuric turned his attention back to me. "He probably had his reasons for doing so," he said.

I stood in front of him opening and closing my mouth like one of the shimmering opalescent fish in the Celestri's pond.

"You can't be serious," I exclaimed as we started walking again. The training yard came into sight.

"Ceridwen, Kai isn't the only one with suspicions. None of us want this fate for you both. Neither of you deserve it." As Meuric spoke, he spared a quick glance at the sky. Perhaps he thought the Fates were listening. Perhaps they were. "At least he's doing something proactive about it."

A flush of shame burned across my cheeks. He was right. What had *I* done? Wallowed for six months, then resigned myself to my fate. I had never tried to find a way around it. Perhaps Kai was right. Maybe I had been going about this the wrong way. Instead of accepting that there was only one way this would end, we should have been working together to find out *why* the Fates frowned upon our union.

"What did Belenos tell him?" Meuric asked.

I blew out a long, discouraged breath. "I don't quite know. Kai said the Fates aren't angry at us, something else is in play." The whispered warnings came back me, rolling over me like waves over shingle. "Can I trust Kai, though?" I murmured, more to myself than Meuric.

Nothing made sense any more. I thought I was doing was I was supposed to do, what *needed* to be done, but everyone kept telling me I was wrong, that I shouldn't give in so easily. Well, everyone except for Sabra, Lady Celestri and Gus. They all thought I should just get out of the way. Perhaps I was never meant to have been born, and that's why I had been orphaned, why the Fates had frowned upon me being Chosen. Maybe I should have succumbed to the freezing fog on the Celestial Bridge before I was ever found.

Meuric interrupted my melancholy thoughts. "Hmm, just as I thought." He nodded and clamped a hand on my shoulder. "We still have a couple of weeks. There is time yet to change the course of fate."

I blinked a few times, wondering if he had heard my thoughts, but of course he was referring to Kai speaking with Belenos. My shoulders slumped. It wasn't that I didn't have confidence in my mentor – I just didn't know what a group of mortals could do against the will of the Fates.

We reached the training yard, and Maxen straightened from the post he was leaning on to walk over to us.

"Ready, Wen?" he asked, skilfully twirling a wooden staff in one hand. He threw another at me and I skipped sideways, twirled, and caught it gracefully in my outstretched arm. Grateful I had managed to catch it without it hitting my shins, I didn't realise the yard had gone silent until I looked up.

Everyone had stopped what they were doing and stared at me with varying expressions of disbelief.

I straightened and gave a wobbly little curtsey. Fates above – I'd hoped to cling to my poise for a few minutes more, I thought with a grimace. But despite my waver, a smattering of applause rippled around the group before it was joined by hollers and cheers. I flushed and ducked my head.

"Well, well, well." Gus appeared from around the back of the group. "Looks like we'll all be saved by dancing. Who knew we had such a formidable weapon amongst our midst?" He struck a pose, obviously thinking it would draw laughs his way.

"Shut up, Gus," Maxen said, starting forward with his staff.

"Max," Meuric warned, and Maxen stepped back with a look of disgust on his face. "Though he is right; do be quiet, Master Novarian. Lady Ceridwen has just demonstrated how fighting – and better yet, winning – isn't all about brute force. Sometimes skill and poise can outwit the most... ah... tough of opponents. Would you like to go a round with our Chosen Lady, Gus?"

Gus's red face turned into a scowl, and he marched forwards to grab the staff off Maxen. "It would be my pleasure."

I gave an inward groan. I wasn't in the mood for Gus to try and best me today, especially now he had been made a fool of. Now, he had something to prove.

I barely I had time to dance back as he came at me with ferocity. Our staffs clunked together, and I gritted my teeth as Gus' weight behind his staff had me sliding backwards. Knowing I didn't have the strength to maintain this for long, I took a deep breath and nimbly sidestepped, ducking as Gus' staff narrowly missed connecting with my cheek.

"Come on, Wen!" someone called from the group, and I realised it was Maxen's cousin, Larissa. At her encouraging words, warmth made its way up my arms and I thrust forward, my staff giving Gus's ribs a glancing blow. I grinned, but hissed out a breath as Gus retaliated with a menacing look on his face. His staff stopped a mere inch from my nose as I managed to lean back, using my own staff as leverage.

"Tired yet, twinkle-toes?" he asked through a smirk.

I pirouetted away and turned back. "No, you?"

Gus gave a roar of rage and launched himself at me. It was too easy. I stuck out my staff, and Gus sprawled onto his back. Winded, he glared up at me. *Hmm, how the tables have turned.*

Everyone else crowded around us, and Maxen lifted me up and twirled me around. "You did it!"

I laughed as he set me back on my feet. His eyes were intense on mine, but I avoided them and went over to offer Gus my hand. He ignored it and struggled to his feet, handing the staff back to an amused-looking Meuric.

With a shrug I turned away. Why I'd thought Gus would behave in a sporting manner, I had no idea. I was heading back to Maxen when Gus's voice stopped me.

"Moonshade? Not bad."

As he limped away, I looked at Maxen in shock.

"Did he… *compliment* you?" Maxen asked with a disbelieving laugh.

"I think so," I replied slowly, shaking my head. Well, that was certainly a first – and one probably never to be repeated again. Happier, and buoyed up on adrenaline, I looked at Maxen. "Race you up the wall!"

"Wait – you have to tell me where you learnt those moves," Maxen shouted.

"Ha ha! Distraction won't work!" I called back, already scaling the wall.

"No, seriously," Maxen panted at my heels.

"Eva," I replied, pulling myself up onto the top of the wall. Maxen joined me seconds later.

"Eva?" he said in disbelieving tones, and I grinned at him.

"She's not simply a pretty face, you know," I reminded him, and he grunted.

"I know that. My *ribs* know that," he added, rubbing them as if the memory of the numerous bruises Eva had inflicted over the years still lingered. "She's even more deft with the staff than you're turning out to be."

I grinned. "Exactly, so who better to teach me – a mix of skill and poise, remember?"

"Smart." Maxen nodded and stared off across the training yard. "I miss those days," he said quietly. His knee bumped against mine.

I did too.

Maxen, Eva and I had started at Meuric's training school together. I, all clumsy limbs and self-doubt, hadn't made a great first impression, but even Gus had kept his opinions to himself at first. Eva had been so protective of me. Having grown up on her family's estate, I only knew her well, but Maxen and Eva were already friends. Max was from one of the noble houses, so they'd had plenty of interactions before. Soon we were a trio of friends, and we always had each other's backs – until Eva had come of age and left training, when the dynamic had shifted slightly.

As if reading my thoughts, Maxen turned to me, his expression serious. "Wen, after this is all over, I want you to know—"

He stopped as I held up a hand. "Max, don't." I knew exactly what he was about to say. I could sense his heart thrumming against his chest, even from the distance between us. If he said the words hovering on his tongue and swirling in his eyes, it would spoil everything. Why did things have to change?

His mouth turned down, and he thrust a frustrated hand through his hair. "Why, Wen? Because you're scared of what I'll say? Scared to think you might actually have a future after all – with someone who *isn't* out to kill you?"

I gasped, and Maxen's expression turned stormy. He looked like he wanted to say more, but instead he grabbed the rope and rappelled down the wall. He was striding away on long legs out of the training yard before I could even utter a word.

The adrenaline rush from the fight and the climb dissipated, and shaky, I lay down on top of the wall, leaving my legs to dangle over the side. Great. What was I going to do now? How could I explain to Maxen that I didn't feel that way about him? I was tied to Kai – I always had been. Even without the Choosing he would be the only one for me. No matter how hard I tried to hide it from myself, my soul would be forever intertwined with his, but never in the way I had hoped it would. The Fates had seen to that.

Being with anyone else wouldn't be fair on them, when I couldn't give them what they wanted… what they deserved. My future was full of heartbreak, something I couldn't thrust upon anyone else.

I couldn't lose Maxen's friendship, though. *What a mess.* Knowing I couldn't hide on top of the wall forever, I clambered down the rope and decided to vent my mood on another training dummy.

Everyone else gave me a wide berth, perhaps sensing the tumult inside me. What I wanted – what I *needed* – was a good Nos storm. One of the ones where the air became electrified with supercharged particles ready to be discharged in lightning that streaked across the sky, chased by big, booming claps of thunder that rattled your ribs and echoed around your mind. *Those* kinds of storms. I had heard there were some people who could manipulate the weather, but they were rumours of those who dwelled in Fog. And I certainly did not want to venture there. No, a good bout of fighting should help dissipate the storm raging inside me.

I only hoped the training dummy was up to it.

Fifteen

"Ugh. Are you really going shopping in that?" Eva's eyes raked me up and down, taking in my dusty boots and trousers and my sweat-soaked tunic.

"You said I had to come shopping; you didn't mention anything about a dress code." I attempted an innocent look, but Eva narrowed her eyes at me.

"If you think I'm going to call off the shopping trip because of the way you're dressed, well, it won't work. Don't forget we're going *clothes* shopping. I can easily pick an outfit out for you if you like."

I gave a nonchalant shrug. "That's all right. Let's get this over with." I hoped she wouldn't make good on her threat and try and dress me up like one of her noble friends.

With a satisfied smile, Eva pushed open the door to the dress shop. "After you," she purred.

Head held high, I entered the boutique and stopped dead. Three similar-looking women looked up from racks of clothes and pursed their lips, wearing identical expressions of disdain.

I backed up and made to escape, but Eva stopped me.

"We made a deal, Wen," she reminded me sweetly. I had to suck it up and follow her meekly over to a rack of glittering, shimmering dresses.

One of the women swooped in, blocking my way to the rack. "Miss Celestri, how wonderful to see you. Let me assist you today. Your – ah – friend can sit there."

I didn't need telling twice, and hopped over to the pair of black and silver high-backed chairs to take a seat. Hopefully any dirt on my trousers would blend in.

Eva rolled her eyes at me and turned back to the woman, making a show of looking at the name embroidered on the pocket of her sleek black sheath dress. "Kari, is it? Well, my – ah – *friend* is actually Lady Ceridwen."

All three women looked my way, and I squirmed like a bug being inspected before being stepped on. "Really?" Kari asked, then gave a cough as Eva raised one perfectly arched eyebrow.

Another of the women stepped in with a simpering smile. "Please, let me get Lady Ceridwen a drink while Kari assists you, Miss Celestri."

Eva let them off the hook. "Eva is fine. I'll have a glass too."

"As long as it isn't cider," I muttered.

A glass of bubbly drink was placed onto the marble side table next to me by the woman – her name tag read Sali – and I smiled my thanks. I wondered if the third woman's name ended with an 'i' too and hid my grin behind my glass.

The next hour – or was it more? – passed in a froth of net, tulle, silks and glitter, all in shimmering Nos shades ranging from stormy pewter, thundercloud purple and midnight sky, with a sprinkling of silver.

Eva finally sat next to me in a confection of tiered black lace and hundreds of tiny ribbons criss-crossing her abdomen and chest. Clusters of stars dangled from her ears.

"Your father will never let you wear that," I observed, toasting her with my second – or was that third? – glass of bubbly.

"And *you* have had too much of that," she replied, removing my glass from my hand and setting it down on the side table.

I thought for a moment I was seeing double – no, make that triple – as Kari, Sali and the other 'i' hovered behind Eva. They pursed their lips in thought. Perhaps I *had* had too much drink. That was unlike me; I always tried to keep my alcohol to a minimum. I was clumsy enough without it.

"You were right, Miss Eva, she does have amazing eyes, and her hair is perfection."

Yep, now I really knew I'd had too much. *Perfection? Me?* Right, time to go home. I stood on slightly wobbly legs and made to leave, but was stopped by Eva's slim hand on my wrist.

"Try on one gown for me, Wen. *Please?*" Eva batted her incredibly long, thick, black eyelashes.

Kari held up the most beautiful gown I had ever seen, and my traitorous heart yearned for just one moment where I could experience what it was truly like to belong amongst the nobles of Nos. It was a shimmering ballgown in a froth of black tulle, overlaid with a shimmering gossamer web of a thousand stars. The bodice was a corset of black satin, with one glittering shooting star wrapping itself around the waist and arcing across the chest to sit in a glowing starburst on the left cup. Was I daring enough to wear it? My fingers itched to touch the creation.

"It has a secret weapon – just pull the hilt out from here." Eva gestured to the top of the corset and smiled her cat-like smile of satisfaction, knowing it would seal the deal for me. She took my hand and led me to the screen in the corner of the room. "Get undressed," she ordered.

As if in a dream, I obeyed her. I shunned my dusty clothes and boots, peeling a layer of the old me away. I looked at the pile on the black plush carpet and wondered if it would be easy to return to them once I had worn a dress that inspired dreams and could make the very Fates cry.

Eva handed me the dress, and I slipped it over my head. The tulle whispered as it brushed my skin.

"Turn around," Eva said quietly, and cinched the ribbons at my back, pulling them taut. I could barely breathe, but it only added to the sense of surrealness. My hair was lifted from the nape of my neck and swept to one side before being fastened. One long, dangling earring was clipped to my ear on the opposite side.

"Turn around," Eva said again, and gasped. With her eyes shining, she led me from behind the screen and over to the ornate, floor-to-ceiling mirror.

"Beautiful! Stunning! Magical!" I heard the three other ladies' exclamations, but I couldn't take my eyes off myself and Eva. We could have almost been sisters. I looked like a true Lady of Nos; my curls tumbled from my head in a side sweep held back by a comb of moonstones and crystals. The one long earring was a shooting star matching the one on my dress. I was mesmerised. Was this *me?*

"Maxen won't be able to keep his eyes off you," Eva said with a hip bump and an amused smile.

And just like that, the spell was broken. I turned to her in shock. She *knew* I didn't feel that way about Max.

"What did I say?" she asked, her eyes clouding. "I thought you two were getting closer. Max said…" She trailed off as I turned away, and with my heart pounding furiously in my chest, I rushed away from her, my feet sinking into the thick pile of the carpet. Why did everyone suddenly seem to know what or who was best for me? I wrenched open the shop door and with Kari – or was it Sali? – shouting after me, I plunged into the evening light. My dress of darkness was soon swallowed up by the shadows.

I didn't care where I went; I only cared about getting away from there. What had I been thinking? I could never be a part of Eva's world. My bare feet padded along the cobblestones, and soon I was heading out of the city. The dress floated around my ankles, and I hitched it up to stop myself from tripping over it.

As soon as my feet touched the mossy grass leading up to the old temple ruins, I slowed my pace and allowed my breathing to even out. The crisp air filled my lungs and my head cleared. *Much better,* I thought, as I hopped onto a broken wall and stared out across the sea before me. The crescent moon hung low in the sky and reflected onto the calm water. The waves themselves whispered as they rolled into shore far below me.

"Am I dreaming, or has Arianrhod herself come down from the stars?"

Goosebumps rose along my arms, but I refused to turn. He did not deserve my attention. Not after what he had done last night.

"Ah, her earthly presence stops her from uttering a word. That is the price to pay for leaving her castle in the sky."

A smile twitched at my lips, but inside my heart raced. How did he have this power over me? The power to turn my resistance around with merely his presence and a few humorous words?

Kai stepped up close beside me on the wall, his movements graceful. He didn't touch me, but I still felt the heat radiating off him through the tan tunic he wore. I finally met his eyes, and they lit with an inner glow.

"You look beautiful, my lady," he said reverently.

I looked down at the dress. Eva was going to *kill* me. I groaned and climbed down from the wall to sit on a mossy stone.

"Hmm, my compliments don't usually get that kind of reaction," Kai said. His tone was light, but his lips had flattened into a worried line.

"What?" I said distractedly, before shaking my head. My curls whipped around my face. With a huff of annoyance, I withdrew the clip anchoring them and tossed them back. "I am still angry at you, you know," I told him with narrowed eyes.

"I know," he said, now smiling, "but I had my reasons."

Huh, exactly what Meuric said. "Would you care to share them with me?" I asked pointedly, but he strolled over to me and crouched down, apparently in no hurry to answer the question.

His face close, he looked at me seriously. "I don't want to put you in any danger. There are things happening in Sol... and Nos, but I need to confirm a few matters" – he held up a tanned hand as I opened my mouth – "and then I promise to tell you everything."

I sat back and searched his face. "Fine, but as soon as you know what is happening, you tell me straight away."

Satisfaction rippled across his face, and he clapped his hands to his thighs as he stood. "I promise," he said, his white teeth flashing.

So why did a ripple of unease skate across my back? I shrugged it off as he held out a hand to me.

"Why are you so dressed up?" he asked. "Not that I'm complaining."

I gave a self-conscious smile. "Eva talked me into it. We were shopping – well, she was shopping..."

"Well, thank goodness she did, or I might never have seen you in a dress," Kai said. He twirled me around. "But – and it's definitely a look – why are you barefoot?"

"Ah, well..." How could I tell him I had left in a hurry because Eva had said Maxen would like me in the dress? Kai already disliked Max. Perhaps it wasn't the best idea, but the words were tumbling out of my mouth before I could stop them. I had to know what Kai truly felt. "I left in a hurry; I was meeting... someone."

I instantly regretted it when Kai's face dimmed, like the sun slipping behind a cluster of ragged clouds.

"And that someone obviously isn't me." He stepped back and gave me a mocking bow. "Then, my lady, I will leave you, as my presence is so clearly unwanted." He turned to go.

No. This was all wrong. I didn't want him to go like this. Thinking I was angry at him for yesterday was one thing, but believing I had moved on with my affections was another thing altogether.

"Kai, stop," I said, catching up with him. I placed my white hand on his bronzed wrist. His hand flexed before he turned around.

"Wen," he started, but his eyes shot to something behind me. "*Go!*"

"I'm sorry. I'm not really meet—"

Kai cut me off as he shoved me behind him, his hand going to the thin sword at his hip. Foggy tendrils snaked around our feet.

Something was seriously wrong.

Sixteen

"Wen, you need to go, and *now*," Kai repeated as four shadowy figures stepped from the fog.

"No! I will fight by your side," I told him, and was grateful my voice shook only minimally.

He cast a look my way, and a thousand unspoken words spilled from the depths of his blue eyes. I wished I could reach out and cradle them in my palm, to pocket them to listen to later when the moon would be at its fullest and my doubts would be screaming their highest. Instead, I gave him a look of my own. A look promising so many things if we were lucky enough to get out of this battle.

"You don't have a weapon," Kai said through gritted teeth.

I put a hand to the top of my corset and his eyes widened slightly. I would have found it amusing if the shadow beings hadn't been nearly upon us. I tugged at the top of the corset and withdrew a gleaming dagger, its hilt decorated with star-shaped gems. *Thank you, Eva.*

I spun away to thrust the blade at the closest wraith.

It vanished in a swirl of mist, before coalescing into a figure once again. *What the…?* I threw a look over my shoulder, and Kai met my confused look with one of his own. In all our years of training, none of us had ever been prepared for something like this. We had always been told the wraiths were corporeal. These things were not.

Something long and thin erupted from the mist and tangled around my legs, and I heard the skirt of my dress tear. I was wrenched off-balance by the vicious leather whip and tumbled into Kai. He righted me with a grin.

"Hi," he said, before he was gone in a swirl of mist and gleaming blade.

I shook my head and cursed the fated dress. *Who could fight in this?* I hitched up my torn skirts, freeing my bare feet, and barely had time to react when the whip came snapping out of the gloom again, but managed to duck in time. It hissed past my cheek. A few loose strands of hair floated past me, severed by the cruel bite of the whip.

I twirled the dagger and peered into the mist, acutely aware that my weapon wasn't as formidable as the whip, but knowing I would have to do the best with what I had. My night vision adjusted enough that I could make out the shapes within. Kai appeared to be battling two wraiths, leaving two for me. My instincts sharpened. *Time to dance*, I thought with adrenaline building in my body.

The two wraiths came at me at once, and in the gloom I saw their faces – or lack of faces, I thought with a shudder. No mouths or eyes, just a blank space, but they instinctively followed me as I swerved low and sidestepped.

I didn't have time to waste on questioning why the Shadowwraiths had attacked; my most pressing concern was to simply stay alive. But the terror clawing its way up my throat made it hard to concentrate. I started seeing everything through tunnel vision, and my blade slipped in my sweat-slicked palm.

"Wen, watch out!" Kai called, then let out a moan of pain. I turned in horror to see the other two wraiths glide up behind me. I was surrounded. Kai was slumped on the ground, a trickle of blood running down his temple and his sword arm hanging limply to one side, but in his other hand he held the vicious whip. At least that was one problem dealt with; the rest would be down to me. I had to save myself.

I re-focused, pushing the terror into a tight little box in my mind. Survival instinct kicked in. I made a rapid pirouette, my dagger held outwards as I circled. The swirling fog blurred around me until I could barely make out the four figures cloaked within it, but my dagger scraped across denser fog four times, followed by enraged hisses and puffs of fetid green and grey smoke. The smoke surrounded me, choking me, and I thought for one suffocating moment that my dagger had missed its mark – where the creatures' throats would be. But swiftly the four figures dissolved, and this time they remained gone, leaving only a low-lying blanket of smog behind. The whip that Kai had been clutching dissipated, and he looked at his hand in shock.

Wondering if there was some magic attached the whip that had called it back to Fog, I sagged and dropped my dagger to the ground. I tried to catch my breath, holding my side where a stitch had emerged.

"That was spectacular," Kai said, wincing as he got to his feet.

"Thanks." I straightened. "But what were they? They weren't like the Shadowwraiths we've been warned of. They kept…" My mouth curled in distaste as I tried to think of a better word. "*Reassembling.*"

If it came to a battle, and the wraiths overran Nos and Sol… they would be hard to beat indeed. It was thanks to Meuric that I had managed to. He always said, "When in doubt, go for the throat". Thank the Fates, it had worked.

That knowledge hummed in the air between us. Could we risk taking the time to find a way around the prophecy, or should we be spending time with our friends and family and readying ourselves for the Fate's Day Ceremony instead?

"Wen, this doesn't change anything," Kai said, reaching for me with his good arm. I almost let him, but shouts and movement from outside the temple had me leaning over to pick up my dagger again.

Meuric, Lord Celestri, the Nos Guard, Maxen, Eva, Gus, Larissa, and a few other trainees ran into the temple ruins and looked around. Maxen wouldn't meet my eyes, while Eva's were speculative.

"What happened here?" Lord Celestri demanded, his silver eyes raking across the last tendrils of mist, then over to me in my beautiful, tattered gown.

"Shadowwraiths," Kai said shortly, replacing his sword in its scabbard.

Meuric frowned. "I saw the mist up here and sounded the alarm. How many were there?"

"Four," I said, conscious of the many eyes taking in my dress. I didn't think anyone had ever seen me in one before, and I had to restrain myself from hitching up the corset top. I felt dreadfully exposed, especially with the tears in the skirt showing my legs. Even Gus looked somewhat unsure of himself – possibly I no longer appeared to be such an easy target now. "But they weren't like the ones we've been trained against. They healed themselves back into their forms when we attacked them. It was only when I went for their throats" – *or where their throats would be.* I shuddered – "that I was able to fully defeat them."

"She was magnificent," Kai said, pride colouring his voice, and this time Maxen's eyes whipped up to mine, an unfathomable look swirling within their depths.

Lord Celestri and Meuric exchanged a look. "We must summon the Council. They need to hear about this," Meuric said, and Lord Celestri gave a grim nod.

"Are you hurt?" he asked me abruptly.

Touched by his concern, I shook my head. "No, but Kai is."

"It's just a scratch. I think the temple wall came off worse than me." Kai tapped a fist to his head, making me laugh.

Maxen let out an unintelligible noise and Kai looked over at him, one golden brow raised. Maxen stared back at him, a challenge in his eyes, and I fought to prevent myself from sighing. *Men!*

"Very well. Lord Malakai, if you could return to Sol and ask Sabra and the other Sol Council members to convene at the Chambers tomorrow morning at nine o'clock," Lord Celestri instructed. "I would ask what you were doing in Nos, alone with Lady Ceridwen, but perhaps it's a good thing you *were* here."

"Perhaps they attacked *because* he was here," Maxen said. "Two birds, one stone. Maybe it's better if he just stayed in Sol."

At my intake of breath and Eva's "*Meow*", Kai gave his heartstopping grin. "Oh, you would love that, wouldn't you, Master Mercurius?"

Maxen sneered, and I wondered what was happening to my easy-going, laidback friend. I had feared this would happen. Everything was falling apart.

"I'm tired," I said, and everyone looked at me.

"Of course. Let's get you back to Alys," Lord Celestri said. "Eva?"

Eva patted Maxen on the arm in a 'stand-down' gesture, winked at Kai, and joined me and her father.

"I will collect you in the morning," Meuric told me, and I gave him a jerky nod. The adrenaline had left me, and I really was exhausted. I wanted Lunara and my bed.

"'Night, Wen," Kai murmured. "I hope you'll wear that dress again," he added, only loud enough for me to hear.

I blushed, but murmured a soft "Goodnight" back.

Kai left for Sol, and while the others headed back to the city, Lord Celestri, Eva and I walked back to the Celestris' estate.

"I'm sorry about running off with the dress, Eva," I told my friend.

"Oh, don't worry about it," she said airily, "I had already paid for it. I knew you wouldn't be able to resist it."

"You mean *I* had already paid for it," Lord Celestri put in with an amused laugh, and I flushed bright red in mortification. "Ah, don't fret, Ceridwen. It suits you; we can easily get the damage repaired, and Eva has ruined far more in the past eighteen years. She thinks the Celestri coffers run deep."

I was surprised to see angry hauteur cross Eva's face. "Well, if I am to be paraded about like chattel, then you can at least pay for me to look good."

The good humour vanished off Lord Celestri's face. "Now, Eva, this is not the time."

Eva stopped as we reached the gate to the cottage, two bright spots of colour high on her pale cheeks. "No? Well, when *would* be a good time? When I'm being paired to the highest bidder – or when I have to watch my best friend be killed in order for me to secure a lucrative partner? A partner that should have been *hers*?"

I gulped. I had no idea Eva had been concealing so much; she always hid it behind a cool and collected mask. I reached out a hand to her, but she shrugged it away. Was she angry at me, or the hopeless situation we all found ourselves in? I hoped it wasn't me. I couldn't lose both my best friends tonight.

The door to the cottage opened, and Alys took in the scene before her. "Everything all right?" she asked in her soft voice.

Lord Celestri murmured something to Eva. She didn't respond, so he took a deep breath and walked me up the path to where Alys waited, her eyes curiously on me in my gown. I threw a worried look over my shoulder, but Eva was staring off up the drive leading to her house. I hoped I would get a chance to talk to her after the Council meeting. It wasn't right that she suffered – it wasn't fair. None of this was.

"Good evening, Alys," Lord Celestri said, and despite my emotional turmoil, I sensed the air thrum between them. *Interesting.*

"Cosimo," Alys replied, and I looked at her. She appeared poised, but I knew her well, and I could see she was struggling with containing her emotions. Perhaps I should suggest some chamomile tea before we retired. What was going on with everyone tonight? Usually the full moon heightened emotions, but the crescent cutting a chink out of the sky tonight was working a fantastically surreal style of magic.

"She had a run-in with a few Shadowwraiths at the temple ruins," Lord Celestri explained, and Alys put a trembling arm around me and pulled me close with a gasp.

"Oh my," she said, her eyes running over me, checking for injuries. Her face cleared as if satisfied I was unharmed. And I was – physically. Mentally, who knew? I had so much rushing through my mind, so many things to worry about, as if the Fates knew that I only had these next few weeks to live, and they were throwing a lifetime's worth of concerns at me all at once. I hoped I was strong enough to put things right before it was too late.

"Look after her," Lord Celestri said, and the air thickened with unsaid words and inferred meanings. I looked from one to the other, as Alys's arm tightened around me once again.

She looked straight into his silver eyes. "Always," she said.

Seventeen

"So, are you going to tell me why you were fighting Shadowwraiths in such a beautiful dress – or any dress really – or should I save it until the morning?"

I toyed with my mug of chamomile tea, bringing it slowly to my lips and looking at Alys from over the rim of the cup. Lunara nestled into my shoulder, and I finally felt some semblance of peace.

The 'beautiful dress' had been relegated to Alys's room; she was adamant about mending it. Back in my usual home attire of a pair of soft trousers and tunic, I didn't know what to think about the dress. I should be happy never to wear it again, but the way Kai's eyes had lit up when he saw me in it – well, I was tempted to risk another four hundred Shadowwraiths just to see that look again.

I put my cup down with a clink as a warm flush crept up my neck. "I didn't mean to fight them," I said. "They appeared out of nowhere."

Alys pushed away from the sink and took a seat opposite me. "That is so strange. They must know

Fate's Day is getting close. They always tried to stop the unions happening, but they always came from the bridge, never materialising suddenly. The fogs came first, then the Shadowwraiths. They always had to stay within the fog."

"They brought their own fog with them," I realised, thinking back. "And they kept returning to their form, even after we struck them. I had to go for their throats." I shuddered, hoping the faceless beings wouldn't haunt my dreams, then yawned, my eyes drooping. Through blurred vision, I saw Alys putting on her long, hooded jacket. "Where are you going?"

"I'm going to speak to Meuric and then see if there is any of the fog residue left. I'd like to test it."

I stood on tired legs. "It's not safe – what if they come back?"

"I'll be careful. Go on to bed now." She caught me as I stumbled towards her and helped me up the ladder to my bed, Lunara fluttering ahead of us. "I put a bit of sleeping draught in your chamomile. I wanted you to have a break from nightmares tonight." She laid me down, pulled the covers over me and kissed my forehead tenderly. "Good night, my precious girl," she whispered as my eyes softly closed, and a dreamless sleep welcomed me.

A smash awoke me with a jump, causing Lunara to grumble in her sleep. I stared up at the ceiling, and through the curved window I saw the sun had risen. *The Council meeting!*

Mutterings from the kitchen got me out of bed. I climbed down the ladder, my head surprisingly clear.

Whatever Alys had put in my drink last night had done the trick.

She stood in the centre of the small kitchen, surrounded by shards of glass; her short hair stuck up in tufts as if she had been raking her hands through it. A sure sign she was frustrated. I made to go over to her, but she said, "Stop!"

I hovered on the rug while she knelt down and swept up the shards with a dustpan and brush. When the floor was clear, I joined her and guided her to one of the kitchen chairs. "Have you even been to bed?" I asked, noting the rows of glass jars on the side. They were filled with what looked like various shades of mist, ranging from barely-there white to bruised purple and endless black.

"No, not yet... I must have lost track of time," Alys said wearily, resting her head on her arms.

I placed the kettle on the stove and lit it. Now it was my turn to care for her. My gut twisted as I looked at the curve of her eyelashes as they fluttered against her pale cheeks. If I didn't survive, she would be alone. Hot tears pricking the back of my eyes, I turned away to inspect the jars. My hand itched to pick one up and take a closer look, but I suspected Alys had retrieved the mist residue from the old temple, and I certainly didn't want any Shadowwraiths materialising in our kitchen.

I took a deep breath and made some peppermint tea for me, and soothing lavender and chamomile for Alys. I took it into her room and pulled back her covers before going back to help her to her room.

"Drink – sleep," I encouraged, as I pulled her covers over her. "I have to speak to the Council today... you know, about the Shadowwraiths."

She opened her eyes fully to look at me for a long moment. "Be careful. There are those within the Council who are not what they seem." Her words were slurred, but I leaned over to listen. What did she know?

"I'll be careful." I squeezed her hand as her eyes fluttered closed. I watched her for a moment before a knock at the door galvanised me into action.

I opened the door to Meuric. "Come in, I just need to finish getting ready," I told him. He looked at his watch and raised an eyebrow. "I know, I know." I quickly poured him a cup of peppermint tea and took my own up to my room.

After I had downed my tea, nearly scalding myself, I had a quick wash and got dressed in a pair of black leather trousers and a clean black tunic. I looked around for my boots. *My boots!* I groaned. I'd left them at the dress shop the day before. The shopping trip with Eva seemed like light years ago. With no time to address the frizzy state of my curls, I tamed my wild hair into a thick side braid, while scouring under my bed. I spotted a pair of old battered boots – they would have to do. I grabbed them and pressed a kiss to a slumbering Lunara.

In the kitchen, I left a bowl of frostberries for my mothling before shoving my feet into the boots.

Meuric sipped his tea, before saying, "I see Alys has been busy." He gestured at the jars. "I went with her to collect the mist. I didn't want her wandering about alone, not with Shadowwraiths on the loose."

"Thank you," I said. "I wanted to talk her out of it, but she gave me a sleeping draught."

"You know Alys. She'll do everything in her power to keep you safe. Even if it means investigating magical fog in the middle of the night." He set his cup down, and I thought about his words.

Everyone was trying so hard to 'save' me, but could I even be saved? Or was my story already written, my path already set? The Fates didn't favour me as their champion, that was for certain. I stared into the swirling fog, becoming lost in the uncertainty of it all. Maybe it was time to take my destiny into my own hands. I shrugged into one of my smarter jackets and felt a new sense of determination come over me. I needed to speak to Kai. I had made my decision; a truce was in order.

"Let's go," I said, and Meuric gave me a long look of appraisal. Did my voice sound stronger? I certainly felt it.

On the walk to the city, conversation was minimal. I was grateful Meuric seemed absorbed in his own thoughts; it gave me time to formulate my plan. If I was going to work with Kai, I needed to set down some rules. We had mere weeks to do this – we had to stop playing games and get serious.

Utterly absorbed in my ideas, I realised we had arrived at the Council chambers. Butterflies immediately clamoured in my throat, desperate for release, but I tamped them down. I had to be on my guard. Alys had the same suspicions Kai did… that some high-up Council members had ulterior motives. *But who, and why?*

"Ready?" Meuric asked, and I nodded.

We entered the building and were greeted by a clerk, who took us to the meeting. Everyone else was already there; the Celestris were in their seats and Kai and Sabra sat amongst the Sol members. Meuric and I joined Nos's, but I was careful to hold my head high and avert my eyes from Kai's as we passed him. I knew now what I had to do.

"Right, if we are all here?" Lord Celestri looked around, then carried on. "We are meeting today to discuss why Shadowwraiths were able to leave the confines of the Celestial Bridge mist and venture into Nos… to attack our Chosen pair."

Murmurings and exchanged looks passed through the Council members. Gus's father raised his hand.

"Yes, Council Member Novarian?"

He shot a glare my way before demanding, "*Why* were the Chosen pair together after we had *expressly* told them the dangers?"

Shouts of agreement filled the hall, and Lady Celestri met my eyes with a smug grin. She was enjoying this, but I refused to react. I clenched my fists on my lap, and slowly looked away.

Lord Celestri banged on the desk before him with a small black marble gavel. His deep voice rose above the din. "That is not the issue here."

Immediately the clamouring stopped, and all eyes turned to him.

"I will ensure it is revisited, but I will allow it… for now," Master Novarian said grudgingly. "Then how *were* the Shadowwraiths able to leave their domain?"

A small, bespectacled Nosian stood. "I have a theory," he said in a birdlike voice.

"Proceed, Master Nimbus," Lord Celestri said, sitting back in his chair. Immediately, Lady Celestri rested her hand possessively on his arm. As always, she was dressed immaculately, down to her long nails painted the exact same shade as her fitted jacket.

Master Nimbus cleared his throat. "I believe the realm of Fog is becoming stronger. My instruments measure the fog generated on the Celestial Bridge, and it is at unprecedented levels. It may be down to the unique situation of our Fated Pair, and possibly will resolve itself after the... ah... um..." He trailed off, his cheeks flushing, unable to look in either my or Kai's direction.

"After Fate's Day, Master Nimbus?" Lady Celestri asked with an innocent look my way.

Master Nimbus looked relieved. "Yes, exactly; after Fate's Day."

"But you cannot be certain?" Meuric asked. "That Fog is becoming stronger because of Lady Ceridwen and Lord Malakai's situation, *or* that it will resolve itself after Fate's Day?"

Lord Celestri leaned forward and steepled his fingers; his silver eyes shone in speculation. Lady Celestri pouted.

Sweat beaded between my closed fists, and Kai's eyes burned in my direction. I could almost hear him. *Look at me, Wen.* I shook my head slightly, as if he had actually spoken the words.

Master Nimbus opened his mouth but Sabra, who had been watching the proceedings with hooded eyes, stood and declared, "Enough of this. I do not see why we are wasting our time on trivial matters." *Being almost killed by Shadowwraiths is trivial, is it?* "We *all* know that

Fog will retreat to its dormant state when the prophecy is fulfilled, and those within will no longer have the opportunity to break free and threaten our realms."

Master Nimbus sat down and clutched at his grey robe as he looked in awed apprehension at the luminous Sabra. He started nodding, and I had to fight to stop from huffing in exasperation.

"Thank you, Mistress Sabra," Lady Celestri said and stood, appearing to revel in the attention as all eyes locked onto her. She adjusted the lapel of her silver trouser suit and spread her arms wide. "My dear Council members, it appears we have come full circle. Why, Lady Ceridwen, were you hosting a clandestine meeting with Kai – I mean Lord Malakai – in Nos when you have been told over and over again of the risks? The prophecy *must* be fulfilled… or else the Shadowwraiths will attack us all. You have now seen first-hand what they are capable of." She paused, and her gaze sharpened. Her tone softened in contrast, but I could feel the thorns beneath it. "You wouldn't want that to happen now, would you, my dear?"

I stood, meeting her on equal footing. And finally, I looked directly at Kai. I willed my face into a serious expression. I *had* to be believable.

"No, I wouldn't want that to happen. I agree with you." I flicked a look her way, and saw with satisfaction I that had thrown her, before returning my gaze to a poker-faced Kai. What was he thinking? My heart ached. "The prophecy *will* be fulfilled. I will make certain of it."

Eighteen

As exclamations filled the hall, and my heart pounded in my ears, I sat and gripped the edge of my chair. I could sense Meuric's confusion, and I desperately wanted to look at Kai to explain, but I had to follow through with this course of action now. The Council *had* to believe I was serious. I didn't know who we could truly trust. If they thought I was readying myself for Fate's Day, then I could work in secret to perhaps – no, *hopefully* find another way. I only hoped Kai was still interested in working together.

"Well, Lady Ceridwen, I must say I am impressed. You are showing a degree of maturity some others are lacking," Sabra said with a sideways glance at Kai. "I assume there will be no more night-time visits to *either* of the realms?" she continued pointedly.

"Absolutely," I promised. *No* night-time *visits, at least.*

"We should double our guard patrols until Fate's Day is over," Lord Celestri said brusquely to both the Nos and Sol generals, who nodded. "And warn them

163

that these Shadowwraiths appear to be able to re-coalesce unless you go for their throats." He looked up at me, his mouth a grim line.

I shivered at the look in his eyes; he appeared to be holding back his anger. I bit my lip. Was I doing the right thing? Perhaps he was still having problems with Eva. I hadn't seen him like this before. Usually, Council matters were dealt with quickly and satisfactorily and then the Celestris went back to their idyllic lives. ...*Or maybe not so idyllic.* I watched Lady Celestri take Lord Celestri's arm, but he didn't look at her, and her eyes narrowed to slits as they walked away from their seats and led the Council members from the Chambers. With a start, I saw the meeting was over.

"Come on, Ceridwen," Meuric said. I realised we were the only ones left in the room.

I got to my feet and winced as my old boots pinched my toes. "I'll meet you at the training yard. I need to collect my boots from the dress shop," I told Meuric as we headed out of the chambers.

"Just don't wear a dress to training," he quipped, and I did a double-take. *Jokes, now? Really?* He glanced at my face. "Sorry – trying to lighten the tension."

"Thanks, Meuric," I said, limping slightly down the steps and along the road.

As I passed an alleyway beside the dress shop, urgent whispers coming from inside it stopped me. I flattened myself against the wall. I knew those voices, and I had to bite my tongue to stop myself from gasping aloud.

"You told me this would work," Lady Celestri hissed.

"I was right, wasn't I?" Sabra returned coldly.

A Nos alleyway was the last place I expected to find Salomé Celestri, but perhaps that was the point. I peeped around a stack of boxes and watched the two ladies standing closely together, deep in conversation. Sabra had the hood of her cloak up, while Lady Celestri kept to the shadows.

"Barely," she spat back. "But I didn't expect her to look so reconciled. What if she wins? I can't afford to have everything go wrong. I've trusted you for this long. Do not let me down now."

"When have I ever let you down, Sal? If this works out the way I've planned, we'll *both* get what we want. Now, go about your normal day-to-day life of being Lady of the Twin Realms and leave the important stuff to me." Sabra patted Lady Celestri patronisingly on the shoulder; she pouted and inspected her manicure. "Oh, and remember just *who* you owe your perfect little life to."

Footsteps echoed towards me, and I froze. They were coming this way. I willed my legs into action, but they stubbornly refused to start working.

Someone gripped my wrist and yanked me around the corner of the alleyway, along the street, and into the set-back doorway of a boarded-up shop.

"Are you mad? They almost caught you!" Kai hissed. His momentum had thrown us together, pinned against the wall, his face against my hair. I pushed myself off him and met his warm but slightly wary look.

"I panicked," I said defensively. "I was going to get my boots and I overheard them." I nibbled my lip. "Did you hear what they said?"

Kai looked as though he was having an internal debate. He nodded. "Sabra told me she had to run an errand and asked me to wait in the carriage. I was only too happy to oblige so I could be alone with my dark thoughts." He looked at me pointedly, and I flushed. "But then I saw Lady Celestri slip down the same alley after her, and shall we just say that my interest was piqued. Then I saw *you*, and I knew you'd be getting yourself into trouble... and I was right." He crossed his arms, waiting.

"Well – look, Kai, before we get into what Sabra and Lady Celestri were doing, I want you to know I didn't mean what I said in there."

He raised one golden eyebrow.

"I still want to work with you. I need to try and see if there's another way where this doesn't end badly for one of us" – *both of us,* I added to myself – "but I needed the Council to believe I'm taking the prophecy seriously. That allows us some freedom."

A smile worked its way across Kai's face until he was beaming. He pulled me into his arms. "That's my girl," he said. "Listen, we need to come up with a way of communicating with each other. Is there someone you can trust implicitly?"

My immediate thought was Eva, but the way things were between us, I didn't really know... and it was a conflict of interest where Kai was concerned. I shrugged helplessly. "No one I want to drag into this. It could be dangerous for them." I was beginning to understand who Alys suspected.

"All right, leave it to me. I'll find a way of getting a message to you if I find anything out. But I'd better go before Sabra comes looking for me." He looked me deep in the eyes before giving my hand a squeeze. My fingers tingled under his heated touch. He hesitated, looking reluctant. "I'm glad you don't want to kill me," he said softly, before ducking out of the doorway.

I watched him weave across the road, avoiding carriages, carts and horses, to the white and orange official Sol carriage. My hand inadvertently went to my chest, over my heart. Fates above – I hadn't stipulated my rules for working with him. But he was right about one thing. I didn't *want* to kill him... but I would if it was the only way to ensure the safety of countless Nosian and Solian lives. Ultimately, I knew he would make the same decision too. That was why he was so desperate to find another way.

The knowledge didn't make it any easier; in fact, it made it worse. If only we didn't care so deeply, if only we could be apathetic towards each other... but no, that wouldn't really change anything. It would still be *wrong.* This whole situation was wrong!

Still, morosely, I wondered if Alys had some kind of potion she could give me. Maybe a tonic for hardening the heart. Nervously, I realised I was only half joking. Before I could spiral into dark thoughts myself, I remembered I had to retrieve my boots and get to the training yard.

Sabra was getting into the carriage; it appeared her errand was complete. I hoped Kai would be able to discover what she was up to and send me a message soon. Maybe I could spy on Lady Celestri, I mused. I hadn't seen her pass by. Either she had gone home, or else she had errands to run too.

I pushed off from the wall and headed to the dress shop; it was time to eat some humble pie and apologise. The bell above the door tinkled as I entered, drawing the attention of the four women inside. I stopped dead, framed in the doorway, as Lady Celestri smiled her cat-like smile and waggled her fingers at me.

"Lady Ceridwen," Kari said, and hurried over to draw me inside. "We were just telling our wonderful patron Lady Celestri about your beautiful dress."

Her smile was a little forced, and I guessed she was urging me to not say anything about running off with it. They did have a certain prestigious reputation to uphold, I presumed.

"Oh yes… it is, um, beautiful," I said lamely.

Lady Celestri rolled her eyes. "Well, of course it is. This is the finest dress boutique in all of Nos… and Sol," she added with a conspiratorial laugh. "But don't tell Stefania."

Kari's hands fluttered about her chest. "Oh, but Mistress Stefania's dresses are breath-taking – did she not create your union gown, Lady Celestri?"

Lady Celestri inclined her head, and I squirmed, wondering how on Nos I would be able to make my excuses and leave. "That she did. In fact, Lady Ceridwen, I hear she is making Lord Malakai's Fate's Day clothes. She is working on an outfit suitable for the Ceremony *and* combat."

A small, surprised squeak left me at this new piece of information, and Lady Celestri smiled in triumph.

"Oh, Lady Ceridwen, you simply must allow us to make your Fate's Day clothes too! It would be our gift to you." Kari beamed at Sali and – I squinted at the other lady's name embroidered on her dress – Tori. *Ha, I was right.* "We are especially skilled at adding little surprise details to our clothing." Kari gave me a wink, and I remembered the intricate corset dagger. It was now hidden in my bedroom drawer.

I didn't feel up for another dress shopping excursion, but Lady Celestri didn't look at all pleased at the offer, so that cemented my decision. "I would be honoured," I announced proudly. *One all.*

Kari, Sali and Tori clapped their hands together and surrounded me like little chirping mothlings, whipping out tape measures and holding colour wheels against my cheeks, then pulling out shimmering silver bolts of fabric. Their enthusiasm was infectious but overwhelming. Flustered, I stepped back and said, "I only popped in for the things I left here yesterday."

The three ladies drooped in disappointment.

"But Mistress Eva took them with her yesterday," Sali said.

I groaned inwardly as Lady Celestri turned shining eyes my way. I knew exactly what she was going to suggest.

"Oh, how *perfect*. You can come in the carriage with me. I am ready to head home myself now; it has been a most trying day."

The last thing I wanted now was to be trapped in a carriage with Lady Celestri… but perhaps I could turn it to my advantage and do some sleuthing too. Kai wasn't the only one who could think on his toes.

I smiled a wide smile of my own. "Thank you, Lady Celestri, that would be *wonderful.*"

Nineteen

"Now, where did Cos tell me the carriage would be waiting?" Lady Celestri mused as she scanned the busy street.

I wouldn't be able to interrogate Lady Celestri if Lord Celestri was in the carriage, but her next words allayed my fears. "Why he couldn't have waited for me, I have no notion. But one thing you'll learn about important men is that they like to keep busy. Especially noble men – they are rarely idle. Cosimo is off to the vineyard and orchard to check on our new venture." She gave a sigh of contentment, before glancing my way. "Well, what I meant to say is that you *would* have learned, if your fate had been different, of course."

I bit down on my inner lip. Hard. For a moment I wondered if she'd had special training at being tactless, but I was sure she didn't choose her words without them being calculated and weighed up to see which would be the most effective. And Fates above, she'd hit her mark – again. I sighed. Perhaps I should sneak off to the training yard instead.

"Ah, there it is. Come along, Ceridwen. I'm sure Eva will be most delighted to see you." Her tone implied that while Eva would be, she most certainly wasn't. She trotted off along the cobblestones in her four-inch purple stilettos, and I jogged to keep up with her.

I hoped Eva *would* be delighted. Our quarrels were usually short-lived, but she was obviously carrying so much pain and stress that seeing me might add to it. I hoped she would let me in. I really needed my trusty boots back. The ones I had on were killing me.

Lady Celestri was helped aboard by her footman, and I clambered in after her before I could be assisted. Being fawned over made me uncomfortable.

As the carriage set off, I pondered on the best way to interrogate Lady Celestri, but she presented me with the ideal opportunity herself as she stared out of the window up at the cloudy sky.

"Ugh, I do miss Sol's sunshine," she muttered.

"I bet it's hard having to move away from your own realm," I said sympathetically.

She looked at me sharply; I kept my face impassive. After a moment, she inclined her head. "Indeed. I've lived here twenty years now. And while it does have its obvious benefits…" She stared down at the giant moonstone on her ring finger with a satisfied smile, and I wondered if she was thinking of Lord Celestri or the jewels that had come with her position. "You cannot beat the sun warming your skin as you sip a drink at one of Sol's numerous outdoor taverns. My sister and I had the most wonderful coming-of-age party on the beach, a few days before my union." Her eyes clouded reminiscently, and my interest spiked.

"You have a sister?"

Lady Celestri's eyes went wide, and I was surprised to see her skin pale beneath her usual golden hue. "S-sister," she stammered, and I leaned in closer. I had never, ever seen Lady Salomé Celestri flustered before. "Did I say sister? I meant best friend, of course. How silly of me." She gave a tittering laugh.

"Of course," I murmured.

She was lying. But why?

She resumed her appraisal of the sky, but her hands twisted nervously on the hem of her jacket. Interesting. I filed this bit of information away for future use. Perhaps Alys would know more about Lady Celestri and this best friend; she had been a candidate in the same Choosing year as the Celestris. I would ask her later.

"Ah, here we are," Lady Celestri said with forced brightness. She barely allowed her footman to help her alight before she was out of the carriage and jogging up the steps. I followed more sedately and took a seat in the foyer as Lady Celestri headed up the grand staircase, calling, "Eva, darling."

I loosened the laces on my boots and rubbed at my feet where they had pinched.

"Hi." Eva appeared before me, her arms full of my things, including – thank the Fates – my boots.

"Hi." I gave her a tentative smile.

"Oh, don't look so worried." Eva dumped my stuff onto the bench beside me. "I'm not angry with *you*. It's just…" She blew out a frustrated breath and leaned against the wall, throwing her hands up helplessly.

172

"I know." Standing, I pulled her into a tight hug. *It's everything all at once. It's not knowing what your future holds, or fearing a future that is picked for you; it's all of it, and it's terrifying.*

We drew apart, and Eva sniffed. "You'll ruin my carefully created 'I-haven't-got-a-care-in-the-realm' make-up."

We looked at each other and burst out laughing. She gave me a shoulder bump and said, "Come on, let's have a cup of tea. Mother has gone to lie down with one of her headaches."

"Argh, I can't. I'm sorry, but Meuric is expecting me. Can we meet up later?"

Eva pouted, looking very much like her mother, though I wouldn't dare say it. "All right. But meet me at the tavern later?" She saw the hesitation in my eyes and added, "*Please?*"

"All right, all right." I held up my hands. "I'll join you, but I can't stay long. I need to get serious about training."

"Well, that's why you have me, remember; dance instructor, combat specialist – you name it, I'm your girl." She gave me a curtsy before twirling into a fighting stance, and I was laughing again.

"Thanks, Eva." *For being there, for understanding, for not making me feel bad about possibly having to leave you.*

She smiled back in understanding.

I sat back down and swapped over my boots. They fitted like a second skin, and my toes groaned in relief. "Much better. See you later." I grabbed the rest of my things and left the manor, feeling somewhat lighter.

As I neared the cottage on my way to the training yard I debated going to check on Alys, but I was already late, and if I wanted everyone to think I was taking the prophecy seriously then I needed to make sure I was seen training hard. Especially with Gus watching – no doubt he would be reporting back to his father.

I swiped up a cluster of lavender and was bringing it up to my nose when I saw the cottage door start to open. Clutching my bundle of clothes and old boots, I instinctively ducked behind a bush as Lord Celestri appeared, followed by Alys. She was pulling her robe around her shoulders tighter.

What the...? I couldn't believe what I was seeing. Not one to immediately jump to conclusions, my mind whirred with a multitude of reasonable explanations, but the memory of Alys returning from a midnight walk with a basketful of fresh pears from the place where I'd seen Lord Celestri waiting kept fighting for prominence. I shook my head, trying to make sense of it all. Lord and Lady Celestri were a *Fated Pair*... so what was he doing with Alys?

Through the leaves, I saw Lord Celestri's hand flex before gripping the doorframe, as if he were trying incredibly hard to stop himself from reaching out to Alys. She stared up at him, and the look that passed between them was unmistakable, even from a distance. Bile rose up in my throat. I didn't like Lady Celestri, but there was something very wrong about this whole situation. They were a Fated Pair. *Fated Pair, Fated Pair, Fated Pair.* The words flew around my mind like angry, buzzing bees. They were meant to be together; it was *Fated.* Fated Pairs failing in their union was unheard of – it just didn't happen!

Everything I thought I knew about the realms had just been shattered. My breath came in short gasps.

Dizzily, I turned to stumble my way along the hedges, out of sight, until I reached the small woods bordering the Celestris' estate. I kept walking, sucking in air until I found a fallen log and staggered down onto it, my clothes and boots falling from my numb hands.

What did it all mean? Was the reason the realms were at risk because the *Celestris'* union had failed? I needed to speak to… *who*? Who could I trust with this information? I didn't want to put Alys at risk; Lady Celestri would destroy her. No – perhaps, I should make sure my suspicions were correct. Maybe there *was* a reasonable explanation. Alys had always been trustworthy and honest. I shouldn't doubt her now.

My breathing had finally evened out, so I pushed my fears away, hefted my things and made my way to the training yard. I needed something to distract me, and the poor training dummy was just the thing. That or Gus.

Maxen met me at the archway.

Not now, I thought ungraciously. I knew we needed to put things right, but my mind was too full of making up with Eva, and the situation with Lord Celestri and Alys. I was drained before I'd even started training.

I gave myself a moment to prepare for this next confrontation by placing my things down on one of the stone seats, then took a deep breath and turned around.

"Look," Maxen said, "I don't like him, and I don't like this whole" – he waved his hand around to encompass the training yard – "scenario, but I will help you. You're my friend, that will never change, so I'll help you do whatever you need to – but I don't like him…"

"You said that already," I told him, but relief had begun to sink through me. He was back. I hadn't realised how the thought of not having Eva or Maxen on my side had felt like a big hole in me.

"Well." He ran a hand along his tightly braided hair and gave me a sheepish grin. "I don't." He shrugged.

I rolled my eyes and pulled him in for a hug, closing my eyes and breathing in his familiar, reassuring scent of leather and the black pepper and tobacco soap he favoured. Alys always made it for him. It was nothing like being close to Kai, where the heat would curl deep in my belly, and I felt a momentary pang of grief that I couldn't be what Max wanted. My fate was inexplicably tied up with someone else's. I hoped he would eventually be able to come to terms with that.

He might have held on to me a fraction longer than necessary, and his eyes might have been a touch wistful when we pulled apart, but I was just happy to have my friends back. I couldn't do this alone.

"Aww, isn't this a touching scene. Forgotten about your Sol boyfriend already, Lady Ceridwen? My, my, we are a fickle one."

"Shut up, Gus," Maxen and I both said, before sharing a grin.

Gus looked down his long nose at me. "Right, well, I would love to stand around and gossip all day, but some of us have important work to do guarding the realm." He strapped the sword he was holding to his thigh, and I realised he was dressed in the uniform of the Nos Guard. I looked at Maxen in confusion.

"But you haven't come of age yet. How can you join the Guard?" I asked.

Something flickered in Gus's eyes. Fear? He blinked and it was gone. "Thanks to your escapade with the Shadowwraiths, they've doubled the guard, but they don't have enough, so they're calling on those who are nearing the end of their training." He looked over at Maxen. "Oh, didn't they ask you, Max?"

Max grinned, flashing his straight white teeth. "They did, but I asked to train with Wen instead. The Council were only too happy to have extra people protecting the Lady of Nos."

He bowed at me, and I laughed – not that I needed protecting, but I was so relieved Maxen wouldn't be joining the guard yet.

"Well don't worry, Max, you'll only have to suffer through that for the next few weeks. After that, she won't be a problem anymore." Gus patted Maxen on the shoulder in a fake conciliatory gesture.

The laughter died on my lips as he passed me by with a satisfied smile.

Twenty

I hate him. Punch. *I hate him.* Punch.

"You know, that's the third training dummy I've had re-stuffed in as many days." Meuric filled my vision, and the red mist receded.

I wiped the sweat off my brow with the back of my hand. "Sorry," I said, but I wasn't really. Not when it was so satisfying to imagine Gus's face on the dummies. I was fed up with his digs and self-righteous looks anytime I encountered him. That, paired with the fact that I hadn't heard from Kai, was starting to fray my nerves.

"Take a break." Meuric drew me away and sat me down before handing me a cup of cool, clear water.

I gratefully downed it, and Meuric refilled it before looking critically at my knuckles. Without a word, he walked over to his hut and returned moments later carrying a small cobalt jar. He took my hand and slathered on a gold-hued cream, smelling of calendula and honey.

"Alys special?" I asked.

Meuric nodded and handed me the jar. "Keep it. You need it more than me."

I stuffed it into my trouser pocket.

Mentioning Alys made me think of breakfast that morning. I hadn't been at home much these past few days. What with the long training days and trying to spend more time with Eva and Maxen, I hadn't had time to sit and talk to her. When I'd returned home the day I'd seen her with Lord Celestri she had appeared her usual self, and I didn't know whether to say anything. So I hadn't. But this morning, I'd caught her going through a box of memorabilia. As soon as I appeared she had stuffed it into the kitchen dresser, and now I was itching to know what was in there. I had to keep reminding myself that her personal life was none of my business, but I still needed to ask her about Lady Celestri and whether she knew about a sister. Time was running out to find another way out of this mess.

"Everything all right?" Meuric asked as he took a seat next to me.

Inspiration struck. "What happened at the last Choosing – I mean, the one before mine?"

Meuric looked around the yard at the others going through their manoeuvres. He turned back to me, his eyes wary. "It's only natural you're interested in what usually happens. I'm surprised you haven't asked before."

That stumped me. *Why* hadn't I asked before? Deep down I knew the answer: I had been so caught up in my grief at my own Choosing going so horribly wrong, I couldn't focus on anybody else's happily ever after.

"Everyone believed Master Mercurius, Maxen's father, would be Chosen that year, so it was quite a shock when Lord Celestri was. He'd appeared to be Fated for another," Meuric mused. *Alys?* "The names took an age to be revealed, and everyone was surprised when Cosimo's name came out after Salomé's."

"Was Sabra there?" I asked. She must have been too young to be a candidate mentor then.

"Oh yes, their mother was a mentor back then," Meuric explained, and my brain paused for a moment. "But Sabra wasn't put forward as candidate; she had already come of age."

"Wait, what? *Their* mother?" My brain caught up. *Of course.* It all made sense now.

Meuric looked as if he had said too much. Casting a wary look around to make sure no one else was listening, he leaned in close to me and whispered, "Yes, Sabra and Salomé are sisters. But it isn't common knowledge."

"Why?"

"Because their mother disgraced herself soon after the Choosing. She used an ancient magic to try and contact the realm of Fog, but it ended badly, and she disappeared one night. There are some Council members who believe Sabra can't be trusted, that she only cares for Sol, and a few who were uneasy Salomé had been Chosen. They thought Sabra would have too much influence over her."

Fates above, I should have spoken to Meuric sooner. This was interesting information indeed. "So have people just forgotten they're related?"

"No, but it isn't widely talked about. Time has a funny way of pushing things under the rug. Lady

Celestri especially wants to distance herself from any questionable origins."

Questionable origins. "Meuric... what do you know about the night I was found?" I wasn't sure why I asked. Alys had always suggested I wait until I came of age before I went looking for answers, but time was running out for me. It was obviously a day for revelations, and Meuric was in a talkative mood. What harm could it do?

He paused, lost in thought, and I worried for a moment he wasn't going to answer, that I had asked too much. But surely I had a right to know about my birth, when the spectre of my death hovered ever closer.

"It was a week before Fate's Day – two years after the Celestris' union. A guard had been patrolling near the Celestial Bridge when he heard your cries. At first, so the story goes, he believed it was a Shadowwraith, but your cries persisted, and he realised it was a baby. Despite his fears that you had come from Fog, a father himself, he knew he couldn't leave you there; you would have perished, so he took you to the guard house and the Council was called. Cosimo Celestri appeared suited to his new position and had taken to the role well. Immediately, he decided you were a citizen of Nos, thanks to your colouring, and suggested you be placed with Alys. She had shown remarkable promise at becoming a great Healer, so he thought you would be safe with her, if any health problems arose for you in the future."

"And Alys agreed to this? Didn't she want a family of her own?" I asked, trying to understand why a young woman would take on an orphaned child.

"She did. She said Healing was her calling and had no plans to marry." Meuric nodded. "She loved you immediately – it was plain for all to see."

For a fleeting moment I wondered who my real parents were and why they had abandoned me, but I only allowed myself a second to dwell on it. Alys and Lunara were my family. *And* I had a secret benefactor, whoever that was.

"Thanks." I stood and stretched my stiff, sore muscles.

Meuric stood too, his expression worried. "Ceridwen. A word of warning: do not underestimate Lady Celestri. She might come across as insipid and self-absorbed, but she can be ruthless and motivated when she wants to be. She was raised by two powerful women."

"I can handle her," I said, injecting faux confidence into my voice. I made to walk over to the armoury, but Meuric stopped me with a sinewy hand on my arm.

"I'm serious. She wanted to put you back on the Celestial Bridge. She was absolutely resistant to Lord Celestri's suggestion. It was the first time I had ever seen a Fated Pair disagree so heatedly." He looked deep into my eyes, his grey irises swirling like a storm. "She is a dangerous woman… she wanted you to be claimed by the Shadowwraiths as an offering."

If Meuric hadn't been holding onto me, I would have fallen. I sank slowly back to the seat, and he let me go.

I'd known Eva's mother hated me… but wanting me dead?

What if she wins? I can't afford to have everything go wrong. I've trusted you for so long... Lady Celestri's words to Sabra in the alleyway came back to haunt me. Was she plotting against me even now – or was she afraid of me winning simply because it would scupper her plans for Eva's future and the lucrative connections they could gain in the Ostaras? What was even real anymore?

"I have to go." I stood on trembling legs and hurried out of the yard, Meuric calling me back.

Instinctively, I headed in the direction of the orchard. It was the one place where I could forget about being Lady Ceridwen of Nos and just be a girl who loved pears and daydreaming on hay bales.

I climbed up the tallest tree and found the crook in the branches which fitted my back perfectly. As I scooted along the branch, my eye alighted on a rolled-up piece of parchment. Could it be from Kai?

I unrolled it, but inside was only a sketch of a pear cut in two with juice dripping from it. Whatever did *that* mean? About to toss the paper back into the knot where I'd found it, casting it off as some child's drawing, I remembered Kai telling me about a secret method of communication he and his sister had come up with when they were children.

I smoothed out the paper and looked closely at the drawing, imagining two tiny, golden-haired tots scribbling notes to each other while eating pears and giggling. Inspired, I reached over the branches and plucked a ripe pear from where it hung. I took a bite, savouring the tart taste for a moment before smearing the juicy flesh over the note. Immediately, words appeared. *Huh, ingenious* – ink activated by pear juice.

My heart pumped faster as I scoured the note. Fates above – it was from two days ago. I wished I'd thought to come here sooner, but I hadn't wanted to risk bumping into Kai and someone catching us. Remembering the blonde-haired girl snitching on us to Sabra, I frowned. I'd never asked him about her…

I shook my head. *Focus, Wen.* I had friends of the opposite sex; why couldn't he too?

Wen – I need to meet with you, I have news. I'll be in the orchard in two days. Meet me at our tree.

I groaned. Was he out of his mind? We'd get caught again – that was just my luck. I scrabbled in my pocket and withdrew a stubby pencil, courtesy of the list I had written that morning as Alys recited her foraging requirements. *Oops!* I clapped a hand to my head. I had been so caught up, I had forgotten to go into the woods and collect what she needed.

I was scribbling a reply to Kai when a rustling had me peering anxiously through the branches. *Too late,* I thought as a pair of warm blue eyes pinned me through the leaves.

"You got my note," Kai said, sliding along the branch over to me. Immediately, the huge tree felt tiny.

I held it up. "Only just," I told him, and he looked crestfallen. "Kai, I can't come here on the off chance you may leave me a note. It isn't safe."

"But this is *our* place. I come every day. I feel close to you here."

His breath warmed my face, and I struggled to concentrate on why I had come here in the first place. *Why was it again? Oh yes, that's right. My best friend's mother wants me dead, and I will never have the man I want.*

But when the man in question looked at me like he was doing right now, I believed I could have everything I ever wanted.

"Let's stay here… like old times." The words were out of my mouth before I could even stop them.

A slow smile worked its way across Kai's face. "Now you're talking." He plucked two pears from the tree, leaned in next to me, and handed me one of the fruits. We toasted to ourselves by bumping them against each other with a laugh before biting in deep.

It *was* like old times as we sat huddled on the branch, legs tangled in companionable silence, munching on the pears. Juice ran down my chin; Kai brushed it from my skin before sucking the juice from his thumb.

My mouth dried up.

Our eyes met, and he leaned towards me.

Twenty-One

My eyes widened as his lips almost claimed mine, and I realised we couldn't do this. I jerked back and accidentally hit my head on a low branch.

"Ow," I groaned.

"Are you all right?" Kai asked in amusement, rubbing the back of my head.

I looked across at him sheepishly. The moment had passed. I couldn't help feeling disappointed, but knew I couldn't give into my emotions; if I did I would fall, and fall all the way. And I couldn't risk it. I couldn't risk my heart... or his.

"Look, Kai—"

"Uh-oh," he said, and I grinned in spite of myself.

"We need to be serious. Time is running out. Have you found out anything to help us?" I needed to step back into reality. As idyllic as it was, imagining we could stay here in our leafy bower, it wasn't possible. Not for us.

"Yes. I found out why Sabra and Lady Celestri were speaking in the alleyway – they're sisters!"

"I know," I said, and his eyes dimmed. "I mean, I just found out today. Meuric told me. I asked him what he knew about the last Choosing before ours."

"Smart." He nodded.

"But knowing they're sisters doesn't actually help us. Unless it relates to what Belenos told you?" I hoped he would finally confide in me.

He nodded. "Belenos said there are those in Sol that have betrayed their realm and made deals they shouldn't have. That's why our Choosing was different."

"Then if we find out who and what deals they made, we can stop it?" I gripped a branch to pull myself up to my knees and felt the first chink of light appearing in the dark, sorrow-filled pit in my heart. "Why don't you look more excited?"

Kai scrubbed a hand across his face. "Wen, I didn't tell you because I didn't want to get your hopes up. I suspected it was Sabra, but I've been following her and searching her office – you saw me – and nothing. She does everything by the book, and I mean *everything*. It's actually been kind of boring tailing her."

Comprehension dawned like the sun spearing through dark clouds. "So *that's* why you blamed me for taking the Sunstone. You didn't want her to suspect you were looking for another way around the prophecy." I should never have doubted him.

"Exactly. I'm sorry, but she had to think I was Sol's Lord through and through. I couldn't have her thinking I suspected her, when I didn't even know if it *was* her."

I nodded. "But if it isn't Sabra, then who else?"

"I've been narrowing down the list of Council members, but aside from liking *Celestara* cider a bit too much, most of them are squeaky clean. How about you? Do you have an idea of someone in Nos that would do a shady deal with Sol?"

Maybe Gus's father, Master Novarian? I mused, going with gut instinct. He – and his son – always seemed to have an abnormal dislike of me, but there wasn't anyone else I could suspect. "I'm not sure... leave it with me."

"The Festivale is next week."

We both fell silent at that. He squeezed my hand and pushed back my curls with his other hand.

I usually looked forward to the week-long Festivale, when the shared fields were filled with brightly coloured tents housing fun games and delicious food. But now, I couldn't drum up any enthusiasm for it.

"We still have a little time then," I said at last.

"If it takes until the last second, I will do whatever it takes," Kai vowed, and falling into his blue eyes, I believed him.

"Me too," I whispered.

He dropped his forehead to mine, and we sat like that for a few time-frozen moments, until the sun dropped low in the sky.

"I'd better go; I have a few things to collect for Alys," I said reluctantly. "Let me go first, then wait a bit until you leave, in case we're being watched."

"Make sure you're home before dusk," Kai said, moving out of the way so I could get down.

"I will. You too," I told him, mindful that Shadowwraiths preferred the twilight hours, when the sun kissed the horizon and the moon had yet to reveal herself.

"Leave me a note if you find out anything," Kai called after me as I started shimmying down the trunk.

"Likewise!" I called back, and snagging a couple of pears, I headed off across the orchard, Kai's eyes burning into my back.

Maxen suddenly appeared in the forest and jumped over a nearby log, nearly making me drop the basket of mushrooms I was holding. "Where have you been? I've been searching the whole of Nos for you."

"You nearly gave me a heart attack!" I complained, before holding up my list. "I've been foraging for Alys."

I didn't meet his eyes. While things were better between us, I didn't think that would last long if he knew where I'd really been.

"Well, your disappearance nearly gave *me* one. I came back to the training yard where I had left you annihilating another dummy, and Meuric told you had gone." He looked at me sternly. "You're supposed to tell someone where you're going."

I felt like giving him an Eva pout, but restrained myself. I hated being treated like a child. I was the Chosen Lady of Nos; I did *not* need a babysitter.

"I'm fine – it's fine," I said soothingly. "Here, have some frostberries. Freshly picked." I handed him a handful. He loved them almost as much as Lunara did.

"Mmm," he managed around a huge mouthful, trying to take a few more, but I held them out of reach.

"Save some for Lunara!"

He popped one more in his mouth, then sat on the log. Voices coming through the trees had us turning to each other quizzically.

"You are my Fated Partner, Cos – start acting like it!"

It was Lady Celestri, wearing a long, loose dress and carrying a towel. It looked like she and Lord Celestri were heading from the lake nestled amongst the trees in the centre of the woods. *Time to make a smooth exit.* I gestured to Maxen with my head.

"Yeah, well, maybe the Fates got it wrong," Lord Celestri shot back.

Maxen and I froze in our escape as Lady Celestri turned to him angrily. I prayed our dark clothing would camouflage us against the ebony frostberry trees.

"Oh no, my Fated Partner, the Fates got it *exactly* right," she hissed, and I shivered. Meuric was right; Lady Celestri *was* a dangerous woman. Maybe Meuric wasn't the only one who'd been surprised when Lord Celestri had been Chosen. Maybe Lord Celestri himself had questioned it… and apparently still was.

He looked positively defeated as he stared back at her for a few tense moments, then stormed off through the trees, Lady Celestri trotting after him.

"That just happened, right?" Maxen asked, looking bemused.

I laughed nervously.

"Poor Eva," he said, picking up my other basket. "Are you finished?"

"Yes, and I know. I wouldn't want Lady Celestri for a mother. Eva has to put up with a lot." I grimaced as we weaved our way through the woods and back to the cottage. The sun had almost reached the horizon, and I looked about nervously, but no ominous wisps of fog crept along the ground.

"Do you want to come in? Alys would love to see you. She's probably got some more of the soap you like," I said, hoping we could cling to the normality we were carefully rebuilding between us.

"I'd love to, but I actually promised to be Eva's support person later. Her mother is hosting another dinner party. I need to get home and get changed." He didn't look at all pleased at the prospect of spending the evening with the Celestris, especially after what we had just witnessed.

"Oh?" I tried for an innocent look. "More business partners?"

He gave me a suspicious glance. "Yes... from Nos."

"Oh," I said, and hoped I didn't sound too relieved. "All right, well, have a lovely night. Be careful." I gestured at the sky, where the sun had almost gone.

"I will. Night." He handed me the other basket and jogged off down the path.

I entered the cottage and placed the baskets on the counter. The table was already set and a plate of fresh bread sat in the centre of the table, a pot bubbling merrily on the stove.

"Hi, sweetheart," Alys said, coming in from the small kitchen garden at the back of the cottage. "Great, you have the mushrooms." She kissed my cheek and handed me two bowls. "Dish up the soup – I just want to put these things away."

"Sure," I replied as Lunara fluttered down from my room. I grabbed a few frostberries before Alys took them away and placed them in a small dish. My mothling deviated from her path towards me and instead made a beeline for her fruit.

"Cheeky mothling," I said affectionately. Lunara shook her wings and grumbled up at me, her tiny mouth smothered in berry juice.

As we sat down to eat, Alys looked over at me with a smile. "So, what did you do today?"

My spoon stopped halfway to my mouth. *Oh, I don't know – obliterated another training dummy, was privy to more revelations about Lady Celestri than I cared to know… Oh, and met with my Fated Partner, the one I am supposed to kill, not kiss!*

"Not much," I said, and filled my mouth with the delicious leek and potato soup. "How about you?"

Her eyes trailed over to the dresser for a split second, then back to me. "Not much," she replied.

Touché. We finished eating in silence.

I spent the evening helping Alys sort out what I'd foraged that day, and it was exactly what I needed. For this evening I would pretend I was just a normal girl, helping out her mother with methodical, menial work. A normal girl who was looking forward to the Festivale and hoping to share a dance with the man she… no, I couldn't even bring myself to *think* the word.

"There, that'll do," Alys said, wiping her hands on a cloth. She stood up, collecting the jars and bottles and boxes. I picked up the remaining ones and followed her into her pantry. We stowed them on the shelves, and I was grateful once again for the distraction of finding the right spots for them all.

"Tea?" Alys asked once we were done.

I plumped for a cup of elderberry and took it up to my room. Lunara had gone to bed early – apparently sorting out healing ingredients bored her. I pressed a gentle kiss to her furry head before readying myself for sleep. Snuggling into my bed, I sipped my tea in contentment. The waxing quarter moon beamed down at me, and I counted the stars until sleep laid its mantle over me.

My contentment didn't follow me into my dreams.

I crawled along the Celestial Bridge as a mewling baby's cries rent the air. I saw a bundle in the centre of the bridge, and two tiny, pale fists fought their way free of the blanket to wave around in the mist-shrouded night.

The fog thickened. Dread surrounded me. There were figures in the mist. Faceless figures, and they were aiming for the baby. I wouldn't get there quickly enough, I understood with dismay, but it didn't stop me from trying. I crawled faster, my hands and knees slipping on the damp bridge.

No. You cannot have her, I cried out.

As the figures reached the baby, a light burst from the bundle – a light so bright it blinded me. I cried out and shielded my eyes, rocking back onto my heels.

The light cleared and I opened my eyes, blinking furiously to refocus my vision. A scream tore from my throat.

The baby and the Shadowwraiths were gone.

Twenty-Two

The day before the Festivale grand opening dawned bright and clear. With no snaking mists emanating from the Celestial Bridge, even Nos was warmer than usual.

I stood before my mirror and surveyed myself critically. A box from the dress shop had arrived first thing, and Alys had made me promise to wear the outfit inside to the Festivale opening tomorrow. It was a matte black suit studded by thousands of tiny silver stars. It was a beautiful suit, and though it wasn't what I would normally wear, I'd promised Alys – and right now I would promise her anything. Kai and I only had a week left, and we were still no closer to figuring out who had made a deal they shouldn't have, and to what end. I'd even been tempted, for a brief moment, to try and steal the Moonstone to speak with Arianrhod. But the memory of Belenos's reaction didn't fill me with confidence

So today – today I was going to do something probably a little bit stupid and more than likely a lot dangerous. Thankfully, Maxen was busy today, so I wouldn't have my shadow. That left me free to sneak into the Novarians' townhouse and see if I could find anything. Aside from Lady Celestri and Sabra, he was the only other person who really disliked me... and I was running out of options. My dreams were getting worse, and they were beginning to morph into harbingers of doom.

Kai had fared no better. Despite ruling out Sabra, we kept circling back to her, so he was going to follow her today. She had told him she had 'official business' to attend to in Nos. It was a risk, him following her here, but we had little choice. We hoped to reconvene tomorrow at the Festivale opening. With crowds of Solians and Nosians mingling, hopefully we would go unnoticed.

I removed the suit and hung it up for tomorrow, before donning my usual uniform of leather combat trousers and cotton tunic in my signature black. I pulled my hair back and secured it, hoping it would stay put. I didn't want my curls springing loose and giving me away – there wasn't anyone else in Nos with black and silver curls like mine. Grabbing a hooded jacket, I went downstairs.

Alys had already left – she had a few tonics to deliver – so I grabbed the frostberry muffin she had left, crumbled up another one for a slumbering Lunara, and made my way outside. It was so warm by Nos standards that I didn't really need the jacket, but I donned it anyway, zipping it up ready to pull the hood up if anyone saw me near the Novarians' house.

The Novarians lived in an opulent house in the same street as Maxen's family – the nobles all lived in the same area. The houses were made from the same black stone as most of the city, but they were adorned with moonstones and glittering silver tiles. Thankfully, the Novarians lived in the end house, so I could slip down the side and over the wall into the garden without being seen.

I crouched behind a row of rose bushes. The black blooms were abundant and the perfect camouflage. Thanks to Alys, I knew that Master Novarian's wife and daughter had a shopping trip planned to Sol, and Gus would be on Guard duty. As tradition dictated, his servants would have been given the day off to prepare for the Festivale the next day. Master Novarian should have been alone – but I gripped the rose bush in front of me in surprise as I saw him exit the house onto the terrace... with Sabra. He poured two drinks from the glass carafe on the table; from here they looked like two old friends simply catching up and enjoying the mild weather.

Fates above! I winced as a thorn pierced my skin and brought my finger to my lip to suck the pain away. When I looked back up they appeared to be having a heated discussion, but I couldn't hear what they were saying. After a moment, Sabra passed something to Master Novarian. He pocketed it in his jacket before they both re-entered the house.

I needed to know what she had given him. Keeping to the fence, I sneaked up to the terrace and sidled along the wall to the house. Without thinking of the consequences of what would happen if I got caught, I cast a furtive look inside before slipping in through the unlocked terrace doors.

I made my way over the plush black carpet and into the hallway, across the black-and-silver checkerboard floor. The silence in the house was only broken by a deep baritone voice singing from upstairs, so I assumed Sabra had gone. I hoped I was right. I *really* didn't want to witness any more clandestine meetings.

I sidled up the stairs and ducked as Master Novarian walked along the landing into a room at the end. Steam poured from within, so I assumed he was heading for a bath. *Perfect!* I waited a few minutes until I was sure he wasn't going to reappear before ducking into what looked to be the master bedroom. I pushed back the unpleasant sensation of being Gus's father's bedroom. I had to work quickly; I couldn't afford to let my disgust take over.

I saw the grey jacket he had been wearing and hastened over to check the pockets. They were empty. I looked around in dismay. Now what was I going to do?

A pouch on the dresser caught my eye. Slowly, I walked over to it. It was made from buttery yellow velvet, embroidered with a gold sun insignia. *Sol!* I carefully untied the ribbon and looked inside; the pouch was full to the brim with large gold coins. Now why would Sabra be paying Master Novarian a large sum of money? A bribe? But what for, I had no clue. It was so frustrating; I was still no nearer to finding out what was going on. This proved he was corrupt, but it wasn't as if I could tell the Council. I couldn't explain I'd been inside his *house*.

I blew out a breath and decided I had better leave before he finished with his bath and discovered me. I certainly didn't want to encounter Master Novarian in a bathrobe, or worse yet, a towel.

Shuddering to myself, I made a quick exit, the singing from the bathroom following me as I left the way I had come. Back in the street, I removed my hood and unzipped my jacket. It had got warmer. I wished I could speak to Kai and see if he had any ideas.

I jumped back as a cream-and-orange-striped carriage hurtled past me. I was about to shout after the driver for nearly running me down, but a face beaming at me from underneath the carriage made the words die in my throat. *Kai.* So he *had* followed Sabra! Fates above, he was going to get himself killed. The way the driver was manoeuvring the carriage, he'd be lucky to make it back to Sol with his bones intact.

I shook my head and carried on along the street. Reaching the dress shop, I thought it only polite to go and thank the ladies for my Festivale outfit before I met Eva for lunch. Meuric had insisted I have a day off from training; I'd resisted as much as I could before remembering I could use the day for some investigation. So far, it hadn't gone that well.

Three excited squeals met my ears as I entered the shop. "Oh, Lady Ceridwen, you're just in time!"

"Time for what?" I asked nervously as I was pulled over to a seat and settled into it.

"You are going to *die!*" Sali enthused.

You could have cut the air with a knife. Kari and Tori shot daggers at Sali, and her face paled even more than her usual milky white complexion.

"I mean, I just…" She trailed off.

I came to her rescue, hating to see her so obviously distressed. "It's all right, Sali, I knew what you meant. What have you got to show me?" I injected enthusiasm into my voice and leaned forward in the chair.

With one final disgusted look at Sali, Kari clapped her hands together. "Tori, if you would?"

Tori's eyes gleamed as she swept behind a screen to wheel out a mannequin wearing a long silver robe, the bodice encrusted with glimmering moonstones in the shape of the emblem of Nos – a crescent moon. The garment had splits to either side, and underneath I could see pewter leather leggings.

"Your Fate's Day ceremony clothes. There is a fitted armoured top underneath, with concealed weapons in the bodice – just press the moon pearl to release them. You can remove the robe when it's time for..." Kari left the last words unsaid. We all knew what she meant.

In the tense silence, Sali brought out a pair of low-heeled knee-length silver boots. "There are weapons in there too," she whispered, pointing to a catch near the heels.

"Thank you," I murmured, "and thank you for my Festivale suit too. It's lovely."

"You're welcome," Kari said, her eyes shining with sympathy. "Oh, but that's not all. We have one more surprise for you, but you'll have to wait for that one. We'll have everything delivered to the cottage."

I nodded, unable to speak. It was all becoming rapidly real, but these ladies were showing me a kindness and compassion I hadn't expected. They usually dealt with the nobles, not some orphaned, Fate-discarded nobody.

"I have to go – I'm meeting Miss Eva," I explained through a throat that refused to work properly.

"Oh, wonderful, have a lovely time," Sali trilled. Kari walked me to the door and pulled me in for a quick hug.

Touched, I hugged her back before I left, blinking stinging eyes.

"Fates above, Eva, could you have chosen a shabbier place for lunch?" I picked my way across the sticky floor. I certainly wasn't a snob, but even I had my eatery standards.

"Shh!" Eva hissed, and pulled me into the booth in a darkened alcove. "No one knows me here, and that's the way I like it."

I did a double take. "What *are* you wearing?"

"Oh, this? It's one of Maxen's old jackets. He left it at my house last summer. Don't tell him I've got it; it comes in handy when I want to keep a low profile."

My brain tried to catch up with all this. "All right, what gives?" I demanded.

She took a drink of a suspicious-looking beverage and barely hid her grimace. "What, can't we try somewhere new for a change?"

I waited.

"Oh, all right," she burst out. "Did you know about that dinner party the other night?" I remembered Maxen telling me he was going to be Eva's support person and nodded. "Well, I may have had a few too many drinks, and now the son of the family thinks I'm interested in him." I tried to keep my face neutral. "So I can't go to any of my usual places, in case I bump into him."

"Ah, I see." My lips twitched. "Just because your parents own a vineyard doesn't mean you should take advantage of it."

She groaned and laid her head on the table, before sitting sharply back up, a placemat stuck to her forehead. "Ugh," she said, peeling it off her skin.

"Come on," I said. "I'll make you a sandwich at the cottage. Lunara misses you." I stood, pulling her up after me.

"*Thank* you," she said, "this place really is terrible."

I looked at her and we burst out laughing. Arms linked, we left the gloomy tavern.

"So, did you get your outfit from Kari?" Eva asked as we ambled out of the city in the muted sunshine.

"Which one?" I replied with a laugh. "I've been spoiled. It was quite overwhelming, actually."

"You deserve it," Eva said seriously.

"So, what are you wearing?" I didn't want to dwell on what I deserved or not. Different people had differing opinions on that. I was only glad I did have a few people in my corner.

"Oh, you're going to love it. It's a trouser suit. It's a deep lavender colour, overlaid with swirls of dark purple. I was thinking of having my hair up for a change." She swished her silky waterfall of black hair effortlessly.

I loved seeing her back to her usual self; carefree, and excited about the Festivale. "That sounds lovely," I murmured.

At the border of the Celestri Estate, we met Lord Celestri coming the other way.

"Dad!" Eva exclaimed. "Where are you going?"

Or, I thought, as I watched the startled expression ripple across his face and a shuttered look come into his silver eyes, *where have you been?*

Twenty-Three

"Just taking a walk," Lord Celestri said, but his eyes flicked away from Eva's.

I was sure he was lying, but Eva was apparently oblivious as she slipped her other arm through his, linking us all together. "Why don't you join us? That's all right, isn't it?" she directed at me, before continuing, "Wen is going to make us a sandwich at the cottage."

I was interested to see how he would get out of that, but to my surprise he gave a genuine smile as he looked from Eva to me. "That would be lovely."

All right then. This was going to be interesting.

I pushed open the cottage door, calling out quickly, "Alys, we have guests," to give her warning.

Eva looked at me weirdly. "Guests? More like family." She laughed as she moved into the room and scooped up Lunara from her perch. As she peppered the little mothling with kisses, making her grumble in delight, I watched Lord Celestri's face. The shuttered look was back in his eyes, but not before I saw a spark of something like grief flicker in their molten depths. I filed that away for later.

Alys came out of her room and stopped short. "Oh, Eva, Co— Lord Celestri." She just stopped herself from saying his name, a flush staining her cheeks. Even more interesting.

Eva looked up and gave Alys a grin. "I hope you don't mind us stopping by. Wen and I decided to eat here instead."

"Of course, you're always welcome." Her glance shifted across to include Lord Celestri too.

He inclined his head with a small smile, before going over to the sink and washing his hands. "Right, I'm starving."

I rolled my shoulders back. *All right, so we're actually doing this.*

I thought it would be awkward, but soon we were all pitching in: shredding up lettuce, slicing tomatoes and cutting fresh bread before piling up huge cheese-and-ham-salad sandwiches. We sat around the small circular kitchen table, our knees bumping, and ate in companionable silence.

"All we need now is a few nice cool glasses of *Celestara* cider," Lord Celestri said as he pushed back from the table in satisfaction and wiped his mouth with a napkin.

I almost choked on the last of my sandwich. *Kai!* I hoped he'd made it back to Sol in one piece.

Eva nodded. "This is nice – we should do it more often. Alys, we never see you any more." She pouted. "Mother says you're always too busy with your healing to join us for dinner."

Alys opened her mouth, her eyes crinkling in confusion. "Oh, yes. I am *extremely* busy…"

I wondered why she was lying. Perhaps Lady Celestri was lying; I couldn't remember the last time Alys had actually been invited up to the manor. Maybe Lady Celestri didn't like her either. As I looked from my adoptive mother to Lord Celestri, I wondered if she had good reason.

"You work too hard, doesn't she, Dad?" Eva said, and the tension in the room grew. Alys looked uncomfortable as Lord Celestri's captivating gaze took in her face.

"That she does, Eva, but for good reason. Where would we be without her?"

Where indeed? I smiled at the woman who had raised me and stood to collect the dishes. Lunara rolled over in the little basket she had claimed, her belly distended from all the tomatoes she had eaten.

"I'll help you." Lord Celestri joined me at the sink while Eva and Alys talked amongst themselves. "How are you doing?"

I didn't need to ask what he meant. Fate's Day was all anyone could think or talk about. That day and what occurred within its hours would determine what happened to all the realms, Fog included. I plunged my hands into the hot water, enjoying the tingling in my fingers. Any chance I had to feel *something*, I took. I didn't like being numb, but sometimes it was the best armour.

"I am…"

What? Fine, not fine, resigned, not resigned? No, none of it was how I truly felt.

"*Terrified*," I whispered, then clamped my lips shut in horror. How could I say that out loud? *And* to the Fated Lord of the realm! But Lord Celestri had a way of making you confide in him, as if he could make every bad thing go away, and slay the monsters under the bed for you.

But no one else could actually slay them. It was down to me.

"Of course you are," he whispered back kindly. "For too long the Fates have toyed with our lives, as if we're mere pawns in their games of power."

From the way he spoke, I knew he was talking about his own situation too. "It's not fair." I shook my head.

Lord Celestri fell silent, and we carried on washing and drying the dishes together. As he stacked the last plate, he said quietly, "I think you should take an offering to Arianrhod tonight. Go alone."

With a meaningful look, he patted me on the shoulder and went over to Eva. "Come along, miss, I think we should leave these two lovely women. We've intruded on their hospitality long enough."

I stared after him. Why had he suggested I go to the shrine? Did he know something? I balked at the idea of going back there and facing the Fates' wrath. Caught up in my thoughts, I had to pull myself together as Eva waved a hand in front of my face. "Nos to Wen," she said with a smile.

"Oh, sorry. What did you say?"

"I said I'll see you at the Festivale opening tomorrow?"

I gave her a hug, my eyes meeting Lord Celestri's over her shoulder. The strength I saw in his eyes gave rise to my own. "I'll be there," I said, although I wasn't sure if I was talking to him or Eva.

"Perfect. Thanks for lunch!" She blew me a kiss, hugged Alys, and tickled Lunara before leaving with Lord Celestri.

Alys stared after them before blowing out a long breath.

"Sorry if we sprang that on you," I said warily. Alys had always encouraged me to bring friends back; there was always plenty of food to spare, so she'd never minded in the past. But that was before…

"Oh, it's fine," she said, her voice pitched higher than usual. "I… um… I have some work to do in the garden." She placed a cool hand on my arm before grabbing her apron and heading outside.

I watched her through the window for a few minutes, but she appeared to be all right as she yanked some weeds from the flower beds. She always self-soothed with weeding, so I left her to it. I had my own soothing to do.

I picked up Lunara from the dish in which she had decided to take her food-coma, settled her against my neck, and climbed up the ladder to my room. I lay down on the bed, meaning only to think the day's events through, but Lunara's tiny, rumbling snores lulled me to the point of drowsiness, and soon I was slumbering too.

When I awoke, my blanket covered me, and a stubby blue candle burning on my nightstand lit the darkened room. Lunara now dozed in her nest. I couldn't believe I had slept so long. I rolled over and looked out the window. The moon was up, and with a start I remembered Lord Celestri's suggestion.

I sat up and leaned over to blow out the candle – blue for protection. I smiled. Alys looking out for me, even in my sleep. My boots were next to the bed, so I put them on and crept down the ladder. I found a note on the kitchen table.

Wen, I tried to wake you for dinner, but you must have been exhausted. There's stew in the saucepan when you want it. I'm having an early night too. See you in the morning.
Love you, Alys xx

I looked from the note to her closed door and felt my heart lurch. Going back to the shrine might be a terrible idea, but it was the only one I had right now. I hoped it would work.

Shrugging into my jacket, I picked up an empty wide, glass jar with a lid, and silently left the cottage. The air was still and mild. The velvet sky was pinpricked with thousands of sparkling stars, and I enjoyed the walk beneath the almost full moon.

I stopped next to a cluster of moonflowers and took my dagger from my boot. With a whispered thank you, I cut the stems and made them into a posy, wrapping them together with a long blade of grass and tying it off. I took a deep breath of the fragrant flowers and hoped they would be a good enough offering for the Moon Fate.

At the opening to the caves, I paused. I had never been here alone, and it felt eerie. A shadow detached itself from the wall and I gave a start, dropping the posy and immediately going for my dagger.

"I'm glad to see your reactions are quick," Lord Celestri said with a laugh, his white teeth flashing in the moonlight.

I lowered the dagger. "Sorry." I picked up the posy again.

"I'm glad you came," he said, "but you're going to need this." He opened his hand to reveal the duck-egg sized Moonstone.

I gaped at it, then at him. A vivid flashback to Kai showing me the Sunstone made me step back. I was not going there again. "I thought you said to just bring her an offering."

"I did, but you need to speak to her too before the ceremony. Without Belenos there – he can be overbearing sometimes." The stars above twinkled as if laughing at his statement. I thought he was treading on dangerous ground, but what did I have to lose?

"All right." I nodded, holding out a hand for the stone. He lowered it reverently into my palm and I clutched it tightly. It pulsed coolly against my skin.

"Do you want me to come with you?" he asked in a gentle voice.

"Would you?" The water would be even darker now.

"It would be an honour," Lord Celestri said quietly, and together we entered the cave. I toed off my boots and placed my jacket on top. Lord Celestri did the same; I noted he favoured well-worn boots too.

I placed the posy of flowers inside the glass jar and stoppered the lid to keep them dry. Clutching the jar in one hand and putting the Moonstone into my pocket, I slid into the water, Lord Celestri behind me.

Spears of light crisscrossed the dark water, and I wondered where they were coming from. I didn't dwell on it; I was simply thankful they were there to guide our way.

I pulled myself out of the water and stood dripping before the statues of Belenos and Arianrhod. Lord Celestri joined me, and we stared up at the stone faces. Arianrhod appeared serene in the moonlit radiance coming in from the open roof, while Belenos' face was all sharp angles and fierce edges. I half expected him to come to life and berate me.

Not wanting to linger longer than necessary, especially shivering from the cool water, I pulled off the lid and withdrew the flowers. They glowed softly. I placed them at Arianrhod's feet before pulling out the Moonstone.

When I hesitated, Lord Celestri asked, "Would you like me to place it?"

"No." I shook my head and firmly set the stone into the indent. This was something *I* had to do. I understood that now.

We stepped back to better see Arianrhod's face. For a moment nothing happened, then the statue gave a delicate yawn and opened her eyes. She blinked her long eyelashes a few times before looking down at us.

"Oh, isn't this interesting," she said in a cool, clear voice, looking from me to Lord Celestri, a knowing look in her eyes. "I would ask why you have summoned me, but I think I already know."

"You do?" I asked, thankful my voice didn't shake with nerves. It was intimidating to be in the Fate's radiant presence. While Belenos' manifestation had felt raw and uncontrollable, Arianrhod was otherworldly, ethereal, and I immediately felt connected to her. Would she be able to help?

She smiled serenely.

"Oh yes. You want to know who your parents are."

Twenty-Four

I gasped at the Fate's declaration. *Did* I want to know who my real parents were? That wasn't why I had come – but if she could tell me... Would I be happier going to my possible grave after learning who they were? Would it change anything? Surely if anything it would make it harder, knowing who I was leaving behind.

As I debated, Lord Celestri spoke quickly. "That isn't why we came – Lady Ceridwen wants—"

"Wants, needs," Arianrhod interrupted him. "Sometimes what mortals want and what they *need* are two extremely different things." She sighed and focused her luminous gaze on me. "Well, if you are sure? I accept your beautiful offering, Lady Ceridwen Moonshade; therefore you may ask me one thing."

I nibbled my lip. It was tempting to ask the question she so obviously knew the answer to, and was evidently keen to share, but I couldn't be selfish. This related to Kai's future too.

"Is our Fate sealed?" I asked. "Is the prophecy true?" *Fates above! That was two questions.* I threw a frustrated look at Lord Celestri, but he smiled back encouragingly.

Arianrhod stared down at me. "I will answer your first question only. Yes, your fates are sealed…"

My legs buckled, and Lord Celestri grabbed me before I fell. He looked up angrily. "Why do you toy with us so? *Please* – help her!"

I had never heard such raw emotion in his voice before. I clung to his arm and barely heard the Moon Fate's next words over the thundering of my heart.

"I had not finished," Arianrhod chastised him. "Yes, your fates are sealed, but it isn't what you have been led to believe."

The whispers I had heard when I had visited the Fates with Kai erupted inside my head once again, but this time I couldn't discern what they were saying. They pounded against my skull like thunder in the night, relentless and unyielding. I thought I would collapse from the pressure, but abruptly they stopped, and I gasped out a breath.

"But what does that mean?" I rasped.

"I cannot say another word." She cast a sideways look at Belenos' statue.

"But *he* spoke freely," I said, gesturing up at Belenos angrily. "He entered Kai's mind and gave him information without us having to bring an offering." I knew I risked offending Arianrhod, but I was beyond caring. I was desperate.

She puckered her brow. "Oh, his arrogance makes his tongue extremely loose. But we are bound by a code, we and the other Fate – of whom the Twin Realms should be extraordinarily wary. There is a promise not to meddle in the ways of mortals… unless they interfere in ours. Now, I have said too much. I wish you luck, Ceridwen Moonshade – you are going to need it."

Her face rippled and was once again stone – but then, without warning, she was back for one final utterance.

"What you and your Fated Partner do on Fate's Day will ripple across *all* the realms. Choose wisely."

As her light blinked out, I sagged in Lord Celestri's hold and he lowered me to sit on the ground. I pulled my knees up to my chest and wrapped my arms around my damp legs, shivering as I laid my head atop my knees and closed my eyes. I wanted to stay here, stay hidden until it was all over. I knew now that we had to follow the path laid before us. There was no fork in the road. Our path was set, the destination clear, but what we would find when we got there was still down to the choice we would make upon arrival.

I needed to speak to Kai.

"Ceridwen… Wen. How can I help you?" Lord Celestri crouched down next to me. I turned my head.

"You can't." *No one can.* I pushed myself to my feet. "I have to go," I told him. "I need to think. Thank you for your kindness."

"Wen, it isn't a *kindness*. If only I could—" He broke off and ran a hand through his hair.

Silver eyes met, and I nodded in understanding.

"I'll see you at the Festivale opening," I said, before turning and diving into the pool.

I swam as if a band of Shadowwraiths were on my tail, thinking only to put distance between me and the Fates. If only I could distance myself from my own fate as easily.

I barely stopped to pull on my jacket and boots before rushing out of the caves and into the night. I huddled into my jacket and ran along the moonlit path, only to trip over my loose lace and tumble headfirst into a mossy mound. I lay with my face pressed into the dew-soaked vegetation before, with a scream of anguish, I flipped over and cursed at the moon.

It beamed down at me, mocking my plight. I couldn't do it; I couldn't pretend anymore. The uncertainty, the not knowing what to *do* was killing me – I wouldn't make it another week. My heart would simply give out. Everyone who doubted me was right. I wasn't strong enough to be the victor in a challenge the Fates had set. Because I *didn't know the rules!*

Another cry tore from my throat, this one anger-filled. I kicked my heels into the ground and pushed myself up to a sitting position. Alys's soft voice entered my mind. *You are a Lady of Nos; you will hold your head high.*

I shoved my wet curls off my face and stood. She was right. What was I doing wallowing like this? I needed to get home before Lord Celestri came along. I couldn't bear to see pity in his eyes. It would undo me.

I bent to re-tie my lace before I made the peaceful walk home. The still night was at odds with my pounding heart and whirling thoughts, but at least I walked with my head held high, my stride eating up the ground as if I could carve a path that would last for millennia to come. *Here walked Lady Ceridwen Moonshade, Lady of Nos.* Moths and fireflies flitted in the garden as I opened the gate, and I couldn't wait to hear Lunara's grumbling snores. She always centred me.

Back in my room, I towel-dried my limp curls before shoving them in a loose bun – too tired to salvage them now – and changing into soft, dry clothes. When I lay down, Lunara opened one tiny black eye and fluttered over. As if instinctively knowing I needed her, she burrowed into my neck, her fluffy body warming me up.

"Thank you, Lu," I whispered. This time I didn't fight back the tears; I let them come. They tracked down my face, and Lunara grumbled in concern at me.

"It's all right," I whispered, over and over, until sleep came and I dreamt I was drowning in a sea of tears as waves of whispers claimed me.

"Oh, sweetheart, you look lovely." Alys looked me up and down, pride shining in her smoky eyes.

I adjusted the lapel on the tight-fitting suit and grimaced. It followed every one of my curves as though I was wearing a second skin.

"But you are a bit pale – did you sleep well?" She came over to run a hand across my brow. "Here, have some orange tea, it'll pep you up a bit."

I shook my head, before taking the cup she offered and inhaling the citrusy scent. As always, she was right; the aroma refreshed me, and immediately I felt more alert.

"Shall I do your hair?" she asked, holding up a clip and a comb.

"I think I'll leave it loose," I told her. "I'm more comfortable with it down." *And more like me.* I'd spent ages on my curls this morning, the methodical ritual soothing me. They trailed, full and shiny, down my back and around my shoulders like a cloak of protection.

"All right. I'll go and get dressed," she said, and slipped into her room.

"And what about you, little mothling, are you going to come today?" I asked Lunara. She grumbled back at me from her perch, before swooping over to settle on my shoulder. "I'll take that as a yes," I said happily, reaching up to stroke her wings. She would be a comforting presence.

Alys reappeared dressed in a long gown. It had a shirred silver bodice and cap sleeves, with a long, flowing, gunmetal-grey skirt dotted with tiny black stars and flowers. Her hair had recently grown out slightly and it waved over her forehead in a few loose curls, a clutch of moonflowers tucked behind one ear. Crescent moons dangled from her ears.

"You look beautiful," I breathed out, and she flushed prettily, giving a little twirl.

"Thank you, Wen. I want to do you proud today." Her eyes turned serious as she joined me. "I have a gift for you."

I gave a surprised laugh. "I'm always proud of you, Alys. And I don't need a gift."

"I know you don't *need* one... but all the same, I want you to have it." She turned away, and I was reminded starkly of Arianrhod with her 'wants, needs'. Alys turned back to me with a small purple velvet jewellery box and opened it to reveal a crescent moon brooch. It was hammered silver with an outline of tiny moonstones.

She affixed it to the lapel of my jacket, her touch gentle. "It was my great-grandmother's. She was one half of a Fated Pair too. She moved to Sol but wore this every day of her rule as a reminder of her birth realm." She stepped back with tears in her eyes. "I think it only fitting you should have it."

"But Alys, this belonged to your family," I protested, touched. If I'd had a normal Choosing, I would have learned all about the past Fated Pairs in my tutelage with the Celestris, but this small bit of knowledge was comforting somehow and made me feel even closer to Alys.

She gave me a look so profound my heart stuttered. "You *are* my family." As tears welled in my own eyes, Lunara grumbled. "And you too, little one," she added with a laugh, turning away, though not before I saw the grief in her eyes.

"Thank you, Alys. I am honoured to wear it." And I was. I would walk into the Festivale grand opening and do *Alys* proud.

She grabbed a basket full of vials and dark bottles, holding out her other hand to me. "Shall we, my lady?"

I blew out a breath and squared my shoulders. Checking Lunara was securely anchored with her talons, I gripped Alys's hand tightly and together we left the cottage.

Sun-and-moon-shaped banners in gold and silver lined the way into the shared fields. Tents lined the edges of the grass, leaving the middle clear for a wooden pallet dance floor, hay bales, and a large pole draped with orange and purple trailing ribbons, ready for the Beltane dance. A makeshift stage was situated at the far end, and that was where Alys and I headed for the Festivale opening ceremony.

Curious eyes followed me, and I tried my best to appear serene and calm; I never enjoyed being the centre of attention. I met as many eyes as I could with a gracious smile, all while my heart thundered in my chest. Alys squeezed my hand at intervals, and I squeezed back gratefully. Not all eyes were kind; some were accusing and judgemental, as if they knew I was weak and a fraud. That I might yet make the wrong decision for the Twin Realms.

I *really* needed to speak to Kai.

My eyes searched the stage and I was relieved to see him there, standing next to Sabra with his parents behind him. He gave me a quick wink when no one was looking and warmth filled me up, displacing the hollowness.

Lord Celestri, who stood in the centre of the stage with Lady Celestri, Eva and another older woman I didn't recognise wearing a Sol-emblazoned robe, walked over to help me and Alys up the steps to the stage.

"Really, Cos, they're not *that* old – although, Alys, is that a few grey strands I see in your hair?" Lady Celestri said with a snappy laugh. Her eyes gleamed maliciously as Alys tensed beside me. Even Eva looked aghast at her mother's tactlessness.

I cast a glance over Alys' hair; what was Lady Celestri talking about? The sunlight picked out a few lighter strands in her hair, but they weren't grey… they were silver.

Twenty-Five

"Really, mother," Eva said in exasperation, and rolled her eyes. "Pay no attention to her, Alys, they're just highlights from the sun. It's been unusually sunny for Nos!" She smiled at Alys, and while still pale, Alys gave her a grateful smile back.

Is that what it is? I wondered, trying to catch Alys' eyes, but she had turned away to speak to the older Sol lady, while Lord Celestri shot daggers at his lady.

"You look so glamorous," Eva said to me as Lady Celestri ignored Lord Celestri and cosied up to the Ostaras instead. I noticed she kept a wide berth from Sabra, who stood apart from everyone else with a bored expression on her face.

I looked Eva up and down. "I can't hold a candle to you," I argued.

She gave me a smile as she ran a purple-tipped fingernail along Lunara's head. "I do look fabulous, don't I?" She winked and I let out a laugh, the knot in my chest loosening.

Meuric jogged up the steps and gave me a nod before taking a place next to Alys.

"If we're ready?" Lord Celestri said, looking as if he wanted the opening ceremony over with. He pulled at the neck of his Nos Guard official uniform before introducing the older woman. "This is Lady Aurelia Summers."

I nodded in greeting, recognising her as part of the Fated Pair who had ruled before the Celestris. The Council usually brought out somebody important from one of the realms to open the Festivale along with the current Fated Pair.

"Well, aren't you a handsome pair," Lady Aurelia said, looking from me to Kai in his gold suit, who had taken his position beside me on the podium. "Such a shame, such a shame," she muttered as she joined Lord and Lady Celestri at the front of the stage.

A crowd had gathered before the stage, but I couldn't concentrate on the sea of faces; I was too aware of the masculine presence beside me. Our fingers brushed. An electric shock shot up my arm, and my lips parted.

"Is your sister going to come this year?" I asked, saying the first thing that came to mind. I had never officially met his family; the prophecy meant it had never seemed appropriate to do so.

"No, she still doesn't like large crowds. She's happier at home. I told her I'd bring her some candied pears back," Kai replied, his voice like warm honey.

I restrained a shiver as my nerve endings tingled at the sound of his voice. It was as though my very being was electrified every time he was near. Calling out to complete the circuit.

I forced a deep breath. Kai's sister never came to the Festivale, so I had never had the chance to meet her. I wished *I* didn't have to attend, but every year I had been made to stand on the stage next to Kai like some sacrificial lamb, paraded in front of all the Twin Realms. *Look, here is the girl whose fate is to either become a murderess or to die so you can all live.* Dark thoughts were creeping in again as I focused on the faces in the crowd, on the tiny tots clinging to their mother's skirts or the elderly men sharing a tankard of cider. Were their lives any more important than mine... any less? *Stop it, Wen.* This wasn't doing me any good.

I realised that Lord Celestri had introduced Lady Aurelia and she was speaking to the crowd. "This is an extremely important Festivale. It has been almost three years to the day since these two young people were Chosen." She looked over at us. Her voice was strong, but her deep blue eyes belied her true feelings; they glimmered with sympathy. I wondered if she was thinking about how she would have felt if it were her and her Fated Partner. "They have an important part to play in the future of the Twin Realms. They will be remembered, and honoured, for a long time, whatever the outcome."

All eyes turned to us, and a solemn silence fell across the field. Even the bees ceased to buzz. Then tankards and glasses were raised in a silent toast to us. An urgent hand gripped mine, and Kai squeezed hard.

"Have faith in us," he whispered fervently, and I nodded back tremulously, a lump in my throat stopping me from replying.

"To Lord Malakai Ostara and Lady Ceridwen Moonshade: they who will save us all," Lady Aurelia said, breaking the silence, and cheers erupted.

She held up a hand and the din subsided.

"Before I officially open the Festivale, I have another announcement. For the first time in our twin history, our current gracious Fated Pair will be opening their house to us all for a grand ball on Fate's Day Eve. They hope you will don your finest clothes and dance the night away with them."

Cheers once again rippled through the crowd and Lady Celestri stepped forward waving her black-tipped nails, a cat-like smile upon her face as she lapped up the attention. I peeled my gaze away from her and looked over the crowd. Kari, Sali and Tori stood near the front in fabulous dresses. They waved at me, and Kari mouthed, "Surprise."

So that's what they had been on about – another surprise outfit. I would stake a barrelful of frostberries that it was a ballgown. I groaned.

Kai nudged me as Lady Aurelia announced that the Festivale was officially open. "I thought you liked dancing?"

"I do... I just don't like *ballgowns*," I replied, watching the crowd disperse to take advantage of the festivities.

Kai released my hand as his mother came over to claim him. "Oh, but you look so beautiful in them," he murmured before he was drawn away.

Lunara grumbled in my ear.

"I know, he didn't have time to speak to you. Hopefully we'll find him later." I rubbed her head in a placating gesture. She chirped back, and then nuzzled my neck.

"Let's go find Max and Rissa," Eva said, linking my arm. "I'm parched."

"Will you be all right?" I looked over at Alys.

"Of course, you go on with your friends. I have some tonics to deliver," Alys told me, breaking off her conversation with Meuric.

Keen to get away from Lady Celestri and Sabra and the cautious looks the Ostaras kept giving me, I let Eva lead me down the steps and into the throng. We sidestepped a pair of jolly Solians and scoured the crowd for Maxen and Larissa.

"There they are." Eva pointed to a purple-and-cream-striped tent. Candied pears were displayed enticingly on a wooden rack outside, and barrels of cider lined the entrance. "Might have known we'd find you here, Riss," Eva told the other girl with a laugh. "The Festivale is the only time I know you to indulge in sweet treats."

Larissa grinned around a bite of the pear-on-a-stick. "Well, Madame Stella would have my guts for garters if I didn't maintain my dancer's physique."

Eva plucked her own pear from the stand and lifted hers in the air in a salute, tossing a coin to the vendor. "That is the truth." She shuddered comically before taking a hearty bite.

Maxen offered me a pear and I took it, not really wanting it. I twirled the stick as he asked, "How are you doing? That was some speech Lady Aurelia gave."

"One of the best yet," I said with an eye-roll. The speeches were usually along the same theme, though in previous years it hadn't bothered me as much. This

Fate's Day had seemed lightyears away, but now it was upon me, it was suffocating.

I handed the uneaten pear back to Maxen. "I'm going to take a walk," I told him. "I want to get Lunara out of the sun."

"Do you want me to come with you?"

"No, I'll be fine," I reassured him. "Keep those two in line." I gestured to Eva and Larissa, who were now giggling over cups of cider.

He ran a hand across his braids, and his steel-grey eyes lit with long-suffering humour. "I'll try."

I meandered along the tent line, keeping to the shade so Lunara wouldn't get overheated. Mothlings didn't do well in the sun; they much preferred the cool stillness of night, as did I.

Seizing my chance, I ducked down the side of an orange-and-cream tent and underneath a group of trees to climb over the fence into the orchard. I passed groups of young people lounging on the grass having picnics, and children playing hide-and-seek amongst the dense trees. Moving further in, I removed my jacket while Lunara fluttered on ahead through the shady canopy. I noted with pleasure that no one else lingered this far in, so I stopped and leaned against the large tree, wondering if Kai would come.

I watched Lunara play chase with a couple of butterflies for a few peaceful moments, listening to the laughter of the children in the distance.

"Happy Festivale." Kai rounded the tree with a posy of bright yellow flowers. I laughed as he presented them to me with a flourish, not bothering to keep out of sight.

"What are you doing? You might be seen!" I took the flowers, a blush staining my cheeks.

"Let them see. I'm just a young man coming across a pretty girl on the first day of the Festivale." He moved closer.

"How much cider have you had?" I joked, but my breath caught as he took another step towards me.

"Not – one – drop," he murmured, his gaze turning molten. "Let's pretend... let's pretend we're not Fated to kill each other. Let's imagine our eyes meet through the trees." He sauntered in even closer and I pressed myself up against the tree trunk, one errant twig scraping the bare skin of my arm. I gasped at the sting, but Kai's eyes lit with heat. "I pick one golden, *juicy* pear... and take a bite." His hand reached above my head and plucked a pear from one of the low-lying branches.

His perfect white teeth sank into the glossy skin, and this time my gasp was nothing to do with pain. What was going on? I could usually resist his advances, but not this time. I wanted to *be* the pear.

He leaned in closer still, his honeyed breath tantalisingly mingling with my own. It was intoxicating.

Abruptly, he stepped back, the pear falling from his hand. He bowed mockingly. "And that is why I would win."

What? Anger burned through me, swift and fierce, and coloured my cheeks. Why would he humiliate me like that?

Out of the corner of my eye, I saw movement and realised that a group of young Solian men stood watching us. *Oh. Well, two can play at that game, Kai.*

My hand blurred. In an instant, I was up against him, my small blade pressed to his neck. This time, *his* lips parted in surprise. I knew there was a reason I tucked my weapon into my boot that morning.

"Do not underestimate me. I'm not the silly, doe-eyed girl you used to know." I shoved him away from me, and he inclined his head as the Solian men whooped and jeered at our show. Well, for me it was a show; I hoped it was for Kai too.

As I turned away, I heard his voice say softly, "I've never thought you were silly." My heart thudded in relief.

The men moved on; I hoped if they spoke of what they saw they would just say they'd seen us sparring in the orchard. Alone again, we turned silently to each other, and I caught up a trembling Lunara who bombed towards me, chittering and grumbling as if telling us off.

"I'm all right – we were only playing," I reassured her. Before I could tell Kai of the events of the last few days – searching the Novarians' house, finding the gold, and what Arianrhod had told me – I realised that the blonde girl, the one who had told Sabra about our meeting, stood at a gate at the far end of the orchard, waving to Kai with a radiant smile on her pretty face.

"Your *friend* wants you," I said, pointing over to her and hating the jealous bite in my voice.

Kai looked over at the blonde girl in confusion. "What?" he said, before throwing back his golden head and laughing a deep belly laugh.

I let out a huff and turned on my heel. "Come on, Lunara, we're going."

I marched away, with Kai calling after me to come back.

Twenty-Six

"Wen! Wait – it's not what you think!" Kai caught up with me and turned me around to face him. The laughter had gone from his eyes. He stroked Lunara as she grumbled angrily at him. "That's Tesni." He looked at me expectantly, but I stared blankly back. "You know, my *sister*."

"Oh," I said. "*Ohhhh*." Fates above! What a fool I was. Of course it was his sister. Now I wasn't looking at her through a veil of green mist, I could see the likeness between them. "I… may need to apologise to her. I was a bit cutting to her after she told Sabra where we were."

"Don't be cross with her. She's very overprotective of me and thought she was doing the right thing. She never agreed with me still keeping in contact with you after the Choosing. She thinks my heart will get broken… in the end," Kai explained honestly as Tesni tentatively picked her way across the orchard towards us.

"Kai…" I trailed off at his vulnerable declaration.

"Later," he promised, as Tesni joined us.

"Ceridwen! How lovely to finally meet you properly," she said, her face wreathed in a wide smile.

Guilt assailed me at how I had thought so badly of her – and Kai. We were a Fated Pair; of course he hadn't given his heart elsewhere. That wasn't how it worked… but a whisper slipped inside my mind, like a creeping vine with poisonous thorns. *What about Lord and Lady Celestri?*

My smile slipped at the thought. What if being a Fated Pair wasn't all sunshine and moonlight? What if, over time, it tainted any true feelings, because you hadn't chosen that person – the *Fates* had?

Well, it wasn't as if Kai and I would ever get the chance to find out. Fate's Day was nearly upon us, and Arianrhod had confirmed our fate *was* set.

"You too," I said to Tesni, zeroing back in on the glowing girl before me. "I'm sorry about before."

"Oh, don't be." She pulled me in for a hug. I was so surprised, I gaped at Kai over her shoulder. Wasn't I the girl who was Fated to *kill* her precious brother? "I should have kept my nose out. Kai is forever telling me I'm too nosy."

"And bossy," he added, and the two shared an identical, white-toothed grin. Was I missing something? Why was Tesni acting like I was her new best friend?

Lunara fluttered over to Tesni, and I felt even worse. Lunara was a superb judge of character; this meant I had nothing to fear from Tesni. She had no ill will in her. She squealed in delight as Lunara nuzzled her neck, her eyes widening at the sight of the tiny creature.

She smiled over at me, one hand holding Lunara carefully on her shoulder. "I have resolved to trust in

Kai… and in you. I know you will find a way. I have faith." She put a warm hand on my cool skin and looked deep into my eyes. "The Fates do not get to chart the course of your lives. You do." Her blue eyes swirled liked a whirlpool and I fell into them, mesmerised.

"Tes." Kai gently withdrew her hand from my arm. "It happened again."

Tesni blinked. Her eyes were back to their warm blue, but her face had paled. "I'm sorry if I scared you," she said. "That's why I don't mix with large crowds. It gets overwhelming at times, and I – I … *feel* things. Only Kai and our parents know."

Shaking off the dream-like sensation, I nodded in understanding. Alys had told me about empaths and seers; perhaps Tesni had some skill in that area. I hoped Sabra never got it in her head to take advantage of Tesni and what she could do. "Don't worry, your secret is safe with me," I told her. Tesni smiled back, some of her colour returning.

"I'm going to head back home. I have a headache coming on," she said to Kai, and he frowned at her in concern.

"Do you want me to walk you back?"

"No, stay with Ceridwen. Enjoy the Festivale." She carefully handed Lunara back to me. "Bye, little one. Bye, Wen."

"Nice to meet you, Tesni."

"I'll see you at home," Kai said. "I'll bring you back those candied pears."

"You'd better!" she threw over her shoulder, winding her way through the trees and out of the gate.

"Right… where were we?" Kai said, turning back to me, one eyebrow raised.

I placed my hands against his chest. Lunara fluttered away and up into the tree — *sensible mothling*. Kai leaned in close, and I gave him a wide grin as I pushed him away firmly.

He staggered back. "What was that for?"

"Oh, I don't know… making me think you were only getting close to me to best me? How about that for a start?" I planted my legs wide and fisted my hands on my hips.

"I didn't have a choice. I was thinking on my feet." He held up his hands in a surrender pose, and I tilted my head.

"All right," I conceded. "But I need to know what you're thinking. It helps if we're on the same page."

His eyes dropped to my mouth. "I'm not sure it's best you know what I'm thinking right now."

He made to move towards me again, but I stepped back, putting distance between us.

"Kai, it's time to be serious. Did you find anything out yesterday? Nice mode of transport, by the way."

He laughed. "I thought it was rather inventive myself — although my back is full of stone chips. Do you want to see?" He made to lift up his dull gold shirt, but I shook my head quickly.

"Um, I'll take your word for it."

His eyes sobered. "The only thing I discovered is Sabra that visited a townhouse in Nos and has a penchant for frostberry truffles. She brought back a whole crateful."

231

My confidence spiralled away like sand through an hourglass. "I know about her visiting a townhouse. I was there—"

"*What?* I saw you on the street, but I never imagined—"

"It's fine, I wasn't caught," I assured him quickly. "I was planning to search Master Novarian's house – he dislikes me, and has a deceptive air about him. I saw him and Sabra talking on his terrace. I checked his room and found a pouch full of Solian gold, but nothing else." I shrugged helplessly.

Kai frowned in thought. "Why would Sabra be paying him off? It's not for frostberry truffles – she picked them up from a shop before she left."

I didn't laugh at his attempt at a joke. It didn't matter why. "Maybe we should stop focusing on them…" I trailed off as Kai strode forward and gripped my hand.

"You're not giving up. You can't!"

My skin burned beneath his touch, and my nerve endings ignited. I gripped back. "I'm *not* giving up, but Arianrhod told me our fate is set."

He let go of my hand. "*Arianrhod?* You went to the shrine without me." The absence of his heat made me cold – so cold.

"It wasn't like that, Kai! Lord Celestri suggested I take her an offering. I thought it might help. But he was there with the Moonstone, and I spoke to her." My voice had taken on a desperate edge. "She told me our fates are set… but it isn't what we think."

"But what does that even *mean?*" he exploded, turning away from me to pace up and down in front of the trees. "Was that it, was that all she said?" I hesitated. "What, Wen?"

"She mentioned a third Fate, one we should all be wary of, and then she warned me to choose wisely, because what we do on Fate's Day will ripple across all the realms."

"Well, we know that. But what *is* our choice? Sabra would have us all believe our only options are either for me to kill you or you to kill me. That it's the only way to hold back the wrath of Fog." He moved back in. "But I don't believe that. I don't believe that what we have together is fated for sacrifice. I believe if we stand together and face what comes, our *union* could hold it back."

"Do you really believe that? Do you think we *could* change the prophecy by accepting that we're Fated to be? That we could be stronger as one?" I so wanted desperately to believe it too: that if we stood together, Solians and Nosians side by side, we could strengthen the realms through the sheer power of our combined belief.

"We must at least try." He pulled me into his arms and held me tightly as I rested my head on his shoulder.

And I believed. Arianrhod had said there was a choice I had to make; well, maybe this was it. I couldn't think of the alternative. I *refused* to think of the alternative.

"You should get back," I murmured. "Or we will truly be caught this time." I reluctantly pulled back.

"You're right. My mother has been getting very anxious as Fate's Day approaches. I bet Alys is the same," he said with a small smile, though it didn't light his blue eyes with warmth as his smiles usually did.

"She's being strong for me. But I know it's tearing her up inside. I'm prepared to do whatever it takes to spare her and your mother from heartbreak," I promised him.

"So, we'll stand together, against the Fates?" He held out his hand. "Are you with me?"

I didn't hesitate in taking it. "Forever."

His eyes lit with an inner fire – one that promised forever and more. He slowly brought my hand to his lips and kissed it reverently, as if worshipping at my altar, and I had never experienced the sensations cascading through my body before. It was as though every cell in my body yearned to be connected with his. The Fates would have a fight on their hands; how could they deny what was so pure and true? It made no sense.

"See you at the ball," Kai said, releasing me.

"I'll be the one in a ballgown."

"I look forward to it." He bowed and was gone.

I leaned back against a tree trunk and called for Lunara. She came sailing down from the tree branch and snuggled on my shoulder.

"Let's go and find Alys," I told her.

"Did you *see* Ric? I did not know he could move like that!" Alys laughed as we weaved our way back home, along the shared fields and through the black-stone-moon-topped archway, with other merry Nosians.

We passed brightly decorated huts and cottages. Star-sprinkled banners and candlelit lanterns bobbed gently in the breeze, and tinkling music followed us home. I gently twirled the purple and silver ribboned wand Eva had impulsively bought for me. We had spent a few childish moments twirling them like we had when we'd been little girls. I gave a small smile as I remembered Lunara chasing the ribbons. It was a memory I would cherish.

Twilight was nearly upon us, but tonight nobody worried; the ambience was light and carefree. Knowing that Fog's mists had dissipated allowed more freedom between the Twin Realms during the Festivale.

A scream cut through the air ahead of us.

I dropped the ribbon wand and thrust Lunara at Alys, and with no thought for my own safety, barrelled around the curve in the path into the fray. A wall of thick fog blocked my view from the revellers ahead. *What?* The mists were gone. *Should* be gone!

"Ceridwen, come back!" Alys shouted from behind me, but I took a deep breath and plunged into the cloying cloud.

Inside, five Shadowwraiths were circling a family with young children. An older male appeared to be on the floor, clutching his side and groaning in pain. Baring my teeth, I removed my dagger and darted forwards. The wraiths turned as one and focused on me.

"Go!" I shouted to the family, and seizing their chance, they helped the old man up, backed away, and left as fast as they could, supporting him.

One wraith lunged, and I vanquished it with a slice of my dagger to its throat. A second and third were close on its heels, but with a sidestep and twirl I had them both. My good fortune did not last. I tripped over a loose stone and ended up flat on my back, winded, while the two remaining wraiths loomed over me. Their faceless heads blurred before my eyes as one mist-shrouded hand crept across my neck.

My vision dimmed, but an unexpected, searingly bright light shot at them, and they disappeared so fast I could scarcely believe they had actually been there. I sat up, coughing and gasping for breath.

Alys stood before me, holding out a large black glass jar. She stoppered the lid, and the light went out.

"That was you?" I croaked as she hurried over to me, her face a picture of terror.

She nodded, but her eyes were on my neck, and I wondered if the wraiths had left bruises there – a vicious tattoo of their attack. "I've been experimenting with the fog. Essence of moonflower works a treat." She gave a grim nod. "No fog – no Shadowwraiths. Now I know it works, I'll have to tell the Council. Come on, let's get you home." She shivered, before opening the cover on her basket and withdrawing a trembling Lunara.

As I cradled my terrified mothling, I began to question my resolution not to fight Kai. There weren't enough moonflowers in the whole of Nos to counteract the legion of Shadowwraiths that would be unleashed if the realm of Fog was freed.

The slaughter would be uncountable.

And I didn't know if was brave enough to test Kai's theory. There were more than our lives on the line. Tonight had cemented that fact for me in a most painful way. I rubbed my throat and remembered the look on the terrified family's faces, fervently hoping the old man would recover from his injuries. I couldn't bear to see those I loved endure the wrath of the Shadowwraiths.

I had some soul-searching to do.

Twenty-Seven

"They must be getting stronger."

Alys placed her basket on the counter and set about making tea. I withdrew Lunara from my jacket and placed her onto her perch. Her trembling had thankfully stopped, but I gave her a few frostberries to comfort her before sitting heavily in one of the kitchen chairs.

"This has never happened before. The week of the Festivale has always been a safe time – it *should* be a safe time. People shouldn't be terrorised in their own realm. It isn't fair!" I exclaimed, taking the mug of chamomile from her.

She ran a hand over my hair. "I know, my darling girl, but this Fate's Day is different. I am sure what dwells within Fog knows this and wants to do anything to thwart you and Kai from fulfilling the prophecy. If you fail, they'll be free." She spoke quietly, her voice gentle, but the words cut me deeply with a blade made of guilt and longing.

I stood abruptly. "I'm going to bed."

Alys nibbled on her lip, her eyes huge in her pale face. "All right, sweetheart. Put some of this on your neck, it'll help heal your…" She trailed off with a shudder. "Do you want a sleeping draught?"

I took the pot of salve and shook my head. No, tonight I would face my nightmares head on. They couldn't be any worse than what I had already endured… or what was to come.

But I couldn't even rely on my nightmares to give me something to fight. Sleep eluded me; I tossed and turned all night. I kept replaying the scene with Kai in the orchard, and then the Shadowwraith attack. I didn't know what to do. Finally, as the moon disappeared below the horizon and the sun took its place, I kicked my tangled covers off and got dressed for the day, enviously leaving Lunara to her slumbers.

"Surprise!"

I nearly tumbled down the ladder as the shout filled our small lower level. I looked around in shock at Alys, Eva, Maxen, Larissa, and Meuric as they grinned back at me, all holding gifts. *Oh, yes – it's my birthday.* Today I came of age. Today I should have been anticipating my union to Kai.

"Th-thanks," I said, ducking my head. Alys must have snuck them all in.

"Here, open mine first." Eva skipped forward with a long, glossy black box wrapped in a silver ribbon. She pressed a kiss to my cheek, before drawing me over to the comfy armchair beneath the living area window.

As sunbeams speared in through the glass, I unwrapped the gift to reveal a beautiful silver and black onyx necklace. The onyx stones were cut into five-pointed stars and dangled from the two long silver chains. "You loop the chains around your neck and leave the stars to drape down your back." Eva winked.

My stomach churned, but I didn't want to spoil everyone's obvious pleasure at presenting me with their gifts. "Thank you," I told Eva quietly. "I'll wear it at the ball."

"Speaking of the ball, this came for you from Kari's dress shop." Alys gestured to an enormous box on the kitchen table.

My nausea intensified, and I hoped I wouldn't retch. I forced a smile. "I'll open it later."

"Happy coming-of-age, Wen." Maxen leaned over to press a kiss to my forehead and dropped his gift into my lap. His fresh, clean scent comforted me, and I opened his gift to reveal a set of matching blades. I grinned as sharply as the edges on the daggers. These would be perfect in a Shadowwraith attack. "Thank you," I said, and meant it.

"A pleasure," Maxen replied, and his eyes flashed with meaning. I didn't think he had intended the gifts to be used on Shadowwraiths – he had someone much more luminous in mind. I had no intention of using them on Kai. But was the plan I'd made with Kai still really the right thing to do? After the Shadowwraith attack, I didn't know any more.

Larissa presented me with a basket of candied pears and frostberry truffles. I had to keep the smile pasted on my face; the truffles made me think of Sabra. I didn't want her ruining my day... Well. Her declaration almost three years ago had ruined my *life* – one more day wouldn't make a difference. But I remembered my manners. "Thanks, Riss."

Larissa smiled back at me in delight and allowed Meuric to take her place.

"Lady Ceridwen," he said formally with a small bow. His smile didn't reach his grey eyes as he handed me a sheet of rolled-up parchment and a small purple velvet box. "I officially declare you graduated from my training school. You have been an honour to teach."

I opened the box to reveal a medal shaped as a crescent moon on a thick satin purple ribbon. Meuric took it and placed it formally over my neck, and my breath hitched. This was the end of an era in so many ways. Tears fought for release, but I pushed them back.

I stood and pulled my old mentor in for a hug. He tensed, but after a moment his strong, sinewy arms snaked around me and hugged back tightly. I closed my eyes, and images of the past few years raced through my mind. Of Meuric patiently threading arrow after arrow into my bow as I sent them wide, one after the other; of him picking me up when I dropped from exhaustion. No, gestures of affection weren't his style, but he showed it in many other ways. I was so grateful for him.

I pulled back and looked around the room as they clapped and said, "Happy graduation, Wen!" *I'm grateful for all of them.*

"And here's mine." Once Meuric had awkwardly backed away, Alys handed me a large square box.

I opened it curiously and withdrew a hand-etched leather belt. Runes and symbols decorated the length of it, and holsters along half of it held tiny black glass bottles. I looked up at her curiously; she stared back at me pointedly.

"Essence of moonflower," she murmured, and I remembered the Shadowwraiths fleeing from her light. She had made me a weapon.

"I love it. Thanks, Alys." I did. But if Kai and I decided to fight against the prophecy, we were going to need a lot more.

She smiled and clapped her hands together. "Let's eat!"

It took both Meuric and Maxen to remove the dress box from the kitchen table and place it on the sofa. We then helped ourselves to pancakes and fruits from the counter, and glasses of elderflower punch.

To my surprise, I actually managed to eat two pancakes, and even let out a genuine laugh when Lunara came barrelling down from my room. She made a beeline for the mound of frostberries, and Alys had to catch her before she dived into the whole bowl.

"What are your plans for the day?" Eva asked. "I'd love to spend it with you, but I have to do the rounds with my parents for official Festivale business." A knock came on the door. "In fact, that's probably my father now."

I nibbled my lip. I hadn't spoken properly to Lord Celestri since the night of the shrine visit – it wasn't as if we could have had a chat yesterday on the stage.

"I'll walk you out," I said. Eva waved her goodbyes and thanked Alys for the food.

Outside, the gentle sunshine warmed my arms. Lord Celestri hovered in the garden. "Happy birthday, Lady Ceridwen," he said formally, handing me a small box. "Open it on Fate's Day."

Touched, but slightly apprehensive, I tucked it into my pocket.

"I hope you have a lovely day full of celebrations," Lord Celestri added, his silver eyes swirling. "Come along, Eva, we don't want to be late."

She pulled me in for a quick hug, before joining her father and heading off down the path. "Thanks," I called after them wistfully, a pang of envy surprising me. I gave myself a mental shake, shrugging off a life I could never have, before re-entering the cottage.

Maxen and Larissa were helping Alys wash up while Meuric and Lunara were playfully fighting over the last frostberry. I took in the scene for a moment, then – hardly realising what I was doing – stepped back out into the garden and started walking.

I needed a moment alone.

I headed up to the old temple ruins and sat on a broken wall looking out across the sea. I breathed slowly, in and out, in and out, letting the crisp sea air fill my lungs and ground me. After a few peaceful moments, my senses started to tingle and I became aware that I was no longer alone.

A hand caressed my shoulder, and I inhaled the warm, spicy scent I knew better than my own. "I thought you said I'd see you at the ball," I said huskily, secretly pleased he had risked coming to see me on my birthday.

"Well, I wouldn't want to spoil the surprise, would I?" Kai said, turning me around to face him. He handed me a bouquet of bright yellow flowers, intermingled with moonflowers. A perfect partnership of the Twin Realms. *Like us?*

I took them and breathed their scent deeply. "Thank you," I murmured.

"That's not all," he said, in the most nervous tone I had ever heard from him.

He knelt before me, and I got to my feet with a gasp. In his hand he held a ring. It was a twisted band of gold and silver, with a moonstone crescent inlaid upon a sunstone sun.

"Ceridwen Moonshade, I pledge myself to you in this realm and all the ones beyond. Please accept this ring…"

He trailed off as I shook my head.

"Kai, we can't. Do you know how close my heart is to breaking right now? There was another Shadowwraith attack last night." I yearned to accept the ring, to slide its cool shape over my ring finger. To pledge myself to him too.

"Then that's exactly *why* we should do this." He stood. "I don't need a formal union to know I belong to you, and you to me. We're two halves of one whole. You *complete* me."

And I was undone.

I slowly sank back onto the stone wall, my head in my hands. I wanted to agree with him so badly, but what would happen if I did? Would the Fates smite us down right here? No, they couldn't – the prophecy must be fulfilled – but would our unofficial union put that at risk? I had thought I could do as Kai suggested and fight against our fate, against a prophecy only one person – Sabra – declared was truth. But this had to end now. What if that old man had died yesterday? If the prophecy wasn't fulfilled, it wouldn't be just one man's death on my conscience – it would be countless others in both realms. I couldn't risk their lives… and I couldn't prolong the heartbreak.

"Kai… I cannot express how much I want to accept, but I can't. We must not do this. It's time we faced the fact that, no matter what we try to tell ourselves, there is no other way out for us."

The hand holding the ring dropped. Kai's face fell, and as he staggered back it felt as though I had stabbed him through the heart.

"Wen, don't do this… *please*. You'll kill me. Only the thought that we'll find a way around this has kept me going. I *can't* hurt you." He dropped to his knees and wrapped his arms around my legs, resting his head in my lap. Shudders cascaded through his body and through me until they felt like my own.

I can't do this. Pressing my trembling lips to his golden hair, I inhaled his familiar scent one last time before gently removing his arms and standing.

He slumped against the wall and watched me with dimmed eyes, like the sun trying to filter through the gloom. There was no spark left. I had killed it.

My heart beating sluggishly in my chest, I walked away, and heard the chink of metal as the ring dropped to the stone floor.

Twenty-Eight

Despite it being Festivale, and my coming-of-age, I spent the next couple of days training. Eva had grudgingly agreed to take over my instruction now that I was no longer expected at the training yard.

I barely ate and slept. I could see that my friends were worried about me, but I couldn't tell them what had happened. Eva would have thought it was romantic, and Maxen would have been disappointed I had let my emotions come before the good of the realm. I couldn't even speak to Alys – not without completely falling to pieces. No, it was time to reinstate the armour around my heart. That was the only way I could get through the days.

The Guard had been kept busy with more random Shadowwraith attacks, and Alys had been working all hours to prepare more essence of moonflower. The attacks only solidified my decision. A guard had been killed, and every time I thought about her suffering, I felt sick with guilt. I avoided the ruins, the orchard and the caves; my world was slowly shrinking. If it shrank small enough, perhaps I would cease to exist.

"Enough, Wen!" Eva caught me as I staggered and fell.

I threw the sword to the ground with a clatter and pulled out of her grip, then took a long drink and finally met her narrowed eyes.

"This isn't healthy," she said quietly, and I looked away. What did I care? It didn't matter. All that mattered was doing the right thing for the good of the Twin Realms.

"Let's go again." I bent to pick up the sword, but she stood with her hands fisted on her hips.

"Nope. I have an appointment at the salon. It's the Fate's Day Eve ball, remember?" She looked critically at her hands and pouted. "Look at the state of my nails." She held them out to me.

"Seriously, Eva?" I couldn't keep the anger from my voice. "You do know that tomorrow evening, I might *die*!"

Her face paled, but I didn't feel a shred of remorse. "Your stupid hair and nail appointment. Doesn't. Matter!"

Eva stormed towards me, tears welling in her eyes. "Do you think I don't *know* what tomorrow is? Do you think I don't have to listen to my parents arguing every night because my mother is planning my wedding for when you lose?"

When, not if. "Of course, Lady Eva Celestri and the golden boy. What a perfect match for the Twin Realms," I sneered.

"You think I want that?" The ferocity in her died. She faded before me, a glimmer of her usual luminous self. "I love you, Wen. You're like a sister to me."

Finally, the red haze parted, and I saw what I had done. Was I really pushing everyone away now, when it mattered the most?

"I – I'm sorry," I choked out, and left her standing like a broken doll in the small cottage garden, the way I left everyone. Hurt and disillusioned.

I stormed into the cottage, thankful Alys wasn't home, and headed up to my room. Lunara raised her tiny head and grumbled at me. Her tone was chastising as I slammed drawers shut and kicked a box underneath my bed. *What was that?* I thought, momentarily distracted as I pulled out the huge box. *Oh, the ballgown.* I had told Alys I would open it later, and after she had helped me to take it up to my room, I had shoved it under my bed and forgotten about it.

Since my final moment with Kai, I hadn't been myself. I had severed our connection, and it felt *wrong*. There was something within me that kept searching, searching, but there was nothing there. I floundered; a ship without an anchor, the moon without the sun's light to help me glow. I was adrift, my light reduced to a mere flicker.

I was pushing the box back under the bed when Alys' head popped up from the ladder. I hadn't even heard her come in. "Oh, lovely, you're going to open it. I've been longing to see what's inside." She climbed all the way up and sat on my bed, looking at me expectantly. "I saw Eva; she looked a little peaky. Everything all right with her?"

"She's just preoccupied." I turned my face away, making a show of untying the wide purple-and-black striped ribbon. I didn't want to open the box. I wanted to join it beneath the bed and gather dust.

Alys knelt next to me and helped me remove the lid. We pulled away the gossamer thin silver tissue paper. My fingers trembled as I ran my hand over the dress inside. It was a galaxy, a mystery, a question mark all in one. What would I be once I put it on?

At Alys's urging, I lifted it from the box and spread its fullness on the bed. The sleeveless boned corset-style top had a hammered silver sideways crescent moon overlaid on top of its crushed black gem bodice, with the two points set so they would accentuate the clavicle. The full skirt was created from numerous layers of petticoats, covered with shimmering black satin down to the floor and overlaid with a twinkling layer of silver, star-strewn tulle. The final touch was the wispy black lace that flowed from the top of each of the corset straps to trail along the floor, leaving my shoulder blades bare. They reminded me of wings. Perhaps they would allow me to fly away.

It was the midnight sky. It was Nos. It was… *me?*

"Oh, Wen. It's exquisite." Alys dabbed at her eyes with a handkerchief she had pulled from her skirt pocket. "Oh look – there's more." She pulled out a velvet pouch and a shoe box.

I was numb. The dress was everything I couldn't have. It should be Eva's. Would it sting my skin to put it on? Would it burn where it whispered against my legs? I hoped so. I wanted to feel *something*.

I took the box and looked inside to see a pair of black strappy heels: an accident waiting to happen. The heels themselves were made from four stacked stars in varying sizes, from tiny to big at the top, while the shoes were crafted from wide black satin ribbons, which continued into ties that would be knotted on my calves like ballet shoes. The velvet pouch held earrings, a choker and a bejewelled hair clip.

I slowly and carefully placed everything onto my dresser, where they sparkled and shone mockingly.

"I'll run you a bath." Alys placed a hand on my arm, and I realised my silence must have been worrying for her, but I couldn't form the words to tell her what was going through my mind. I hoped she thought I was merely overwhelmed by the dress.

"Thanks," I murmured.

She disappeared down the ladder, and the sound of running water drifted up from the lower level. I carefully pushed the dress aside and sat down. Finally, I dropped my head into my hands and closed my eyes. A warmth burrowing in at my neck had me putting my hand up to stroke Lunara as she grumbled at me.

"It's all right," I soothed. I just wanted to shut everything out for a few moments. If only I could do the same with my thoughts too.

"Are you sure you don't want me to stay and help you get dressed?" Alys plucked at her long, puff-sleeved lavender ball gown. Its skirts were a froth of floaty organza that shimmered when she moved. It had been her own mother's dress; unable to justify the cost of a new gown, she had adjusted it to fit her. She would look ethereal on the dance floor.

I shook my head. I needed to do this alone. "You go on."

"Very well." She hovered, as if not quite believing I would attend the ball. "I'll see you soon." She picked up her velvet drawstring bag, which I was pretty sure clinked with tiny bottles, put on her purple half-cape, and blew me a kiss before venturing out into the evening.

I sighed as the tension left my body. The lavender bath had settled me somewhat, but as soon as I had seen Alys ready for the ball, my anxiety had spiked once more. Now I was alone, I could stop pretending. Drop the fake smile.

I looked at the dress I had brought down from my room – I didn't fancy trying to clamber down the ladder in it. And as for the shoes? I would rather go barefoot. I couldn't stop the hysterical giggle that burbled out of my throat as I imagined Lady Celestri's aghast face.

Knowing time was running out, I removed my robe and stepped into the dress. Thankful the corset had a side opening instead of straps, I zipped it up and walked into Alys' room to take a look in her floor-length mirror.

It fitted perfectly. The points of the crescent rested coolly against my collar bone. I looked like me, but an otherworldly version. Instead of the choker, I added Eva's coming-of-age gift; I wrapped the lariat necklace around my neck, leaving the two stars to dangle between my shoulder blades. I liked the weight they added there.

The star and moon clusters were surprisingly light and delicate at my ears. I pulled my curls back off my face and carefully braided the top in four rows from my forehead to my crown, coiling the rest of my hair into a thick knot at the nape of my neck, securing it with the shooting star clip. I added a few star jewels to my cheeks and some ruby-red colour to my lips. Finally, back in the living area, I stepped into the shoes, and was surprised at how stable I felt. Kari, Sali and Tori were masters in their craft.

"Lunara," I called, and she came wheeling down to me. "I'll be back soon. I've left you a bowl of frostberries." I showed her the large bowl. I was sure she would eat herself into a stupor and settle down for the night.

I knew I was stalling. I wanted to leave it until everyone else had already arrived and I could slip in unnoticed. Perhaps I could just not go at all. Would anyone even miss me? But my plan went out the window when a knock sounded at the door. My heart beating fast, I went to open it.

"Max," I exclaimed. "What are you doing here?"

Maxen's throat worked a few times as he took me in, and I blushed self-consciously. "I – um – I thought I would escort you to the ball."

I gave an inward groan. *I thought we were over this.* He awkwardly adjusted his fitted black jacket, the silver shirt beneath accentuating his muscular neck. His black hair was loose except for one braid down the centre of his head. He looked so handsome – but his cool, mysterious look didn't spark in me the glow Kai did.

"As friends," he added at my hesitation.

Slowly, I nodded. "All right." I pulled the door closed behind me and locked it, sliding the key into my dress pocket.

He tucked my arm into the crook of his, and together we left the familiarity of the cottage garden and walked the long path to the Celestris' manor. Bright, star-shaped lanterns lit the way, and a few latecomers straggled ahead of us, talking jovially amongst themselves.

"Moved on fast, I see," a voice slurred to my left, and I turned with a start to see Kai staggering towards me, a half-full glass in hand.

Twenty-Nine

"Kai, are you *drunk*?" I asked, appalled.

"Not quite enough," he declared. He offered me his glass with a grin and I shook my head, stepping back before he could slosh it on my dress. The last thing I wanted was to go into the ball smelling of alcohol. That would really satisfy Lady Celestri.

"Come on, Lord Malakai. I think you've had enough." Maxen released my arm and moved to take the glass off Kai.

"Oh, so you want my drink as well? Anything *else* you want to take from me?" As abruptly as if a switch had been flicked, Kai looked at me with clear eyes.

I turned to Maxen. "Give us a minute, please."

"No. I am not leaving you with him, especially in this state," Maxen said with a curl to his lip.

I put a hand on Maxen's arm, and Kai hissed out a breath. "I'll be fine; he won't hurt me."

"Not today, he won't," Maxen said angrily, and I gasped, while Kai cursed under his breath. Maxen paused, then added, "If you're not inside in five minutes, I'm coming to look for you."

I nodded and waited while my friend stalked away.

"You don't belong with him," Kai said softly from close behind me.

I turned and found myself pinned against his chest. His soft golden jacket felt warm on my skin.

"I know," I said before I could stop myself. But knowing this route would only cause heartache for us both, I disentangled myself and stepped back. "But I can't be with you either."

He tossed back the last of his drink and stared unseeing for a moment, as if deciding what to say. "Then at least take this as a token of what could have been." He gripped my hand tenderly and placed something inside it, closing my hand into a fist over it. "You look enchanting," he said hoarsely, before walking unsteadily the last few yards up to the house.

I tried to catch my breath, but it was lodged somewhere between my lungs. I thought for one dizzying moment I would pass out, but I tilted my head up and focused on the almost full moon. I counted the stars surrounding it until my breath evened out. I opened my hand.

The ring glinted back up at me.

Slowly, I slid it onto the upper part of my thumb. I couldn't put it on my ring finger; I couldn't see it sat in the place where it should always sit for eternity.

Taking a deep breath, I walked up the steps and nodded at the footman. Feeling as though I was observing the scene from above, I entered the dream-like ballroom and stopped in the doorway as all eyes turned to me.

Black silk banners draped from the ceiling, and luminous moonflowers hung in clusters, giving the illusion of the night sky. Lady Celestri looked me up and down, her eyes wide and calculating, while Lord Celestri gave me a full smile – a smile that, if I wasn't mistaken, had a touch of pride to it. I couldn't see Eva or Maxen, or Kai for that matter, but Alys floated over to me and took my arm, drawing me inside.

"Oh, my darling, I knew you would look beautiful, but you could be Arianrhod herself."

I winced, fancifully expecting the Fates to smite me down at her blasphemous words. She led me over to a drinks table and pressed a cup of clear cordial into my hand. "Thank you," I said, taking a sip as something to occupy myself with. "Have you seen Eva?" I needed to apologise. Again.

Alys looked around the room. "She was with Larissa, but I haven't seen her in a little while. Oh, but there's Maxen."

The string band struck up a jaunty tune. Couples took to the floor, and Alys was whisked away by an elderly bewhiskered Solian. She giggled as he spun her into the dancing crowd.

Maxen joined me. "Are you all right?"

I put the cup down and nodded. "Of course. Aren't I always?" I attempted a joking tone, but Maxen's expression remained serious.

"Dance with me?" he asked, holding out his hand.

After the briefest of hesitations, I slipped my hand into his, and he led me into the throng. We joined the end of the upbeat dance, and then the music slowed to a haunting melody. The dancefloor thinned as a few couples stepped away. I placed my hand on Maxen's shoulder, and together we waltzed to the lilting music.

As he twirled me near the ballroom doorway, I saw Kai standing there, as golden as Belenos himself. His eyes burned into me, almost branding my very soul. The look on his face crushed me, the weight of it hitting me like the moon tumbling from the sky.

I faltered, missing my step, as Kai tore his eyes from me and turned to walk away. Maxen righted me, gripping my hand tighter. His finger slid over my thumb, and he glanced down. I watched his eyes darken as he saw the ring there.

"Seriously, Wen?" His face like stone, he whirled me around the dance floor, stopping to usher me out of the terrace doors and onto the empty terrace. "You're wearing his *ring*? Why – *why* do you keep returning to him?"

My heart and head pounded. What could I say? I walked away from him, trying to put together a cohesive sentence, while Maxen brooded behind me, waiting.

A giggling rang out as a couple staggered around from the side of the house. The young woman clung to the man, and she leaned in to try and press a kiss to his full mouth.

"Eva?" I did a double-take. "*Kai*?"

They both froze and looked up. Eva wobbled away from him, her face horrified.

"But... but." I couldn't believe what I was seeing. "I *just* saw you," I said blankly to Kai. It had been only mere moments ago, surely?

"It's not what it looks like," he protested. "I found her collapsed on a bench. I helped her up, I swear." His eyes pleaded with mine.

I wavered, knowing I had no right to be angry at him. I had just turned him down – but that didn't stop me from feeling betrayed. As I looked to Eva for her explanation, Maxen hurtled past me, fists raised.

"I've had enough of you, golden boy," he spat, and before anyone could react, he'd landed a blow on Kai's cheek.

Kai's head snapped back. Time seemed to freeze, but then a slow smile worked its way across his face. My stomach dropped.

"No," I breathed out.

Time rushed back in. Eyes lit with a furious gleam, Kai gripped Maxen and plunged a fist into his stomach. Maxen groaned and doubled over, but straightened and lunged at Kai. Even in his inebriated state, it quickly became obvious that Kai was the better fighter.

Eva squealed and stumbled away from them.

"Stop!" I screamed, darting forward. Caught off guard, Maxen took a punch to the side of his face and lurched into me.

"Wen, are you all right?" Kai gasped, immediately coming to my side, but I shrugged him off, trying to catch Maxen as he crashed to the floor.

Larissa ran out of the terrace door. Taking in the scene, she helped Eva, who stood clutching her head, to one side. "The musicians are taking a break. You'd better stop, or they'll hear you," she warned.

Maxen staggered to his feet. A cut split his cheek, the blood dripping slowly down onto his shirt.

I tossed a furious glare over at Kai. "Look what you've done," I accused. Why did everything have to go wrong?

Kai looked around – at Eva sobbing into Larissa's neck, at a bloody Maxen, and finally at me.

"I'm sorry," he said. His blue eyes bored deep into mine and I sensed the pull. The torn threads that had been searching stood to attention, as if one more touch could reconnect us.

"Just go," Maxen spat, and the strands recoiled.

"I'll go if Wen tells me to go, not you," Kai shot back angrily.

I nodded sadly. "Go," I whispered. I slid the ring off my finger and handed it to him. "Please."

He looked down at the ring. His hand jerked as if he wanted to fling it away, but instead he clenched it tightly in his fist, spun away, and strode around the side of the house to be swallowed by the night.

"Finally," Maxen said. "You should have told him to go a long time ago."

I whirled on him. "Do you think that was *easy*?" I pressed a trembling hand to my chest before blindly stumbling down the terrace steps into the garden.

"Wen—" Maxen followed me down and turned me to face him.

I gave a weary sigh. "You asked me why. Why I kept returning to Kai." I paused, considering my words. "I know this is hard for you to hear, Max, but you asked me, so I have to tell you, to make you understand… I'm drawn to him – it's this invisible pull. We're connected, two halves of one heart. It's undeniable."

As I spoke, Maxen's eyes filled with pained acceptance. I could see he knew I spoke the truth: Kai and I were Fated.

"I am the moth to his flame."

He gave one jerky nod and stumbled back to sit on the steps.

"That's what it is to be a Fated Pair – a *true* Fated Pair," Larissa said. She and Eva had followed us. "I've researched the lore; I find it fascinating."

"Then why doesn't that sound like my parents?" Eva asked quietly, to my surprise. I hadn't even realised she was aware of what was going on.

Larissa looked troubled.

"It isn't only one man and one woman. It can be two women, or two men – it doesn't even have to be one from each realm. Fated Pairs can happen even without the Choosing. They're unofficial, of course, and can't rule the Twin Realms, but you know it when you're in the presence of a *true* Fated Pair. It's unmistakeable... the air around them thrums..." she babbled awkwardly.

Time slowed down as I registered what she said. *The air thrums... it's unmistakeable.* Visions swamped my mind like suffocating mist before it parted to reveal what I already knew. A hand clenching on a door frame, a charged look... Alys and Lord Celestri. They were a true Fated Pair. Not him and Lady Celestri.

"Are you all right, Wen?" Larissa asked with concern.

My vision had tunnelled into tiny black pinpricks. I gasped for air, and the light rushed back in. And I knew – I knew what deal had been made.

"Ris," Eva moaned. "I feel sick."

Larissa looked helplessly at a silent Maxen, his head in his hands. "Max, can you help me?" she asked, looking rather green herself.

Maxen roused himself and looked morosely over at the two girls.

"I'm sorry, Max, truly I am," I told him, before striding away from them, nearly tripping over my voluminous skirts.

"Where are you going?" Max found his voice.

I turned and blew out a breath when the skirts flapped around me, trapping my legs. *Fates above! Secret weapon, time to reveal yourself.* I patted down my bodice. *Aha!* I pressed on a notch in the corset, and the side panel popped off to reveal a small folding knife.

"I. Am. Making. A. Dignified. Exit," I said through clenched teeth as I cut away the bottom of the skirt, freeing my legs. "Look after Eva." I was angry, but I didn't want anything to happen to her.

Maxen stared at me, and I knew we were saying a kind of goodbye. For him, it was the end of possibilities; for me, it was knowing things would never be the same between us again.

"I will," he said, finally, and turned back to Larissa and a groaning Eva.

I made longer strides now that my legs were finally free; the shortened skirt floated around my legs as I hurried down the path to the cottage. I needed to think.

Everything was in darkness when I entered, which threw me momentarily. A whirring warned me of Lunara's arrival, and I put my hand up for her to land on.

"Hi, precious," I murmured, and she grumbled at me. I waited until my eyes adjusted before walking into the kitchen to light the stubby green candles on the table. I glanced at the dresser then back again, remembering Alys' memorabilia box. *Should I?*

"I know, I know, don't judge me, but I have to know," I told Lunara, pushing aside the scrying bowl and pulling the box from the dresser. I'd never asked Alys about the scrying; I wondered if I would ever get the chance.

The box was a beautiful, glossy black, embellished with moonstones and star-shaped opals. I flipped open the lid and was immediately assailed by the aroma of the scarce moonshade flower. I recognised the scent from when Alys had taken me, as a girl, to a distant meadow where we had found some for her stores. She had placed one behind my hair, saying it was 'a pretty moonshade flower for a pretty Moonshade girl'. Blinking back tears, I saw a dried posy tied with a silver ribbon nestled on top of a pile of letters. I saved those for later; my eyes were drawn to a small portrait. Slowly, as if compelled, I picked it up.

It was like looking into a mirror. The girl looked to be about my age, with long, tumbling black and silver curls, and dancing eyes. Only the eyes were slightly different: light grey rather than silver. Dread curled in the pit of my stomach. I knew those eyes; I knew that face.

I flipped over the portrait and read the inscription on the back. *Alys, age twenty.*

Now I thought *I* was going to be sick. I dropped the portrait and pushed back the chair, Lunara fluttering away from me in alarm.

Alys was my *real* mother.

Thirty

The statement crashed into my mind. Alys was my mother... and she had *abandoned* me. I turned in a circle before grabbing the sink to steady myself, then retched and dashed into the bathroom.

My stomach emptied itself of what little I'd eaten that day. Alys was my *mother*. She'd always referred to herself as Alys as long as I could remember; why had she wanted to create this distance between us? Why had she hidden the truth? I groaned and lay on the wooden floorboards. I wanted to die. What game had she been playing all these years? Have a baby, only to abandon it – and then take it in and raise it as her own... Did I even really *know* her?

Well, I wasn't about to stick around and listen to her excuses. I pushed myself off the floor and splashed my face with cold water. Untying my shoes, I left them at the foot of the ladder and hurried up to my room. I wrenched off the dress, stuffing it into its box and pushing it out of sight under my bed, then dressed in the first pair of trousers and tunic I came across before adding my hooded jacket.

I picked up my Fate's Day ceremonial clothes and my weapons and put them into a bag. Lunara landed on my shoulder and let out a stream of grumbles and chitters. "I have to go," I told her, and she fell silent.

My hand hesitated over Alys's belt. Pushing emotion aside, I grabbed it and added it to my bag. The essence of moonflower was a formidable weapon, and I would be a fool to leave without it.

I donned my trusty boots and took one final look around the place I had lived my whole life. Whatever happened tomorrow, I would not be returning. Tears threatened to fall as I hefted my bag. *No! She does not deserve your tears.* I choked them back and descended the ladder for the last time, Lunara safely on my shoulder.

Taking a glass bottle full of water and some frostberries for Lunara, I made my way out of the cottage and strode away, my head held high. Just as Alys would have wanted.

I didn't know where I was going; I simply knew I couldn't stay another night at the cottage. It had changed for me. No longer a home full of love and light, it was now a cage of secrets and misery.

Out of habit, I began to traverse the familiar path up to the temple ruins, but my heart clenched and I swiftly changed course, instead making my way through the shared lands towards the caves. Lunara trembled, and I put a hand up to comfort her.

I should have felt trepidation too, but I wore my numbness like a cloak, sailing in through the opening and settling down behind a rock near the entrance. I tucked Lunara safely into the collar of my jacket and closed my eyes. I didn't want to be in the land of the conscious a minute more. Dreams were where I could look for answers, and respite from the life that had become worse than a living nightmare.

No sooner had I closed my eyes than the whispers started.

Ceridwen... choose... choose wisely...

My eyes popped open. I looked into the gloom at the eerie lights flickering below the water of the pool. They danced mesmerically, and I was drawn to the edge of the water, crawling forwards on my hands and knees. Lunara nipped me on the ear. In shock, I leaped back.

"Ow!" She had never done that before. She chittered at me, and I looked down, realising how close I was to the pool's rim. "Oh, I'm sorry, Lunara." The lights beneath the water vanished, and I skirted backwards and over to our hiding place.

Maybe this wasn't the best place to see out the rest of the night. It didn't matter to me, but I had Lunara to look after. I held her close and tried to find a comfortable position on the ground. Something dug into my hip, and in surprise, I reached into my pocket and withdrew the small box Lord Celestri had given me on my coming-of-age day. It had sat forgotten in my pocket. My worry about staying in the caves vanished as I focused on the box. Lord Celestri had said to open it on Fate's Day – well, in a few short hours it would be.

I held my breath as I flicked open the lid, feeling unprepared for whatever was inside. It was a full moon locket on a silver chain, with three stars inlaid upon it. I pulled it out from the velvet pad and, my heartbeat kicking up a notch, opened the catch. The whispering rushed back into my mind like a crescendo, and a sob caught in my throat. My suspicions were true. A tiny black and silver curl lay coiled inside. A baby's curl. Mine.

Alys was my mother and Lord Celestri was my father.

I thought the sobs would tear me apart; they burned in my throat and raged against my ribcage like a torrent waiting to be unleashed. But I wouldn't let them come; I battled them back with every last bit of my strength. The cave swam dizzily around me. With Lunara's concerned chirruping buzzing in my ears, mingling with the harsh whispering, I surrendered to the starless darkness.

The shame of being a product of a deception that mocked the very Fates smothered and battered me until I was broken in my dreams, a thousand eyes upon me and a thousand fingers pointing in my direction. I stood on the Celestial Bridge, exposed before the untainted.

I awoke with a gasp as a voice called my name.

Ignoring the call, I guzzled water from the bottle and dripped the rest onto a dip in a stone for Lunara to lap up. The locket lay on the floor. Keen to hide the evidence of my disgrace, I clasped it around my neck and shoved it out of sight underneath my tunic as my name was called again.

I lay back against the cool stone wall, not planning to reveal myself, but Lunara had other ideas. Before I could stop her, she flew out of the cave with a happy chirrup.

"Come out, Wen. I know you're in there."

Eva.

With a long sigh, I pushed myself to my feet, ready to confront my... *sister*. My mouth dried up. No, I couldn't tell her. I couldn't tell anyone.

Outside, I blinked in the watery sunlight. Eva and I stared at one another for a long moment. I took in her clear eyes, fresh face – free of makeup, I noted with surprise – and leather trousers and plain tunic. She was even wearing boots. Her long hair was tied up in a high ponytail.

She rushed at me and caught me up in a tight hug. "I am so sorry, Wen – *so sorry*. You have no idea how I felt when Larissa told me what you and Maxen saw last night. I would never intentionally hurt you. *Never!*"

I rubbed her back soothingly before drawing back. *And I you*. But the knowledge of our parents *would* hurt her. No, I couldn't do that to her, not when I had made a decision about my choice today. Nobody need ever know the truth.

"I am never drinking again," she vowed, and I could see in her eyes she meant it.

"All right," I said, and just like that we were back to normal again. Well, as normal as two girls could be with one knowing they were half-sisters, and the other blissfully unaware.

"You, on the other hand, look dreadful. Alys looked so pale when I went to the cottage this morning. She told me you hadn't been there all night."

I winced. "I needed to be on my own," I hedged. Lunara grumbled from her perch on Eva's shoulder. "Well, alone with Lunara," I amended with a sad smile.

"I'm sorry if I was the cause." Eva rubbed my arm, and I swallowed back the quick denial. Yes, she had hurt me when she'd tried to kiss Kai, but Alys and Lord

Celestri's betrayal was so much worse. Eva had been drunk; what was their excuse?

"I've got a lot on my mind. I need to prepare myself for this evening." I looked away over the clifftop, focusing on the rolling waves in the distance. "Will you do me a favour?"

"Anything," she said quickly.

"Don't tell anyone where I am. I don't want to see anyone."

"Wen – if this is about last night" – I looked at her sharply – "about Kai and me…" She trailed off as I tensed.

"It's all of it, Eva. I feel everything and nothing all at once! One moment I could explode like a thousand shooting stars; the next I'm hollow like the vacuum of space. Just an empty vessel to be used by the Fates." I resumed my gazing at the sea, ashamed of my outburst.

She placed a gentle but firm hand on my shoulder, coming to stand behind me. "Then take command of it. Take command of what you feel and wield it to *your* bidding." She turned me around to face her. "You are a Lady of Nos – one half of a Fated Pair; you will stand tall as you walk onto the Celestial Bridge. You'll show everyone what you're made of. Even the Fates will bow down to you." Her eyes flashed, and an ominous rumble rolled across the sky.

"Careful, Eva," I muttered nervously, looking up. She was taking a big risk. It was Fate's Day, after all – the day when the Fates could walk among us, if they so chose.

She smirked. "I'm not afraid of them," she said, and I wanted to clap my hand across her mouth.

"I'm not afraid, but I respect their power," I told her wryly.

She rolled her eyes but didn't argue. An awkward silence fell.

"I'm going to clear my head and get ready," I told her.

"Is that your Wen way of telling me to go?" Eva asked, crossing her arms.

"It's better if I'm alone today." I reached out to stroke Lunara. "Can you take Lunara back h... to the cottage, please?"

"Wen, promise me something? Don't do anything stupid today. Don't give up. I need you." Eva gripped my hand as it hovered over Lunara. We linked fingers, and I looked down at the ground.

She wouldn't feel this way if she knew. She would despise me.

I gave her hand one final squeeze before releasing it and stepping back. "I'll see you later. Bye, Lunara."

Lunara chirruped at me, and my heart broke at the thought of never again seeing my precious mothling. But this was the way it had to be.

Eva gave me one long look before saying pointedly, "I'll see you afterwards."

I turned away. I couldn't watch them leave; I would crumble. I made it into the caves before my legs gave out. I crawled behind the rock and let out a silent scream, my fists pounding weakly against the rock.

"Your sister is brave." The voice was so warm it flamed.

I looked up in shock as Belenos and Arianrhod stood before me. Their otherworldly glow lit up the pool behind them, making it appear to move.

I staggered to my feet. "You knew?"

Arianrhod gave a cool smile. "Of course, we knew. Why do you think I offered to tell you?"

Belenos frowned at her.

I shook my head. "Of course." My stomach clenched as I remembered Lord Celestri jumping in smoothly. He'd known; he'd stood next to me, he'd comforted me, and he had *known*.

"Mortals and their emotional suffering," Belenos said in disgust. Then he fixed me with a heated gaze. "So, Lady Ceridwen Moonshade of Nos, have you made your decision?"

Thirty-One

"Bel, we are not to interfere," Arianrhod admonished.

"Oh, you are a fine one to talk. You gave her more information than was permitted," Belenos shot back. He waved his hands in annoyance, flames flickering from his fingertips.

"I gave her exactly what was permitted. It is so frustrating, being bound by these rules! He knew exactly what he was doing when he made that deal."

I looked from one Fate to the other. "He?" I asked.

"Ari," Belenos hissed, but Arianrhod ignored him and glided towards me. Her long silver gown brushed the floor, and her knee-length black hair rippled with the light of a thousand stars.

"Yes, *he,* but per the rules of the deal he made, we cannot tell you what choice you should make. It must be your own free will. That is one rule we all must abide by. Whatever we Fates set in motion, ultimately, mortals can keep their free will. Whatever choices they make, whatever they *choose* to accept, will be because they deemed it so." Arianrhod looked at me intently, as though she were trying to give me the secret meaning to her words.

I sat wearily on the rock, the lack of food catching up with me. "I know what I must do. For the good of the realms, and especially for those within Nos."

Belenos let out a snort. "Mortals. Suffering and sacrifice – is that all you are good at? What about seizing life? What about *love*? You get such a finite time; I do not understand why you do not live every moment as if it was a gift. Because it is! When you have existed as long as we" – he cast a searing look at Arianrhod – "you get to appreciate what *really* matters."

"I don't have the luxury of *love!* And as for seizing life – well, I shouldn't even have been born!" I shouted back, not caring that the Fates could literally blink me out of existence with one touch.

Arianrhod and Belenos exchanged a look. Arianrhod made to reach out to me, but dropped her hands to her side. "Oh, my poor child," she murmured. "Bel, she is in pain…"

Belenos shook his head, his golden mane of hair rippling around his brown face. "No, Arianrhod, we cannot help her. This part is up to her."

Arianrhod's face flickered with sadness. "We must go, but we will be watching over you." She turned away, then back. "Over *both* of you."

I knew she meant Kai too.

Their glow faded until they vanished, and I was once again alone. Not even the whispers intruded.

I was resigned to my fate. I was so tired of the Fates' double-edged meanings and insinuations. I intended to carry out my plan; there was no other way out for me.

A strange sense of peace came over me, and I methodically went about the rest of the day in a state of surreality. I ate the leftover frostberries; I bathed in the pool and meditated on a rock overhanging the crashing waves below before donning the Fate's Day ceremonial clothes. Again, they fitted flawlessly. I slowly and carefully braided my hair from my crown into a thick rope and tied the end with a silver ribbon I found with the clothes. I added the moonflower essence belt in case of an attack on my way to the Celestial Bridge. Forgoing the knee-length boots included, I slipped Maxen's daggers into my own trusty boots. I wouldn't need them, but I felt better with them there.

Finally, I was ready. I sat in the mouth of the cave and watched until the sun began its descent into night.

Purposefully, I stood, and for the briefest of moments an otherworldly hand gripped my shoulder and the scent of moonlight and starshine surrounded me. *Choose well.* The whisper floated through my mind and was gone.

Head held high, I walked through a silent Nos. Only the nobles would be at the Celestial Bridge; everyone else would, as tradition decreed, be at home celebrating Fate's Day with their families.

I thought of Alys alone for all the years to come, but I refused to allow even a shred of guilt to throw me off my stride. I had to become numbness itself, to act as if I were already gone and this was only an echo, a memory.

The steps to the Celestial Bridge came into sight, two guards stationed either side of it.

"Ah, we were just taking bets on whether you would show up," Gus said in a conversational tone. "My good friend here was adamant you wouldn't flee from your responsibilities, that you were no coward. I, on the other hand…" He trailed off meaningfully.

"Shut up, Gus," I said without breaking my stride. The other guard sniggered.

"I would say die well, but I don't actually care as long as you die," Gus said spitefully.

His words were like a dagger to my back, but I kept going: down the steps, one foot after the other, not even stopping on the platform. I could hear murmurs and shouts, but I didn't acknowledge them until my foot hit the pathway to the bridge. Then I finally looked up.

"Ceridwen, where were you? I've been so worried about you!" Alys raced over to grip my hands, her face pale and her hair dishevelled. "We need to talk before you do this."

I couldn't even bring myself to look at her. "No, we don't." I kept my words quiet. "I know everything, but don't worry – your sordid secret will die with me."

Alys gasped as if I had struck her. She staggered away from me, doubling over.

Out of the corner of my eye, I saw the group of assembled Nos nobles, thirty families in all, turn to one another and mutter curiously. Maxen stood with his family; he threw me a confused frown before turning away. Eva clutched her hands, her knuckles white, beside Lord and Lady Celestri on the stone dais surrounded by Nosian banners.

I walked away, over to where Meuric waited at the foot of the bridge.

"Wen!" A shout echoed across the bridge. *Kai*.

I couldn't look over at him. The pain in his voice almost unravelled me, but I focused on Meuric instead.

"Are you ready for this?" he asked, his face set.

"Of course she is, Ric; she's been waiting her whole life for this moment of glory." Lady Celestri sauntered up to join us. Her tone sounded as if *she* had been the one waiting. Well, I would certainly give her what she wanted.

"Salomé," Lord Celestri hissed, but his eyes were on me. He knew that I knew. But surely that was what he'd wanted; why else would he give me the locket to open today, of all days? Did he think it would make me *want* to live? Give me a reason to carry on? Well, it had backfired spectacularly.

I turned away from his fatherly gaze. "Let's get this over with."

Without waiting for them, I made my way across the bridge towards the centre. The crack in the floor rivalled the one in my heart.

I stood on the circular precipice and waited for the Solian contingent to join us. Sabra shot a glance behind me – I guessed at her sister.

Kai skirted around Sabra, angrily shaking off her hand as she reached out to pull him back. He planted himself in front of me, forcing me to look at him. All I saw *was* him; everything else faded away.

"Wen, I am so sorry about last night…"

"None of that matters anymore," I said in a dead tone.

His face crumpled, and he shook me gently. "Don't say that! It all matters. You matter. *We* matter!"

"Kai." Lord Celestri stepped in and pulled him away from me. "You're making this harder than it needs to be."

"Well said, Lord Celestri," Sabra said smoothly, leading Kai away. Lord Celestri looked at her with such intense loathing that I almost reacted in shock.

She ignored him and turned to Meuric. "Shall *I* carry out the proceedings? Everyone else seems a trifle too emotional."

"Oh, Fates, please do," Lady Celestri agreed.

"Whatever you want," Meuric responded coldly. He drew me aside and spoke only to me. "Ceridwen, I don't think what Sabra told us that Fate's Day three years ago was true. It isn't possible for Fates to go against the Choosing. They *chose* you both – remember that. I've been researching the lore. If a Fated Pair harm one another, it has dire consequences. I've come to the conclusion that Sabra was lying. I am going to address the other nobles with my suspicions."

I shook my head. "No, don't, Meuric. It's not worth the risk."

He stared at me, sorrow filling his pewter eyes. He opened his mouth, but I cut off his protest.

"What if they *chose* us simply for this purpose? What if they're putting a mistake right?" *I* was that mistake.

"There is no mistaking a Fated Pair."

As if compelled, my eyes trailed over to Lord Celestri, then beyond him to where Alys stood, gripping the railing. Her eyes flicked from me to him, and the love I saw as she looked at us both was undeniable.

But it didn't change the fact that, even if Lady Celestri had somehow orchestrated herself and Lord

Celestri to wrongly be Paired, my parents had abandoned me.

"No. You are wrong. The prophecy must be carried out," I stated flatly, and walked away from my old mentor.

Sabra smiled in satisfaction as I took my place upon the crescent-shaped stone. Kai stood stiffly upon the sun.

I blinked, and I saw what *should* happen. We should turn to one another, clasp hands, and be joined in union, sealing ourselves as a Fated Pair: the next rulers of the Twin Realms.

The dreamy scene dissolved in my mind as I returned to the nightmare before me. Sabra had started her speech.

"Nobles of Sol and Nos, we are gathered on this Fate's Day to honour the sacrifice one of those young loyal citizens is about to undertake. By fulfilling the prophecy, we will continue to stave back the threats from Fog. Their spilled blood will seal the Celestial Bridge's rift and keep the Twin Realms strong." Her voice rang around the cliffside.

"This is wrong!" a voice shouted from the Sol side.

Kai looked up. "Tesni! What are you doing here?"

Tesni pushed her way out of her mother's grip and raced along the bridge, only to be stopped by Sabra's two guards. "*You* are wrong," she screamed at Sabra. "I've seen it!"

"Miss Ostara, this is no place for you." Sabra gestured at her guards. "Take her away."

Tesni fought against the guards, but she was dragged from the Celestial Bridge and deposited into her mother's arms. "If you do this, you'll kill us all!" she sobbed, her voice reverberating around the bridge.

Kai looked at me, and the first chink of doubt wormed its way into my mind. Would Tesni lie to protect her brother? Of course she would. I had kept the truth from Eva to protect her.

"We must leave the Celestial Bridge now," Sabra instructed Meuric, Lord and Lady Celestri and her guard. Everyone but Lord Celestri started walking away, back to their respective sides.

"Kai's sister is right; I can sense it," he whispered. "Wen, there's so much I want to say – to explain, but you have to look inside your heart and choose wisely."

Choose wisely, choose wisely, choose wisely. It rang in my head until I clutched my temples dizzily.

I looked up and Lord Celestri – *my father* – had gone. Only Kai and I remained on the bridge – for a moment.

"Lunara! What are you doing here?" My mothling fluttered like an arrow in the dark, landing furiously on my shoulder and gripping it with her sharp talons. She couldn't be here, not now. With no other option, I walked back to the Nos side of the bridge. Lady Celestri yawned loudly.

"Eva, take her." I tried to pull Lunara gently off me, but she clung tightly, her claws drawing blood. *"Please."*

Eva's eyes were enormous in her pale face, but she leaned in to try and help me detach Lunara. My mothling made a sound I had never heard her make before: a high, keening warble that caused my heart to skip a beat. It was sorrowful and haunting. It was her version of grief.

Tears finally streamed down my face. "I'm sorry, Lunara. I'm so sorry," I told her.

She stopped the keening cry and nuzzled into my neck, and I closed my eyes. For one moment I believed we had all the time in the world.

"Lady Ceridwen!" Sabra's tight voice had my eyes flicking open again, and my heart sank.

"Lunara," I whispered. "You have to let me go now."

She ruffled her tiny wings and grumbled in disagreement.

"Here, let me." Lord Celestri's large hands cupped around my mothling. Surprised, I watch her comply as he lifted her off me.

I stared up at him, and his eyes met mine. Emotion swirled within their silvery depths, and I swallowed the lump in my throat. "Thank you," I said huskily. "Look after her for me."

"Really, Cos," Lady Celestri said disdainfully.

He whipped his eyes to hers, and immediately she looked away.

Eva stared at her parents. "This isn't the time," she hissed, before pulling me into a hug.

"Love you, Eev," I whispered against her hair. A sob caught in her throat.

Before I completely lost it, I wrenched from her grasp. With Lunara crooning behind me, I walked back along the bridge to where my fate awaited me.

Thirty-Two

The bridge beneath my and Kai's feet rumbled ominously, and a cloud of fog fountained up from beneath us. I stumbled, almost losing my footing, as Sabra screamed, "You must fight, or they will come!"

"Wen, we can unite the realms and fight back!" Kai shouted.

The fog parted. He stood mere inches from me.

I turned away, slowly withdrawing a dagger. "You must fight me," I ground out, the threads of my sanity barely holding together. I had to make him think I would fight him, so he would defend himself. He *had* to defend himself.

I stepped forward with a thrust. Wide-eyed, he held up a wrist, and my blade sang along his metal cuff. The fog whirled around us, cutting us off from everyone else. With every movement I made against Kai, the bridge trembled and rocked.

"*Fight me*," I almost begged.

He caught my dagger hand and pulled me towards him. "I won't." Stronger than me, he pulled the dagger easily from my grip and tossed it over the bridge.

I pulled out the second dagger, and he growled in frustration. "*Why*, Wen? Why have you given up?"

Looking into his devastated eyes, I couldn't hold it together a moment longer. I staggered under the bucking of the bridge. "Because I know. I know who my parents are." He caught me as I fell. "But I wasn't enough. I wasn't enough for them to say, 'she's ours, and we're not ashamed of what our love created'."

"Oh, my darling. Ceridwen, you are more than enough… you're everything."

I crumbled in his arms, armour dissolving. He held me as I wept. The bridge stopped shaking and an eerie stillness came over the Celestial Bridge. The fog hung back as if it was holding its breath, waiting to see what would happen next.

"What's happening?" I heard Alys cry. "Why is Wen on the ground?"

Murmurs and shouts erupted from both sides of the bridge, and I suddenly knew with a stunning clarity that if I killed Kai, or he I, it would not strengthen the Twin Realms; it would tear them asunder. Meuric and Tesni were right.

Kai gave me a tender smile. "I would rather die by your hand than live a life without you. You *are* my life. It is time you forget who you think you should be and remember who you are."

Overcome, I gripped his tunic, leaned up and crushed my lips to his.

He moulded his to mine, and it was everything I ever dreamed it would be. It was the key turning in a lock; it was the moonrise and the dawn all at once. It was a thousand stars arcing across the sky while the sun crested the horizon. The whispers filled my mind, but this time they were a song, a melody that had been sung since the beginning of time. It was the song of us.

I was wrong. There never had been a choice to make: it had only ever been this. I just hadn't seen it, but now my eyes were wide open as the void in my heart repaired itself, sliver by sliver, until it spilled into Kai's. We were two halves of one whole, and we beat as one.

A blazing light shot from our embrace and lit up the whole area. We broke apart, chests heaving, as the light slipped into the crack of the bridge, sealing it, leaving a glistening, crystalline seam.

I barely heard Lady Celestri and Sabra's enraged cries of, "No!"

The fog dissipated, and we lay tangled together on the Celestial Bridge, spent as if we had just fought an epic battle – and we had. A battle for each other.

I looked up in time to see Lady Celestri running towards us across the bridge in her spiked heels.

I scrambled to my feet as she hissed into my face, "Why couldn't you just *die?* You were supposed to die on the bridge, like you should have done all those years ago!"

Eva, Lord Celestri, Sabra, Alys, Maxen and Meuric followed her over. Lord Celestri pulled her back from me and Kai. The other Nosian and Solian nobles made their way over more cautiously, some inspecting the glowing seam in the bridge in shock.

"No, Sal," Sabra said urgently, but Lady Celestri was too far gone.

"Why, sister?" she spat. "Are you scared our little secret will be revealed? Well, I don't care. It's all gone wrong. You promised me she would *die!*"

She pulled out of Lord Celestri's grip and slapped me across the face. Kai caught me as my head snapped back painfully.

Alys wrenched Lady Celestri away, and as I blinked through the pain, I was shocked at the ferocity on Alys' face.

"You. Do. Not. Harm. My. Daughter." She shoved her and Lady Celestri stumbled into Eva, who looked at her mother with disgust.

Alys crumpled into sobs, and Lord Celestri drew her into his arms. A silence fell across the crowd.

Eva was the first to speak.

"Why are you wearing my father's locket?" she asked me slowly, looking from Alys and Lord Celestri to me.

Lunara took the opportunity to flutter over to my shoulder and I held her tightly, taking comfort from her, as my heart began to pound. This was all wrong. Eva shouldn't find out like this.

"*Why?* I'll tell you why!" Lady Celestri threw a furious look at Sabra, who stood frozen, her usually golden face pale. "Because that little harlot" – she pointed at Alys – "and your dear daddy had a child… *her!*" She thrust a finger at me, her eyes wild.

Eva gasped and turned a stricken face my way. Maxen quickly strode over to put an arm around her waist for support as she swayed.

Alys pushed away from Lord Celestri. "No, that is not what happened. *We* were a Fated Pair, not you! We had known it all our lives. We had pledged ourselves to each other, but then it all went wrong at the Choosing."

Sabra shuffled nervously, and Meuric found his voice. "I remember... it was a shock when you two were chosen. That was when the first crack in the bridge appeared."

I stared at him in shock. There had already been a crack? Why had no one ever told us?

"I had my doubts. I should have said something sooner." He shook his head in anguish.

"You always were too astute for your own good," Sabra said bitterly.

"Then tell us what happened, Mistress Sabra, we implore you."

And as if they had always been there, Belenos and Arianrhod materialised. Belenos's hand rested lightly on a gleaming golden sword, and while Arianrhod had a serene expression on her face, her eyes were unyielding.

Sabra visibly cowered. She tried to bow respectfully, but Lady Celestri gripped her arm in terror, and together they wobbled.

"Yes, do," a noble from Sol called out.

Sabra swallowed a few times, her eyes flicking to Belenos's sword. "I simply wanted our mother back, and my sister... wanted another woman's man. So I made a deal..." she faltered.

"Yes. With whom?" Arianrhod asked in melodic tones, but with an edge of steel.

Lady Celestri gripped Sabra's arm even tighter, leaving nail-marks in her skin.

"With *him*. Taranis," Sabra ground out. Arianrhod nodded as if she had already known.

"That was a grave mistake," Belenos said, shaking his head.

"Who is Taranis?" Master Novarian asked from the Nosian group.

Belenos laughed – a deep, warm laugh. "He has influenced so much of your lives, and yet none of you know whom you should fear?" He was incredulous, and Gus's father flushed. "He is the third Fate. You believe there are Twin Realms, but there is a third. Fog is not simply a realm of mist and Shadowwraiths; as you may know, there are people like you beyond the wall. But you are not aware of how they have suffered under his iron fist – as do you all, though you do not know it. We are bound by rules, yet he continues to break them. Now tell me, Mistress Sabra, what were the conditions of this deal?"

Sabra sagged. It was shocking to see her so cowed. She had faded until she looked a watery version of herself. "I don't know. My mother helped Salomé obtain Lord Celestri. Taranis tampered with the Choosing so their names would be Chosen. But our mother had made a bargain with him too, one we never knew about, and soon after he took her."

Belenos and Arianrhod looked at each other as if something finally made sense to them.

It was as though a dam had been unleashed inside Sabra. She continued in a torrent. "But it was wrong. They were never a true Fated Pair, so Cosimo and his true Fated Partner were still drawn together. You cannot deny what is true." Kai and I looked at each other, and he squeezed my hand. "Salomé had her suspicions that they still met, and one night a few months after she'd had Eva, she followed Cosimo and discovered him at Alys' cottage. Alys was giving birth."

Eyes flicked from Alys to me in shock, then back to Sabra.

"She slipped inside the cottage while they slept and took the baby."

Horror startled curdling in my chest; Alys let out a moan.

Lady Celestri took over, her eyes flashing. "I did what I had to do. That baby was an abomination! It should never have been born. He was *my* Fated Partner, and *we* were the rulers of the Twin Realms. I left the baby on the Celestial Bridge as an offering to Taranis, but my dear Fated Partner chased after me and saved his monstrosity." For a brief moment hurt and longing filled her eyes as she looked at Lord Celestri, and I realised she did love him in her own possessive way.

"Do you know the guilt I lived with? I thought I was going mad. My mind said you were my Fated Partner, but my heart and my very being told me otherwise!" Lord Celestri stormed. "You were so devious; you knew the truth, but I still promised to deny Ceridwen to keep you happy. Alys had to renounce her own child." He looked with devastated eyes at Belenos and Arianrhod. "She made us promise to never tell anyone, terrifying us with the thought that Ceridwen would be put to death if anyone found out, because we had broken the most sacred principle of our realms. Fated Partners were never to betray one another."

"You never broke it. Your *love* is sacred." Arianrhod smiled at him and Alys.

"Then it was me," Eva said quietly. "I was the child that never should have been born."

"Eva – no!" I breathed out. I had been feeling so full of joy that my parents never truly had abandoned me that I had never considered what Eva must be feeling.

She cast me a look so full of hurt and wistfulness it hit like a punch to the chest. Pushing away from Maxen, she ran along the bridge towards Nos. I didn't hesitate; I handed Lunara to Kai and ran after her, grabbing her arm to whirl her around.

"Eva, stop!"

"Why, Wen? Everything has fallen apart," she sobbed.

"No! You always said we were like sisters. Well, now we truly are." I pushed every ounce of happiness into my voice, imploring her to be happy too.

She looked past me to the group clustered on the bridge and shook her head sadly. "How can I ever show my face again in Nos? It's like our roles have reversed. You get the man, the loving mother… and now you get my father too. I have nothing left!" She pulled away from me and raced up the steps, not looking back.

"You have me," I said, devastated, but she was already out of earshot.

Maxen joined me. "Let me go after her. Go back to your family."

I searched his face, but his expression was unreadable; a distance seemed to fall between us, one I didn't know if there was ever a chance of closing. Wordlessly, I watched him sprint up the steps after Eva. How could my own happiness come at the expense of my two best friends'… my *sister's*?

Slowly, I made my way back to the centre of the bridge.

"Ah, we were just finishing up the tale," Belenos greeted me. "You, especially, will want to hear this part."

Lady Celestri shot him a look of hatred, before turning to speak to me. "As I was saying, I wanted a way to get rid of you once and for all – you had been a thorn in my side for far too long. I wanted you removed."

Silently, Alys and Lord Celestri flanked me and Kai, who tightly gripped my hand.

"We all knew you were an absolute clumsy fool and terrible at fighting, so what better way to get rid of you than have your Fated Partner do it for me?" She broke off to laugh; everyone was staring at her with varying levels of horror or disgust. Ignoring it, but seemingly relishing being the centre of attention, she carried on, "Sabra discovered you were a Fated Pair, long before it became plain for all to see. So my exceptionally *talented* sister, with a little help from Taranis, wove a teensy prophecy. One that said unless one of you killed the other, then our beloved realms would be overrun with Shadowwraiths – when in fact the opposite is the truth! If a Fated Pair harm the other *then* the bridge would fall. Only the *strength* of your union staves back the darkness," she finished, her chest heaving.

It was what we had always believed, so why had we not trusted in it? Why had we been so quick to believe Sabra and her 'prophecy'?

Lord Celestri had murder in his eyes as he looked at Lady Celestri. "You – you orchestrated all of this?" He waved his hand around in disbelief.

"Well, I can't take all the credit," she said with a meaningful look at Sabra. "In exchange for getting rid of the girl and having the bridge fall, we would get our mother back. Taranis got the run of all three realms, but *we* wouldn't be harmed, of course. We would be treated as the royalty we are." Her crazed eyes took in Lord Celestri as if she couldn't see that he despised the very core of her.

Kai spoke up for the first time. He looked at Sabra with revulsion. "What if she had won?"

Lady Celestri laughed hysterically. "Oh, she could never best *you*, Lord Malakai. You are far superior in every way. That is why I chose you for Eva. Where's Eva? Darling?"

That was the moment I realised she was truly unhinged. She hadn't even noticed – or cared? – that Eva had left, heartbroken.

Kai looked down on Lady Celestri, his face livid. "If you knew me at all, you would know I could never harm a hair on her head." He glanced at me. "She never *needed* to best me. She *is* the best of me."

"Ugh!" Lady Celestri said. "Pretty words, boy." She focused on me. "But your love cannot save her."

And before anyone could stop her, she grabbed hold of me, wrenched me away from my family, and flung me with all her might over the side of the bridge.

Thirty-Three

Shouts followed me down as I was swallowed by the curtain of fog hanging below the Celestial Bridge.

So, this was it; this was how it ended for me, after all. At the bridge where it had all begun. The memory of Kai's life-giving kiss made it so much harder. I had everything to live for now.

I closed my eyes as I fell, the thick fog almost seeming to slow my fall, and pictured his face, then Alys, Lord Celestri, Eva, Maxen, Meuric…. Everyone I cared about. I wrapped myself in their loving expressions and accepted my fate.

Something thumped into me – hard. I somersaulted sideways. A loud grumbling sounded next to my ear, followed by the flapping of large wings. Talons gripped my shoulders firmly, and I winced. Before I could see what was happening, I was being carried upwards.

I burst through the fog, craning my neck to see who – or what – was carrying me. All I could make out was an elongated, furry purple body and large purple feathered wings. I wasn't scared; I was *safe*.

The creature flew away from the bridge on its fluttering iridescent wings and over to the resting place halfway up the steps. It lowered me carefully down to the floor then settled next to me and nuzzled me, nearly knocking me over. I found myself looking into enormous black eyes. *Familiar* black eyes.

"Lunara!" I cried in amazement, taking in her now pony-sized body. She looked like my precious mothling, but so much larger. Her whole immense body glittered and shone with soft moonglow. "But how?"

"Mothlings are fascinating creatures," Arianrhod said, unexpectedly next to me. She put a hand up to a crooning Lunara and stroked her. "She just needed the right circumstances to achieve her metamorphosis."

"You saved me," I whispered into Lunara's fur as I held onto her tightly. "I'll give you a whole barrel full of frostberries tonight."

Lunara grumbled deep in her chest in pleasure. I drew back, gave her one final pat, and looked out over the viewing platform. I waved at Alys, who looked like she was the one who had plummeted from the bridge, not me. Lady Celestri and Sabra were now being held by the combined Nosian and Solian Guard. *But where's Kai?*

I hurried down the steps and over the bridge. "Where's Kai?" I shouted, scanning the area.

Lord Celestri and Alys ran to me, both pulling me in for a tight hug. "You're safe!" Alys exclaimed.

"Where's Kai?" I repeated, unable to focus on anything else.

"He went after you—" Lord Celestri began.

"What?" I shouted. "*Over* the bridge?" I raced to the edge, but he pulled me back.

"No – there's a ladder cut into the cliff face." He pointed, his face creased into a worried frown, and I could make out metal rungs jutting out of the stone.

"Kai!" I screamed into the gloom, but my voice only echoed back to me. *Kai, Kai, Kai.*

Lunara. I had started across the bridge back to her when a cloud of fog blocked my way and two figures stepped from within: one haughty and cruel, the other bruised and bleeding.

"Is this what you were looking for?" The haughty figure pushed Kai at me, and I caught him as he stumbled.

"What happened?" I whispered, taking in his swollen eye and cut cheek.

"I made the acquaintance of Taranis," Kai told me, before kissing my temple. "I thought I had found you, only to lose you." He pulled me into a tight hug.

"I'm here," I promised.

"Well, I can see that your plan did not work out," Taranis said as he stalked past us and over to Sabra and Lady Celestri. The guards held out their swords, but with an arrogant click of his fingers their swords dissolved into fog and floated away.

The other two Fates appeared in front of him. "What are you doing here, Taranis?" Belenos demanded.

"Collecting a payment," Taranis replied languidly. His dark grey hair wisped around his long, pointed face. His eyes, like dark pits, roved over Arianrhod and Belenos. He steepled his fingers. "I was *promised* the run of the Twin Realms."

"They were not Mistress Sabra's to promise," Arianrhod said silkily. "You have no claim over them."

Taranis smiled tightly as Belenos gripped the hilt of his sword. "Hmm. I still demand recompense."

The other two Fates exchanged a look. "He is within his right," Belenos explained to us. "If a mortal makes a deal with him of their own free will, then a boon must be paid if the mortal does not keep their end of the bargain."

"But... but—" Sabra spluttered, her eyes widening.

Lady Celestri looked unconcerned, but Taranis focused on her. "Perhaps Mistress Sabra needs to learn a lesson." He clicked his fingers, and Lady Celestri vanished.

"Not my sister too," Sabra moaned, slumping in the guards' grip.

Taranis floated up to her, his feet concealed by his magical fog. The guards cowered back. "She is to be a permanent guest in my realm. And as for you, I will take back the powers I loaned you." He snapped his fingers again, and a dark mist poured from Sabra. She let out a silent scream, her face leaching of colour until she was a husk of her once formidable presence.

"That is enough, Taranis. Go back to your lair above Fog and leave the Twin Realms to us," Belenos ordered. Taranis threw him a lazy glance.

"Do not doubt for one moment that it will ever be enough, but I will leave you to your narcissistic Fate's Day." A look of disdain crossed his arrogant features. He cast a mocking bow my way; then, with a swirl of fog, he too vanished.

"Take her away," Lord Celestri told the guards holding Sabra after a moment of stunned silence. Shock was evident in his face, but not a tinge of sympathy for the Solian mentor. He swiped a shaky hand across his face and murmured, "How can I tell Eva what's happened to her mother?"

I swallowed hard at the pain in his voice. How must he be feeling? The life he thought he had been living had been a false one. But with Alys by his side, I was hopeful he could find comfort, and I would be there for Eva; we all would.

Sabra allowed herself to be led from the bridge, her feet dragging on the floor so that the guards had to almost lift her.

"And we will leave you to your mortal celebrations. I am sure you have much to discuss," Belenos said.

"Thank you for choosing well, Lady Ceridwen. If you had made any other decision, terrible events would have occurred in Nos and Sol." Arianrhod inclined her head and took Belenos' hand. An intense light surrounded them until they winked out of sight.

In the silence that followed, the nobles took their leave, making their way back to their own sides of the bridge with shell-shocked expressions. Master Novarian demanded a Council meeting. Lord Celestri – my father – placated him with promises of doing just that within the next few days. Finally, it was just Alys, Lord Celestri, Meuric, me and Kai, and Kai's family. Lunara watched from her position on the viewing platform, ruffling her feathered wings every now and again as if she herself couldn't believe the sheer size of them.

Kai drew me over to officially meet his parents, and Tesni caught me up in a tight hug. "I knew you two would find a way!" she cried, drawing back with her eyes shining.

"Thank you, Tesni. You helped me to question what was happening."

She nodded shyly. "I'm so pleased we will be sisters." *Sisters.* My heart thudded in pain as I thought of Eva.

"I am sure she'll come around," Kai whispered, perceptively guessing where my thoughts had wandered.

"I hope so," I murmured, before turning a friendly smile on Master and Mistress Ostara.

"Lady Ceridwen, we are so happy you will be joining our family," Mistress Ostara said, her smile warm and her eyes shining. "Our heart has ached for your unfair situation. We longed to find a way to support you both, but I had faith you would find your own way."

"Thank you," I said, surprised at their instant welcome.

"I must admit, I doubted you," Master Ostara confessed. "I knew my son would never harm you, and I feared I would lose him this day." He gripped Kai's shoulder, and they exchanged a look of respect. "I am so glad to be wrong. Please accept my apologies."

"*I* never doubted her," Kai said, as I said, "No apologies needed!" We all laughed, and Alys came over to link her arm through mine. She exchanged pleasant smiles with Master and Mistress Ostara.

"I hope our two families can meet up soon, but can I steal Ceridwen away for a moment please?"

"Of course, and we would be delighted to dine with you," Mistress Ostara said gracefully.

Alys inclined her head with a smile and drew me to one side and into her gentle embrace. Her head rested on my shoulder, and we stood like that for what felt like a lifetime.

In those precious minutes, it was as if my whole life flashed before my eyes. How could I have not seen that Alys was my mother? Everything made so much sense now – but two things niggled at me.

Slowly withdrawing from her arms, I asked, "How did no one know you were pregnant… or that you were my real mother?" I tugged one of her curls gently, seeing the silver strands mixed in with the black.

She gave a sheepish grin, and swept a hand over my hair. "I've told you about my parents dying when I was young, and being raised by my granny. Well, she was Healer to the Celestri family – I learned at her side. It was just her and me at the cottage, and we mostly kept to ourselves. I had beautiful hair like yours… fancifully, I thought I had been kissed by the moon itself." She broke off to give a self-deprecating laugh. "But your great-granny, although an exceptional Healer, was superstitious. She thought the townsfolk would see my hair and think I was fog-touched. So, from an early age we hid the silver strands with frostberry juice dye." A reminiscent smile on her lips, she looked over at Lord Celestri. "Just before my coming-of-age, she passed and I took over as Healer to the Celestris, living in the cottage alone. I couldn't bear to carry on dyeing my hair, but for some reason it felt disrespectful to *not* do it, so instead I cut my hair. The only person who saw me with hair like yours was your father. Before I cut it, he begged to draw my portrait."

That was the image I had seen in her memory box. I flushed in shame, feeling as though I had intruded on one of their most secret memories.

She rubbed my arm comfortingly. "As to my pregnancy, I hid it – it wasn't the done thing to have children alone," she said simply. "But I vowed to do whatever it took to keep you. I had planned to take an extended break in the far regions of the realm, return with you, and tell everyone you were the result of a sudden marriage with a guard who had passed away soon afterwards. But I never got the chance. You came suddenly, four weeks early." A flush stained her cheeks, but I couldn't feel angry at her; I understood how scared she must have been. "Cos and I gave in to our love only that one night, but you were never a mistake. You were so loved. You *are* so loved."

Tears burned my eyes as Lord Celestri came up beside us and, without a word, enfolded me into his arms. It would take a little time to get used to calling him my father, but his embrace felt like coming home. I leaned into him. In that hug, I felt years of missed celebrations and precious moments. I hoped we would have plenty of time to make new memories to replace the missing ones.

He let me go, and as I sniffed back the tears, Meuric gave an awkward cough from behind us. "I will catch up with you all tomorrow," he said gruffly, and started walking across the bridge.

"Thank you, Ric," I called after him, and he paused. "For always believing in me." His back jerked, and he held up a hand in acknowledgement before carrying on over the strong bridge.

"That was an emotional reaction for him," Alys said with affection.

Lord Celestri looked at her, and the air became charged as she returned his gaze. I could practically see the threads between them intertwining and connecting their hearts, knitting away the erroneous rift.

"I, um, I'll see you later," I mumbled, feeling *very* much like the third wheel.

"All right, sweetheart," Alys murmured.

Hand in hand, they walked from the bridge, Alys saying happily, "We're going to need a bigger room for Lunara."

With a contented smile on my face, I turned around – and saw only Kai. His family had gone, and we were finally alone, in the place where it had all started.

He knelt on one knee and held out the ring. "Lady Ceridwen, I pledge myself to you—"

He didn't get a chance to continue. I knelt before him and pressed my mouth to his. "And I to you."

He slid the ring onto my finger, and we stood together on shaky legs. The moon hit the ring with a kiss of its own and it glowed softly, sealing our union. I smiled with a delighted internal glow as Arianrhod blessed us. Usually a union would be a grand affair, but this private moment was just perfect for us.

A chittering filled the air; I looked over to see Lunara beating her wings in the air, making noises of celebration.

"I think Lunara approves," Kai said with a laugh, before he claimed my mouth once more.

We lay tangled in each other's arms on the floor of the temple ruins, gazing up at the star-strewn sky. The Fate's Day moon hung heavy and full in the sky, and I was the most at peace I had ever been.

Kai trailed a lazy finger up my bare arm. "There's another one." He pointed out a shooting star. He turned to me, his gaze fierce and loving. "Make a wish," he urged.

And I did, because wishes were for the hopeful.

Epilogue

Night tipped into day. Hand in hand, we made our way slowly back to the cottage, following the lengthening shadows.

I felt different. Whole. Nothing could dull my inner glow; I turned to face Kai, and saw a happy smile to rival my own on his golden face.

The cottage was quiet when we entered, until it was buffeted by a huge, rumbling snore. I jumped, then let out a laugh. Following the noise into Alys' room, I found Lunara sprawled out on top of her bed. No wonder my mother had chosen to sleep elsewhere. *My mother.* The thought added another layer of shine to my new happy life.

Giving my slumbering mothling a stroke along her large head, I watched her antennae twitch in her dreams. I hoped they were happy ones; she deserved them. And a whole bathtub full of frostberries!

Humming to myself, I joined Kai at the kitchen table, then faltered at the look on his face.

Silently, he held out a sheet of milky-white paper to me. At once, I recognised it as Eva's stationery; I didn't even have to see the loopy handwriting.

Dear Wen,

Please don't judge me, but I've gone to Fog. Whatever my mother has done, she does not deserve to suffer there. She's still my mother, and she's all I have left now. Please enjoy your new life and don't worry about me — no Shadowwraith would dare touch me, not the way I'm feeling right now. I am sorry I can't be the sister you want. I need time… time to work everything out.

E xo

I dropped the note on the table and gripped the back of the chair as the room swam dizzily around me. Kai immediately came to my side and drew me into his comforting arms.

"She's gone," I sobbed. "She's gone because of me."

"No, not because of you. This is all her mother's doing. Don't forget that. You did nothing wrong." Kai rubbed his hands over my back as I tried to make sense of it all.

The door to the cottage slowly opened, and a cough broke me and Kai apart. Maxen stood awkwardly in the doorway.

Not meeting either of our eyes, he asked, "Have you seen Eva?"

I held out the note to him, and he took it with a frown. His eyes scanned the note once, twice, three times before he looked up, finally meeting my eyes.

"She's gone to *Fog*? Alone?"

I gave a jerky nod.

Maxen turned on his heel, dropping the note to the floor.

"Where are you going?" I burst out.

He paused, a fist clenching on the doorframe. "After her. There's nothing for me here."

My heart thudded in pain. I wanted to go with him and find Eva. I wanted to say, *don't go, it's too dangerous* — but Kai took my hand, a tangible reminder that our paths were diverging, and I knew I had to let Maxen go. Kai and I had the Twin Realms to rule, and I had no claim over Max. If anyone could bring Eva home, it was him.

After a loaded moment, Maxen strode out of the cottage.

I turned into Kai's arms, and he held me while I wept.

TO BE CONTINUED…

Acknowledgements

Much like Wen, I set upon this path as if it was Fated to be, but also like Wen, I understand that you can't do everything alone. You need a loving, supportive team around you to complete your destiny. And so…

Massive thanks to my beta reader, Julia, who not only gave me great suggestions and comments on my early manuscript, but was a great sounding board for all things design and formatting.

Huge thank you to Kate, who answered many queries I had about the complexities of writing YA and NA – your insight was much appreciated.

To Britt of Magic and Moons Press, thank you, for inspiring me to write a piece for your anthology – that piece sparked the idea for this whole series.

Galaxy-sized thanks to my excellent editor, Emma, (and real-life curly-haired girl), who bridged the gap from my Middle Grade series to this one seamlessly. Encouraging me and helping me shape this book into something far better than what it started out. I thank the Fates we met.

To my indie writing fam, you amaze me every day with your talent, tenacity and support – especial thanks to Naomi, Ellie, Nikki, Shauna, E.G, S.V…and of course, my Mystic Sis, Madonna, for championing my books *and* me. I appreciate it more than I can convey.

To my real fam – my mum, my sisters (and their families), thank you for your unwavering support.

And to my beloved children, Adam, Chloe, Nathan, and Jake, and my own Fated Partner, Dean, I wouldn't be able to follow my dreams if it weren't for your constant encouragement and love. I get to do what I do, because of all of you.

Finally, to my readers, I hope you enjoyed this story and that you too chase your dreams…fate isn't *always* set in stone, it is your choices that make all the difference…

About the Author

E. G. Tudor is an award-winning multi-genre author from the beautiful South Wales coast, where she lives with her husband, children, and crazy dog.

She is the author of the well-received *Through the Fairy Door* middle-grade fantasy series, and this is her first book for adult readers. She loves to hear from her readers, and you can connect with her via her Instagram: @from_the_shelf_of_e_g_tudor or Twitter: @E_G_Tudor

If you enjoyed this book, please consider leaving a review.